About the Author

The author is married, with two grown children. He has lived in the wine country of Santa Barbara County most of his life but, currently, he resides in Tucson, Arizona. His business experience is in finance, but his passion is writing.

The Rogue Insurrection

William Congdon

The Rogue Insurrection

Olympia Publishers
London

www.olympiapublishers.com
OLYMPIA PAPERBACK EDITION

A CIP catalogue record for this title is
available from the British Library.

ISBN: 978-1-80439-125-9

This is a work of fiction.
Names, characters, places and incidents originate from the writer's
imagination. Any resemblance to actual persons, living or dead, is
purely coincidental.

First Published in 2023

Olympia Publishers
Tallis House
2 Tallis Street
London
EC4Y 0AB

Printed in Great Britain

Dedication

I'd like to dedicate this book to my children and grandchildren; Jake, Jen, Maggie, Rich, Tucker, and Penelope. Their encouragement and support are a constant inspiration.

Chapter 1

Mike McClintock stood off to the side, watching as the bottles moved along the conveyer to be corked after having been filled with Syrah wine. At 5'11", he was built like a brick. His vineyard was small compared to many in the Santa Ynez Valley, just north of Santa Barbara. That said, he still produced over two thousand cases of high-quality wine every year. This was Mike's third year at the vineyard, after having retired as the Special Agent in Charge of the FBI field office in Chicago. He was burned out with law enforcement and knew that a change was needed. A reduction in the level of stress, as well as a more moderate climate, was what he and the family wanted. His wife, Julie, was firmly on board with the move west, as were his two kids, Zach, nine, and Sam, short for Samantha, aged six.

Julie walked into the warehouse as the last of the bottles were corked.

"I'll bet you're glad this job is done," she said as she walked up and put an arm around Mike's waist.

"It's non-stop. Last year's harvest is now bottled, while this year's crop begins the fermentation process. I never realized how much work is involved in managing a vineyard and producing wine," Mike commented. He watched as the workers moved the bottles from the conveyer to the cases. The last step, in the next few days, would be affixing labels, then sending them off to the distributors for market.

"I think it's time for a well-deserved break. What do you

9

think?" Mike asked as he looked at Julie with her short blonde hair and smiling blue eyes.

"Christmas break isn't for another month and a half. We'd have to take the kids out of school."

"We can work that out with the teachers, I'm sure. Let's get away for just one week," insisted Mike. "Are you in?"

Julie smiled and responded, "I've always been in. What do you have in mind?"

***

October in Montana could be chilly. As the sun set, the temperature dropped. Jason McClintock had the wood ready to go in the fireplace. He lit the fire and stoked it until he had a warm blaze going. Jason, with a Doctorate in Geological Engineering from the Colorado School of mines, acted as a consultant, specializing in mining. With an international reputation, he could be as busy as he wanted. In addition to his occupation, he worked his own gold claim. Two years ago, he exposed one of the largest veins of gold ever found in the state of Montana. To this day, he could count on one hand the number of people that were aware of this discovery. Because of this, his days as a consultant were limited and dwindling each year. His cabin, at the base of the Bitterroot National Forest in the Anaconda-Pintler Wildnerness, was about thirty minutes outside of Butte, Montana, in the southwest portion of the state. Jason, at 6'1', was blonde with blue eyes and looked as though he should be on a beach in southern California. He'd never married, but had a close relationship with Brenda, an artist in Butte. She had her own home with an attached studio, but, more often than not, was at Jason's place in the evening.

Brenda was striking in appearance as well. At 5'4', she was petite, with jet black hair and deep blue eyes. She specialized in oil landscapes and was quickly gaining national attention. She and Jason had been together close to fifteen years and had never had the need or desire to tie the knot. When they wanted a kid fix, they headed to California to see Zach and Sam.

Brenda was preparing dinner when Jason's phone buzzed. Looking at his cell, he spoke to Brenda, "It's Mike."

"Hey, champ, how're you doing?"

"Good. We finished bottling last year's harvest today," Mike replied. "That's the reason for my call."

"To tell me that you're done bottling, or, is there more to the story?" Jason asked as he sipped the Glenfiddich that he'd poured before sitting down.

"Julie and I were talking, and I looked into a seven night cruise out of Los Angeles. We wanted to ask you and Brenda as well as Vladi to join us," said Mike.

"When do you plan on going?"

"It's short notice. Next week. But, because of that, we can get great rates! It's the *Regent Seven Seas Mariner*. The ship has a five-star rating, holds only seven hundred passengers and it's all-inclusive! We leave out of San Pedro and have ports of call in Cabo San Lucas, Mazatlan, and Ensenada. What do you say?" Mike asked.

"Let me talk to Brenda and I'll call you back. I'm not so sure about Cabo," said Jason. "The last time we were down there, it was everything but relaxing."

"This trip will be different, you'll see! I'll give Vladi a call now. It's going to be fun, Jason. We all need a break, right?" asked Mike.

"It does sound like fun, but don't bother calling Vladi. He's either back in Kazakhstan, or on the way," commented Jason.

"When did he leave?"

"I think he planned to leave yesterday. He said he might stay as long as a month," Jason replied.

"Got it. Talk to Brenda and get back to me."

***

Vladi, or, Vladimir Petronovich was once tasked to eliminate Mike and if need be, his family, by a rogue CIA operative. He couldn't do it. Instead, he used his skills as an ex-KGB assassin to assist Mike and Jason in overcoming a dire situation that most people would find insurmountable. Petronovich had become very close to the McClintocks, almost like an older brother. Truth be told, he probably would have chosen the cruise with the McClintocks over Kazakhstan, if he had known about it. The Lufthansa flight had landed in Almaty about forty minutes earlier, and Vladi had just cleared customs. As he made his way down the escalator to baggage claim, he noticed the white-haired couple at the bottom; Andrei and Natalia Mikhailov. They were family friends that Petronovich had grown up with. Their daughter, Marina, had been close to Petronovich as well, though fifteen years younger. He was the reason she emigrated to the United States after having earned her Doctorate in Biochemistry. Unfortunately, she was assassinated last year after exposing a plot by terrorists to attack the U.S. Petronovich and the McClintocks were instrumental in stopping the planned attack. This was Vladi's first trip back home since Marina's death. He knew it would be tough meeting Andrei and Natalia, not having spoken to them since their loss. Both were smiling as he approached. Stepping off the escalator away from the other

12

passengers, Vladi wrapped his arms around the two.

Tears were streaming down the wrinkled faces of his dear friends. Natalia whispered, "Vladi, we are so glad you came to visit us."

Petronovich wiped his eyes. "I'm happy I was able to make it. You two look great." He squeezed Andrei's shoulder, "Let's grab my bag and get out of here."

Chapter 2

The port of San Pedro, on any given day, was busy. But when two cruise ships were in port, to say it was hectic would be an understatement. On this Sunday, *Norwegian Bliss* was docked next to *Seven Seas Mariner*. Bliss was the tenth largest cruise ship in the world. With twenty decks it could accommodate four thousand passengers and one thousand, seven hundred crew members. *Seven Seas Mariner* was much smaller with only twelve decks, seven hundred passengers and four hundred and forty-five crew members. The *Norwegian Bliss* dwarfed every ship around it, especially the *Mariner*.

When you considered turning over close to five thousand passengers in a short period of time, the disembarkation and embarkation process was what one might call controlled chaos. Mike made the two- and-a-half-hour drive south, without any major traffic delays. Jason and Brenda took an Uber from LAX to the port after leaving Butte on the first flight out at five in the morning. The plan was to meet outside the terminal and check in together. Jason and Brenda had cruised before, but for Mike and his family, it was their first time.

***

The level of excitement grew as the lines were dropped from the moorings and pulled in by the deck crew. The ship's thrusters pushed the ship away from the dock as the props engaged and moved the ship slowly forward, towards the mouth of the harbor in the distance. Mike, Julie and the kids were near the rail, by the pool on deck eleven. They looked up and waved at passengers from the *Bliss* as they eased by the monstrous ship. Jason and Brenda brought their drinks over from the pool bar and took in the sight.

"Well, we're off! Zach, Sam, I see an ice cream bar. Do you think we should try it out?" Jason asked as he handed his drink to Brenda and started walking.

"Yes!" replied Sam as she ran alongside Jason with Zach right behind.

***

All the cabins on the *Mariner* were suites. Mike and Julie had a two-bedroom family suite so the kids could have their own space. The family room was nicely appointed with a sofa and two side chairs. The balcony, off the family room, was large, with a chaise lounge chair, table and four chairs. Mike and the kids sat outside on the balcony, listening to the ship as it cut softly through the Pacific waves, while Julie finished dressing for dinner. They had late-seating reservations at Prime Seven, the high-end steakhouse on the ship.

Mike and Zach wore slacks and button-down dress shirts while Julie and Sam were stylish in their dresses. It was time to make their way to deck five and the restaurant.

***

Jason and Brenda were already seated when Mike and the family were shown to the table. The restaurant was decorated in rich, burnished woods with earth-toned colors. They sat at a large round table with white linen and candlelight. The chairs were masculine leather wingbacks, which seemed to swallow Zach and Sam's small frames.

"What are we doing tomorrow, Dad?" Zach asked as everyone perused the menu.

"It was supposed to be a surprise." What do you guys have in mind?" Mike asked as he looked across the table at Jason.

"I think we'll get a day pass and spend time at a resort pool. The place is called Breathless. It's all-inclusive and close to the Marina," said Jason. "I'm not up for much of the excitement Cabo has to offer. So, what's the surprise?"

"I think we'll take the kids to a place called Dolphin Discovery in San Jose del Cabo. It's a thirty-minute cab ride, but the place has great reviews and the kids get to swim with the dolphins. We'll leave before lunch and be back before the ship leaves. I think that's five thirty, so it's going to be a quick trip," Mike explained.

The dinner was as good, if not better than expected. By ten p.m., Brenda was yawning. She and Jason had started their day at three a.m. mountain time in order to catch the early flight from Butte, so they were ready to call it a night. She looked at Jason and he nodded.

"Okay, that does it for us. Thanks for a nice evening. You guys be safe tomorrow and have fun with the dolphins, kids," said Jason, looking at Mike and the family.

***

Almaty was the largest city in Kazakhstan. It was surrounded by the Trans-Illi Alatau mountains, which rose to an astonishing

16

height of almost four thousand, nine hundred meters, or about sixteen thousand feet. The airport was a little over nine miles from town, at the base of those mountains. The Mikhailov's home was in the foothills, about five miles further. Andrei paid the parking fee and merged onto the highway heading away from town.

Both of Petronovich's parents had passed. He was not surprised when Andrei veered off the highway, taking the side road up the hill toward Almaty's Kensay Cemetery.

"We thought you would like to stop here before going home. We'll stop at your parents' grave, then bring you to where Marina rests," Natalia said.

"I'd like that," Vladi replied.

Cemeteries in Kazakhstan are not like the neat, trimmed, rolling lawns with headstones you would find in the U.S. The Kensay Cemetery in Almaty, like most in what was the old U.S.S.R., was overgrown with weeds, trees and high grass. Often, the plot was surrounded by a fence, providing a sense of privacy, or delineating personal space. Some even had a bench or chair for loved ones to use when visiting. Andrei pulled into a parking spot. "Let's take a walk."

"Once a month, we visit your parents, Vladi. We try to keep the gravesite orderly within the confines of the small fence that was erected," Natalia explained.

They wound through the various twists and turns, stopping in front of the well-kept plots.

"It's been over twenty-five years since they've been gone. Not a day goes by that I don't think of them," said Petronovich as he viewed his parents' grave.

"They were good friends, Vladi. They lived a hard life, like many of us did at the time," said Andrei. "Let us show you where

17

Marina is resting."

The three walked further into a newer section of the cemetery, which appeared to be in better shape. Natalia lead the way, wiping her eyes as she approached their daughter's grave. "She was too young to die, Vladi," Natalia whispered.

Vladi put his arm around her and replied, "Far too young. I'm so sorry this happened."

"We all are," Andrei responded quietly.

After twenty minutes, Natalia took Vladi by the arm. "It's time we get you home. I could use a drink, how about you?"

"You don't have to ask me twice, let's go," Vladi replied.

Chapter 3

The harbor in Cabo San Lucas was small. As such, cruise ships had to tender their passengers to the docks to come ashore. It was ten a.m. when Mike, Julie and the kids joined the line to board the waiting tenders. The tenders would work all day taking passengers into port as well as bringing them back to the ship from their day in town. The ride took about ten minutes as the tenders weaved through fishing boats anchored in the harbor. Cabo was known for its billfish tournaments and one was happening over the next four days. All told there were over one hundred and twenty private and commercial fishing boats competing for $1,165,000 in prize money.

Mike was in awe as they passed slowly by some of the nicest yachts he'd ever seen.

"Can you believe these boats?" he asked Julie. "I wonder what the entry fee is for the tournament?"

"I read about it in the ship's newsletter last night. It said the fee to participate was $5,000," Julie explained.

"Wow, you have to have some bucks for a hobby like this," said Mike.

"Well, if you think about it, if your boat team has ten people, that's only $500 per person, so, it may not be that bad."

"All I know is I'm out of their league, for now," Mike replied, wishing he could participate one day. "Maybe someday."

As the tender eased next to the dock, two deckhands jumped off the boat and secured the lines fore and aft. Once secure, they rolled portable stairs next to the vessel and locked it in place, preparing to offload the passengers. Once on shore, Mike led the way toward Marina Boulevard, the busy street in front of the docks. People that had purchased excursions on board the ship waited by the appropriate buses to board. For those who had opted to sightsee or do an excursion on their own, a line of cabs waited to assist. It was busy, with tourists milling about.

Mike walked towards the first cab. The driver hopped out and opened the back door, "Where can I take you, amigo?"

"What's the cost to go to the Dolphin Discovery in San Jose?" Mike asked.

"That's a long way, my friend. But I will take you for $100 U.S."

Mike started to walk away.

"Wait, amigo. What will you pay?" asked the driver.

Mike replied, "$30 U.S."

"$50, and we go? Come on, I will take you," insisted the driver.

Mike looked at Julie and the kids. "Hop in guys, let's go see the dolphins."

***

The cab ride to the Breathless Resort was less than five minutes. The hotel's infinity edge pool looked out over the harbor and created an illusion that the two were connected. The *Seven Seas Mariner* could be seen in the distance at anchor, with a constant procession of tenders shuttling passengers back and forth. Jason stood in the pool. The water was chest deep. He faced Brenda, who was reading a magazine on a chaise lounge under an umbrella. Jason smiled, relaxing for the first time in a long time.

20

He had Brenda with him, a Cussler novel and a Don Julio margarita. Life couldn't be better.

***

The two men watched from their Toyota as Petronovich and the older couple got in the car and pulled out of the cemetery's parking area. One of the men ran the car's plates, noting the owner's address. They were NSC (National Security Committee) agents. The KGB in Kazakhstan had been dissolved in December 1991 and replaced by this organization. At the time, Dimitri Lebedev had been a young KGB agent in the Almaty station. Now, as chief of the station, he had directed his two agents to follow Petronovich after learning Vladimir was on a Lufthansa flight manifest and going to enter the country. Lebedev, like many in 1989, had been furious that Petronovich had defected to the U.S., after receiving an offer to work with the CIA. George Bush, Director of the CIA at the time, initiated the program to attract KGB Agents as the U.S.S.R. crumbled.

In Russia, the foreign intelligence arm of the KGB had been replaced by the Foreign Intelligence Service (SVR) after a failed attempt to depose President Mikhail Gorbachev. Sergey Naryshkin, now Assistant Director of the SVR, had gone through the Moscow Academy, the KGB's top-secret school at the same time as Dimitri Lebedev. To this day, both remained friends. After seeing the flight manifest, Lebedev phoned Naryshkin.

Looking at his phone, Naryshkin answered, "Dimitri, how are you, my friend?"

"I'm doing well, Sergey, and you?"

"I cannot complain. It's not snowing yet, so I'm enjoying life before it begins to freeze, once again."

21

"I know what you mean," Lebedev responded. "Do you still have the list?"

"You are referring to the one we compiled in '89?" Naryshkin asked.

"The very same. There were ten names on that list at the beginning. How many remain unaccounted for?" Lebedev asked.

"Six are outstanding, do you have something to say?" Naryshkin prodded.

"We may soon bring the number down to five. Do you recall Vladimir Petronovich?" Dimitri waited for the answer, knowing it already.

"You know I do, Dimitri. Petronovich had the greatest number of kills. His reputation as an assassin was impeccable, and he was highly regarded. It was as though he stabbed us all in the back when he defected. I've always hated that son of a bitch!" Thoughts of Petronovich brought back gut-wrenching feelings and Naryshkin was close to losing control. "Dimitri, what do you know?"

"He's in Almaty! He came back! I'm having him followed at this moment. I wanted to be sure you were prepared to accept him, at the border, once we take him down," Lebedev explained. "Technically, he has done nothing wrong. But I cannot allow this traitor to remain free. Are the others still at Perm-36?" Lebedev asked.

"Yes, they are there. I have been able to keep it open on a limited basis with funds I've diverted from my budget. As far as the Russian Government, public or the world, for that matter, are concerned, the Gulag system no longer exists," Naryshkin explained.

"But it does at one facility for a limited few, correct?" Lebedev asked.

"Yes, one day, we hope to have ten permanent guests," said Naryshkin.

***

The cab dropped Jason and Brenda off at the marina. Lines for the tenders were growing as passengers returned from their shopping or various excursions.

"I hope the kids had a fun time with the dolphins," Brenda said as they waited their turn to board.

"How could they not? I would have enjoyed watching Zach and Sam play in the water with them. But I must admit, I think the pool at Breathless was probably more relaxing," said Jason as he followed Brenda onto the tender.

They made their way back to the cabins. Mike and Julie's suite was next door to Jason and Brenda's. Before going into their cabin to freshen up, Jason tapped on Mike's door.

"Let's see how their day was," Jason said.

Zach opened the door. "It's Uncle Jason and Aunt Brenda!"

"Let them in Zach," Mike said from the balcony. "Jason, grab a drink and come out. The kids have been waiting to tell you both about the dolphins."

***

It was seven p.m. when the NSC Agents pulled into Mikhailov's driveway. They took the steps up to the porch two at a time and knocked at the front door. Andrei opened it. "Can I help you?"

"Mr. Mikhailov, we would like to speak with your guest, Vladimir Petronovich," said the Agent.

Vladi came up behind Andrei. "I'm Petronovich."

"Can you please step outside for a moment?" asked the agent.

Petronovich looked at Andrei. "Go inside. I'll be just a minute."

Andrei did as he was told and shut the door after Vladi had stepped out.

The second agent stood behind Petronovich with a gun drawn, placed against Vladi's ribs.

"Hands behind your back," he said.

Petronovich complied while he was cuffed and led down the stairs to the car. The agents forced him into the backseat, as Natalia and Andrei watched from the living room window. They wasted no time in starting the car and heading back toward the precinct.

***

The room was sterile with a table and two chairs across from each other. His handcuffs were taken off.

"Sit," commanded the agent as he pointed at the chair.

Petronovich sat. "Why have you taken me? I've done nothing wrong."

The agent ignored the question and stood by the door.

Petronovich looked up as the door swung open and Dimitri Lebedev walked in. "It's been a long time, Vladimir Petronovich."

"I wondered who was behind this. You haven't changed at all, Dimitri," Petronovich said as he watched Lebedev take a seat across from him. "You're just as much a low-life piece of scum now as you were when you left the Academy twenty-five years ago."

"That's all you've got, Vladi? Coming from a piece of shit that betrayed his own country," Lebedev responded. "I'm going to enjoy this more than you know. Do you recall the Gulags?"

"Why? They've been shut down for years," said Petronovich.

"All, but one. There are four inhabitants, soon to be five. You see, Petronovich, we, the old guard, haven't forgotten what you and the other nine traitors did. Our network has kept a constant watch. We have the names of the remaining six, flagged for entry into not only Russia but also the countries that, at one time, were part of the U.S.S.R. As of today, you are the fifth to be captured and your name will now be removed from that list. It's a shame. You had a stellar reputation and you threw it away, for what? Money? You deserve everything you are going to get."

"There were over thirty thousand Gulags back in the day. Where is it that you plan to take me?" Petronovich asked.

"You've heard of Perm-36, haven't you?"

"We used to put political dissidents there that were thought to be the most dangerous," Petronovich responded.

"Precisely! It's fitting, don't you think?" said Lebedev, not waiting for an answer. "Tomorrow, we leave."

Lebedev looked at the guard, "Take him to his cell."

***

There were seven members of the old guard that were recipients of the "list." Ivan Kamarov was one. He had never given it much attention, other than a casual glance. That was, until now. He had recently been promoted to chief of station at the Russian Embassy in Washington, D.C., after having served two years in Riyadh, Saudi Arabia. The memo came as it always did, marked

Confidential-Eyes Only. In other words, to be read only by the twenty individuals designated, no one else. Kamarov noted that there were now only five names on the list, when, for years, there had been six. He scanned it quickly at first, then read it a second time, slowly. The shock hit him as though he'd been kicked in the gut. Vladimir Petronovich, his old partner and friend, even to this day, was no longer mentioned. That could mean only one thing. Vladi had been either eliminated or captured by members intent on bringing the ten traitors to justice.

Kamarov opened his iPhone and dialed Vladi's number. It went directly to voice mail. He then went to his contacts and looked up Jason McClintock. Petronovich had introduced Kamarov to Jason three years earlier. McClintock had been working for the State Department on a mine near Montevideo, Uruguay, at the time. The project had had rogue CIA issues and some very bad actors. Petronovich had been able to help eliminate the problem and get Jason back home safely. Kamarov pulled up Jason's number and dialed.

***

Jason, Brenda and the kids were at the ship's pool when his cell pinged. "Hello?"

"Jason, this is Ivan Kamarov, you're coming in with a little static, where are you?" Kamarov asked.

"In the middle of the Pacific Ocean, on our way to Mazatlan. Something must be wrong, if you're calling, Ivan. What's going on?" said Jason as he rose from the lounge chair and walked away from the pool noise.

"I think we have a problem. I've tried calling Vladi, but can't reach him," Kamarov said. "Do you know where he is?"

26

"He left for Almaty, Kazakhstan, the day before yesterday," Jason said. "Why, is there a problem?"

"You just confirmed my fear. Years ago, when Vladi defected to the U.S., he did so with nine other agents. All were hired by the CIA. A select few KGB agents were furious and pledged to retaliate, no matter how long it took. The names of the defectors were placed on a list. Until now, only four have been eliminated or apprehended. I think that has changed. Vladi's name has always been on the list, but the memo I received today didn't include him."

"The cold war is over, Ivan. How can the government allow this to continue?"

"The government isn't aware of it. If they knew, they would shut it down," Kamarov explained. "There are only seven of us ex-KGB, now SVR or other Intel Agents that are privy to the five outstanding names. I'll do some digging and see if I can find out what happened to Vladi. In the meantime, if you hear from him, let me know. Jason, I may need you and Mike to give me a hand with this."

"Mike and I will do anything we can to help you, Ivan. But, why don't you tell your superiors?" Jason asked.

"I can't. I didn't ask to be a participant in this retribution. But I also didn't request that the memo with defector names stop being sent to me. In a sense, I'm complicit. If we are exposed, it won't look good for us and would probably mean prison. I've never taken an active role in looking for these men. At the time, the Soviet Union was crumbling, and people everywhere were making changes. To me, since the country was falling apart, what these men did was not a treasonous act. In fact, I told Vladi some time ago that I have never begrudged him for making the move to the U.S. I've always felt there are choices in life, and some

27

happen to be more important than others. For these ten men, this was one of those times. I just pray they are still alive."

***

The guards handcuffed Petronovich and escorted him out of his cell. Lebedev was already seated in the front passenger seat of the car when they placed Vladi in the back with one of the guards. The second agent drove the car away from the precinct towards Almaty International. When they reached the airport, the driver turned away from the commercial section and drove toward the FBO terminal used by private pilots. Lebedev had contracted a Learjet 45, which was a midsize business jet, for the trip to Perm, Russia. The flight would take a little less than five hours. Sergey Naryshkin would be waiting on the tarmac for the prisoner transfer. Lebedev planned to remain in Russia only long enough to refuel before returning to Almaty. His part in apprehending the 'traitor' was over and he couldn't be happier to have Naryshkin take responsibility for the subject.

As promised, a black SUV was on the tarmac, waiting near the FBO terminal when the jet from Almaty arrived. The stairs were lowered and Lebedev was first to leave the plane. Sergey Naryshkin waited at the bottom.

"Dimitri, how are you, my friend?" Naryshkin asked as they shook hands. "I can't remember the last time we saw each other."

"Sergey, you look good. It has been a while," Lebedev responded.

"After we process Petronovich, will you have time for drinks and food?"

"Not this trip Sergey. This is a quick turnaround. I need to get back to Almaty. Are you prepared to take on this prisoner?"

28

Lebedev asked.

"Certainly. We have a cell waiting for him with the others. It's been twenty-five years since they defected, but we've only had the opportunity to get these five in the last few years."

"I think, as they've grown older, they've become complacent, thinking nobody cares about them anymore," Lebedev said.

"That may be, but if that's the case, they are mistaken," Naryshkin said as he looked up and watched Petronovich being escorted down the stairs. "Valdimir Petronovich, you don't know how glad I am to see you!"

"Naryshkin, some things never change! I assume you are the same psychotic, narcissistic asshole as you ever were. I've been following your career and understand you are Deputy Director. With your personality traits, I'd expect you to be Director by now," Petronovich said.

"Save your energy, Petronovich. Where you're going, you're going to need it," responded Naryshkin.

"Put him in the SUV," said Naryshkin, looking at the guard.

***

It was five thirty when Jason and Brenda found seating for six in the observation lounge on deck twelve. The seating area couldn't have been any better. Floor-to-ceiling windows overlooking the bow presented an unsurpassed view as the ship cut through the seas and the sun began to set. The cocktail waitress was setting their drinks on the table when Mike and Julie walked up.

"Perfect timing," Jason said.

"The usual, Mr. and Mrs. McClintock?" asked the cocktail waitress with a smile.

"That would be great, Robin, thank you," replied Mike as he and Julie sat in the two armchairs across from Jason and Brenda.

"Where are the kids?" asked Brenda.

"They're watching a movie. I told them we'd pick them up for dinner in about an hour or so," Julie replied.

Once the drinks were delivered, Jason spoke. "We're all concerned about Vladi. I've been thinking that we've got to do more than wait on Kamarov to get back to us."

"We're on the same page, Jason," Mike said.

"Vladi is a CIA asset, still obligated to work for them if needed. As Kamarov said, the others were hired by the CIA as well. I don't have contacts inside the Agency, but we both know someone who does," Mike continued, looking at Jason.

"Are you thinking Schumacher?" Jason asked.

"He's Special Agent in Charge of the Los Angeles FBI field office. He interfaces with the spooks all the time. They've got to know that they have assets missing. They may not know the exact number, since it appears Vladi has only recently been abducted, but they will soon enough," explained Mike. "I'm going to give Jack a call. You guys wait here, I will only be a minute."

Mike left his drink on the table and crossed the room toward a secluded and private alcove. *We're only an hour ahead, so he's probably still in the office,* Mike thought as he dialed. Petronovich had been instrumental in assisting the FBI last year, when the city of Los Angeles had been threatened by a Saudi terrorist cell, intent on detonating a nuclear device in the downtown business district. It was Jack Schumacher's FBI resources that had provided Vladi with a helicopter to transport the suitcase device off the coast where, with only minutes to spare, he had dumped it into deep water before it had exploded. Jack recognized the number and answered immediately. "Mike, what's going on?"

"Jack, you remember Kamarov, right?"

"Sure, his Russian contacts helped us trace the Los Angeles terrorist through the guy's cell phone, why?" Jack asked.

"You also know that Vladi worked for the CIA and was once with the KGB," Mike continued. "Jason received a call from Kamarov this morning. He believes that Petronovich has been taken by a rogue group of old KGB Agents. They appear to have a vendetta against him."

"Did this happen on U.S. soil?" Schumacher asked.

"No, Vladi is, or was, supposed to be on vacation in Kazakhstan. Kamarov said there were ten people that have been targeted, and now five, including Vladi, appear to be in custody, or worse, eliminated. Your CIA counterpart in L.A. must be aware of their missing assets. I know, from my experience that these people tend to be tight-lipped, but sometimes a good relationship makes the difference. Can you contact that person, if you feel it might help and see what they know? Kamarov is working out of the Russian Embassy in D.C. He's using his network, but we may be able to find what happened to Vladi faster if the SVR, CIA and FBI work together," Mike explained. "I think time may be of the essence."

"I'll make the call right now and get back to you," Schumacher said, not waiting for a response.

Chapter 4

Ivan Kamarov sat in his office at the Russian Embassy in Washington, D.C. He knew what he had to do, but didn't want to appear concerned or anxious when he made the call to Dimitri Lebedev in Kazakhstan. Lebedev ran the NSC office in Almaty. If Petronovich was visiting Almaty, it only made sense that Lebedev was involved in his disappearance. Ivan scrolled through his Rolodex, picked up the phone and dialed. Almaty was eleven hours ahead, so it would be two a.m. Kamarov didn't care, he knew someone would answer and at least he could have a message waiting for Lebedev to return his call, day or night. He was reluctant to call anyone else before speaking with Lebedev. The last thing he wanted to do was arouse suspicions that he was concerned about the "list." If Lebedev went to work between eight and nine in the morning, Kamarov expected a call sometime tonight between seven and eight. He had about four hours to wait.

***

The drive from the airport to Perm-36 was a little less than one hour. Petronovich didn't say a word until the SUV pulled up to the fenced complex. A guard came out of the nondescript shack, and, without saying a word, unlocked and swung open the gate for the car to pass.

"Naryshkin, you can't keep me," Petronovich said.

"Where do you think you are, the U.S.? Let me remind you,

you are now in Russia, and in the custody of the SVR," Naryshkin answered. "You betrayed our country twenty-five years ago, and we haven't forgotten. For that, you will spend the rest of your days here, I assure you. Many prisoners, after experiencing the hardship of life in this place, get creative and find ways to commit suicide. Some are quite innovative. You may want to consider that. Or, simply try to escape and we will accommodate you with a bullet to the head."

The black SUV drove toward the back of the seemingly deserted complex and parked out of sight of the main road. To the casual observer, Perm-36 appeared to be uninhabited. Petronovich was escorted from the car, in shackles, and down a series of steps to a solid steel door. The guard rapped on the door with the palm of his hand. After a minute, you could hear the various locks being disengaged and the heavy portal swung open, the sound of metal on metal grinding, with hinges in need of oil. The corridor was dark and damp, lit by a single bare light bulb hanging from the ceiling. The light stayed on twenty-four hours a day. The sound of shoes and shackles being dragged along the concrete floor was all that was heard as they took Petronovich past solid steel doors on either side of the dingy hall. Each door had a small slit, wide enough to pass a tray with a bowl. The cells held prisoners. How many, you couldn't tell. A guard at the end of the hallway held a door open and waited as Petronovich approached. They took off his shackles, shoved him inside, then slammed and locked the heavy barrier. Once inside, Petronovich stood while his eyes adjusted to the slim sliver of light that penetrated the small opening in the door. The cell was maybe eight feet by ten, with a bare cot made of wooden planks and a hole in the ground for a toilet. Petronovich sat on the wood platform and began to shake as the bitter cold infused his body.

***

The CIA field office was only two blocks from Schumacher. Jack picked up the phone and speed dialed his counterpart, Mark (Whit) Whittington. Looking at the number, Whit answered, "What's going on, Jack?"

"Can you give me fifteen minutes, Whit, at our usual spot?" Schumacher asked.

"Sure, I'll be there in thirty."

Both men approached the corner coffee shop from different directions. Schumacher had a table for two in the back, away from other patrons when Whittington walked in. He glanced at Jack, walked to the counter and ordered a large black coffee, which he took to the table.

"What's up, Jack?" Whit asked as he sat.

"I'm going to come right to the point, Whit. Is the agency missing any former KGB assets?"

Whittington looked at Schumacher for probably ten seconds, then responded, "Where did you get that information, Jack?"

"Ivan Kamarov, the guy that helped us last year with the terrorist attack, contacted Jason McClintock. I'm sure you know about McClintock," Schumacher said.

"Right, he helped Petronovich a couple years back down in Montevideo," Whit responded.

"Exactly. Anyway, Kamarov has been trying to get in touch with Petronovich without success. He believes that Petronovich has been taken by a group of rogue former KGB agents. Answer my question, Whit," said Jack, "Are you missing any former KGB assets, like Petronovich?"

"This is strictly confidential, Jack, understood?" Whit asked.

34

"Yes. Go ahead."

"In the last three years, we've lost contact with four assets. They were each traveling out of the country at various times. They simply disappeared. Family and friends have no idea what happened to them or where they might be. What you've said seems improbable, but certainly plausible, since we've come up blank. When these men came over in 1989, it was at the height of the cold war and tensions were high. I can imagine there might be a group of individuals incapable of letting the fall of the Soviet Union go, even after all these years."

"Well, now you seem to be missing five," Schumacher said.

***

Ivan Kamarov fidgeted with his notepad. It was eight-thirty p.m. and the call he was expecting had not come through. *I'll give Lebedev thirty minutes, then try him again,* he thought just as the secure line at his desk rang.

"This is Kamarov," he answered.

"Kamarov, this is Lebedev, returning your call."

"I received the memo yesterday with the list of names outstanding. I was curious about the disposition of the five in custody. Do you know the status?" Kamarov asked.

"I'm not sure you want to know. What do they say, plausible deniability?" Lebedev said.

"I think I'm past that point, Lebedev, being a recipient of the list for so many years. Wouldn't you agree?" Kamarov asked.

"You're probably right," Lebedev answered. "They are being held at a facility east of Moscow. Sergey Naryshkin is responsible for their incarceration. Vladimir Petronovich was transferred yesterday."

"East of Moscow? Where?" asked Kamarov.

"I don't know the location, but it's supposed to be in the Ural Mountains, near the Siberian border. It's in the forest, very secluded, according to Naryshkin," explained Lebedev, choosing not to reveal the exact location. "I wouldn't want to be there. As far as the government is concerned, it doesn't exist. Naryshkin has used a small portion of the SVR budget to keep the facility partially operational."

"So, only a small group of people support it?"

"Yes, as I understand, it's a skeleton crew," replied Lebedev. "Does that satisfy your curiosity?"

"It does. Thank you for bringing me up to speed," Kamarov said, then hung up.

***

The guard finally left, slamming and locking the door behind him. Petronovich looked up when someone in one of the cells called out in a central Russian dialect, "Hey, newcomer, what's your name?"

Petronovich rose from the wood cot, walked to the door, and spoke with an eastern Russian accent. "Vladimir Petronovich, and you?"

"Alexander Sokolov. Where are you from, Petronovich?" Sokolov asked.

"Recently, the U.S. What about you?" Petronovich asked.

Sokolov reverted to English. "Denver, Colorado."

"Dana Point, California," said Petronovich, also in English. "How long have you been here, Sokolov?" Petronovich followed.

"About three months. There are three others who have been here longer. I think two to three years. They hardly ever talk. I

36

did learn that they also have Eastern Bloc backgrounds and are from the states as well."

"That's not a coincidence. Were you KGB, back in the day?" Petronovich continued, "And, if I had to guess, you accepted employment with the CIA, right?"

"Right! We all have the same story. We've been targeted. By the looks of things, we may be here a while."

"You might be right, Sokolov. How often do the guards come around?"

"Twice a day, morning and night. Most of the time it's only one guy. He brings a pot and passes each of us a bowl of broth. I think I've lost twenty pounds. I can't imagine how the other three are looking. My wife wanted me to lose some weight, but this is ridiculous."

"What about water?"

"There's a tin cup somewhere in your cell. They fill that up as well."

"Do they ever let you outside?" Petronovich asked.

"None of us have seen the light of day since we arrived. They never open the door, so we haven't had the opportunity to overpower the guard. Not that any one of us could, at this point, given our physical condition. The bowl and cup are passed through the slot. Petronovich, do you know where we are?" Sokolov asked.

"You've heard of Perm-36?"

"Sure, that's the place where political prisoners that the government feared most were sent. It had the worst reputation of all the gulags," Sokolov answered.

"From what I've seen so far, this place seems to be everything they said it is, and more," Petronovich replied, trying to add a touch of humor.

"I like that, Petronovich. New blood, with a fresh attitude. It won't be long, though, before you begin to live within your mind and pray for physical death, just like the rest of us. I say physical, only because for all intents and purposes, we're already dead. There is nothing more to talk about unless you can come up with a plan to get us out of here."

"Let me think about it, Sokolov," Petronovich replied as he took a couple of steps back and sat down on the wood planks.

***

Julie continued to read as Mike turned the light off on his side of the bed. He closed his eyes and fell asleep almost immediately. Mike's phone buzzed on the nightstand, but he didn't hear it. Julie shook his shoulder.

"Mike, your phone is ringing."

Mike stirred, and rolled toward the nightstand, reaching for the phone. "Hello."

"Mike, this is Jack, I spoke to Whittington, head of the CIA office in L.A. He confirmed they are missing four Russian assets, now probably five, with Petronovich unaccounted for. Whit is passing the information Kamarov gave you on to Langley. Our human intelligence contacts in Russia may be able to shed some light on the men's whereabouts, but that's highly unlikely. I was asked if you or Jason might speak with Kamarov and let him know that we (the U.S. Government) would appreciate any help he might be able to provide in finding them. With everyone's reputation in mind, our coordinated activity would be unofficial, under the radar."

"I think the best shot we have of finding these guys is Kamarov since he's one of the seven that receives the list. I'll ask

38

Jason to talk with him and see if we might be able to work together. As soon as we're able to connect, I'll call you back," Mike said.

With his mind racing, Mike couldn't sleep. It was only a little after ten p.m. He texted Jason, *Are you awake?*

The response was immediate: *What's up?*

We need to talk, Mike typed. *Can we get a drink at the lounge? I can be ready in 5 minutes.*

Sure, Jason responded.

Light piano music was being played as they entered. The lounge was busy with people in groups talking and enjoying themselves. Mike found a table off to the side.

"What's on your mind?" Jason asked.

"I just talked with Schumacher. He spoke with the CIA guy in L.A. It turns out, just as Kamarov said, they are missing four agents. He asked that you contact Kamarov and see if there might be some way for him to work with us," Mike explained.

"By us, you're talking about the CIA, right?" Jason asked.

"The CIA, and maybe you and me. I can't sit and do nothing when I know that Vladi is in danger and needs our help," Mike said.

"If we are going to get involved, we need to decide soon. The ship arrives in Mazatlan tomorrow morning. After that, we're at sea for three days. Mazatlan is where we catch the plane if we're going to do this. I'll call Kamarov right now," said Jason as he looked up the number in his contact list.

***

After the call with Lebedev, Kamarov felt unsettled. Lebedev knew more than he was willing to share. Specifically, the location of the prisoners. The Urals were a mountain range running one thousand, six hundred miles north to south through western Russia. So, to only say the prisoners were being held east of Moscow, somewhere in the Urals, was being quite vague. Kamarov looked at the time. It was approaching eleven p.m., *I'd better pack up and get home,* he thought. Just as he was leaving the office, his cell buzzed. He looked at the phone, turned the office lights back on and sat down at the desk.

"Jason, hello," Kamarov answered.

"Ivan, we spoke with Schumacher, you remember him," Jason responded, knowing he would. "He talked with the CIA and confirmed they are missing five Russian assets, including Vladi. They asked if you would be able to assist them, unofficially, in searching for the men. Given your position, you would have access to information that we could never get."

"Yes and no. Jason, this is a rogue group. I tried to get the prisoner's location, but wasn't able. I was told that Vladi was transferred to a facility yesterday. From where? I can only assume, Almaty. Lebedev, head of NSC in Almaty, is certainly responsible for Vladi's capture, but he's also tight-lipped about the prison location."

"What do you suggest we do?" Jason asked.

There was silence at the other end. Finally, Kamarov spoke. "I cannot leave Washington. But I do have a close contact, also SVR, in Moscow, who may be willing to help us. He knows Vladi. In fact, he helped Petronovich in the Maldives last year."

"I remember Vladi mentioning he had some help. He wasn't specific, though," Jason said.

"His name is Vasily Volkov. He's a younger guy, but very good at his trade. I can probably get him to take a trip to Almaty and pay a visit to Lebedev. I think Volkov may be able to provide enough persuasion to get Lebedev to reveal the location. Do you think you could take some time to assist him? He may need help once we get the prison's location."

"I already told you that Mike and I would not hesitate to help if we could. We'll take a flight out of Mazatlan tomorrow and plan on meeting Volkov in Almaty," said Jason. "I'll text our itinerary when we have it. Thanks for the help, Ivan." Jason put the phone on the table and looked at Mike. "I guess we're on our way to Kazakhstan. What do we do with Brenda, Julie, and the kids?"

"They might as well finish the cruise," Mike said. "There's Mazatlan tomorrow and Ensenada a few days after that."

***

Kamarov was in his office early the next morning. He couldn't sleep, thinking about the conversation he'd had with Jason and the call he was about to make to Volkov. Getting Volkov involved could jeopardize his career since what he was about to propose wasn't sanctioned by SVR leadership. It couldn't be, because of Naryshkin's position as Deputy Director. He'd shut it down immediately and any hope of recovering the prisoners would be gone. It was eight a.m. in Washington. *Volkov should be at his desk,* thought Kamarov. Moscow was eight hours ahead, so it would be four in the afternoon. He picked up the secure phone and dialed Volkov.

"Ivan! It's good to hear from you! How do you like your assignment in D.C.?" asked Volkov after picking up the line.

"It's not exciting, Vasily, mostly politics. It's not my cup of tea, as the Brits say!" responded Kamarov. "How's your position in Moscow? Why aren't you in the field instead of at a desk? Are they still pissed at you?"

"They call it a teaching moment, Ivan. After I helped Petronovich eliminate the three Saudi goons protecting the prince, and then the prince himself, they felt I needed some time in-house, out of the field. I've been here a year and I think they are finally looking to post me somewhere else. I don't know how they could find a place any more subdued than my last assignment. A resort island in the Maldives, running a dive shop, but I believe they are looking for such a place. It may take a little time for them to trust me again."

"I think you are being too hard on yourself. I am, however, glad you brought up the Maldives, Vasily. Petronovich is in trouble. You have some vacation time, correct?" asked Kamarov.

"Yeah, sure, two weeks. What's happened to Vladi?"

"I believe he's been kidnapped by a group still pissed that he left the KGB and joined the CIA," explained Kamarov. "He's not alone. There are four others that have been taken. We don't know where they are being held, but I think I know who does. I want you to have a little chat with him if you know what I mean?"

"The kind of chat that Vladi and I had with the prince?" asked Volkov.

"Not quite that harsh. Just get him to tell you the prison's location, and promise not to tell anyone that you know. Impress him with the fact that if he does, he will face serious, potentially deadly, consequences," Kamarov explained.

"That should be easy enough. Who is this guy?" asked Volkov.

"He's the head of a station for the NSC in Almaty, Kazakhstan. He is ex-KGB. I'm going to send two Americans to help you. They are close friends of Vladi's and I can vouch for them. You will leave once I get their flight plans to Almaty. Any questions?"

"No. I'm looking forward to getting away from this desk. Thank you for the opportunity, Ivan."

"You're welcome. There is one more thing, though. This assignment is not sanctioned. If you are caught, we could both be prosecuted. I understand if you're not willing to take the risk. Just say so now."

"I'm in one hundred percent! Let me know when I fly to Almaty. I'm looking forward to this vacation!" said Volkov with excitement in his voice.

Chapter 5

Mike was up and had his bag packed before the kids woke. He watched from the balcony table as the small cruise ship approached the mouth of Mazatlan's harbor and the city lights in the distance. Julie opened the sliding door and handed Mike a cup of coffee as she pulled a chair out and sat next to him.

"It's a little chilly out here," Julie commented.

"It is, but I like it," Mike responded. "Julie, I want you and the kids to stay on the ship while you're in port. I don't think Mazatlan is the safest place in Mexico. In fact, the headquarters for the Sinaloa cartel is in Culiacan, a city north of town."

"We will. The kids can keep busy in the pool. Mike, I don't like you taking off again, but I understand why you need to do it," said Julie.

"I don't like it either, but we can't sit and wait. If we can help Kamarov's guy find Vladi, we must. He would do it for us," Mike explained. "You have five more days on the ship. Try and enjoy it. Jason and I will be home with Vladi as soon as we can."

"How long is your flight?" asked Julie.

"It's a long one, about twenty one and a half hours. We fly into Houston first, then onto Frankfurt. From there we have a direct flight to Almaty. I texted Kamarov our schedule so his guy, Volkov, should meet us at the airport. I'll phone when we get into Kazakhstan," Mike said.

They sat in silence for the next forty-five minutes, watching as the ship moved slowly up the harbor into the port. Each lost in their own thoughts, worried about the potential danger that might be waiting in Kazakhstan and Russia.

"We'll leave the ship as soon as we can. The window to catch our flight is tight," Mike said as he rose from the table and entered the suite.

***

Petronovich was curled up in the fetal position, trying to retain body heat, as he dozed fitfully. He stirred as he heard the clanging of keys and squeaking of the heavy metal door, from down the hall, as it opened. The guard pounded on each cell door, as he slowly made his way toward Petronovich's hole at the end. This was the prisoner's cue to put their bowl and cup for broth and water through the slot in the door to be filled. Only occasional grunts were heard as the guard lifted the large hot pot and plastic jug of water when he moved. Not a single word was spoken by the inmates.

After the guard had left, Petronovich rose from the cot and spoke through the slot. "Sokolov, can you hear me?"

"Are you getting my hopes up, Petronovich? I told you, there is no need to talk unless you can come up with a way to get us out of here. Have you done that?" Sokolov asked.

"Maybe. I still have my strength. When the guard comes back tonight, I want you to get his attention. Tell him I've been groaning and moaning, as if in pain, all day. Urge him to check on me. When he opens the cell door, I'll try to overpower him, and get the keys," Petronovich explained.

"That is assuming he doesn't call for backup before opening the door," Sokolov responded.

"This is where you need to sell the fact that I'm seriously ill

45

and may already be dead; that I'm in bad shape. If he believes you, he may open the door to check. He won't be able to see a thing through the slot, because I'll have my back to him, lying on the cot. What do you say?" Petronovich asked.

At that point, a whisper from one of the other's cells could be barely heard: "You are fucking nuts. They will kill us all if you fail."

"We're already dead, asshole," Sokolov hissed. "It's worth a shot, Petronovich. I'll do it."

***

Volkov's flight from Moscow landed about thirty minutes before the McClintocks. It was five thirty p.m. The flight from Frankfurt was on time, if not a little early when Volkov walked up to the gate. Passengers from the Air Astana flight had just started coming off. Kamarov had texted Volkov the flight number, arrival time and description of Jason McClintock. Kamarov had met Jason once before in Montevideo, Uruguay a couple of years ago, but he'd never met Mike. Volkov was looking for a tall guy with blonde hair, about mid-forties. The fifth and sixth passengers to exit looked like the Americans he was supposed to meet.

Volkov walked up to the two men. "Would you be the McClintock brothers?"

"So, you are Volkov," Jason said as he shook the Russian's hand. "This is my brother, Mike."

Pleasantries were exchanged and then Volkov suggested, "Let's walk. I'm assuming you carried on?"

"We travel light," Mike said. "Where are we headed?"

"I took the liberty of reserving two rooms at the Holiday Inn.

I hope you don't mind?" Volkov explained. "The website said the hotel is located not more than ten minutes from the airport."

"Sounds good to me. I can't wait for a shower and stiff drink, not necessarily in that order, after spending two days on airplanes," Mike followed.

"I can make that happen," said Volkov as he flagged down a cab outside the passenger terminal.

The ride was as expected. The cab pulled up to a modern looking ten-story structure with a light blue glass façade. *This isn't like any Holiday Inn I've ever stayed in,* thought Jason as he exited the cab.

"This is pretty nice," Jason said. "It looks new."

"Almaty is a growing city. With the oil fields nearby, they are trying to accommodate the executives, from around the world, who are flying in to do business," Volkov explained. "You're right, this is a newer facility. I'm sure they will have an upscale restaurant and bar. It may not be like the Ritz, but it will be nice."

The three checked in and promised to meet in the bar at seven.

***

Schumacher's intercom buzzed with his secretary saying, "I have Mark Whittington on the line."

"Send him through," said Schumacher.

"What have you got, Whit?" asked Schumacher.

"I have eyes and ears in Kazakhstan and Russia. They are aware of the assets we are looking for. If this is a small cell of rogue agents, as your guy has intimated, it will be like looking for a needle in the proverbial haystack. But, if Kamarov's guy

47

can get the prisoner location, we can assist by providing exfil transportation, using private contractors we have available in-country," Whit said. "I can't promise manpower for the snatch and grab operation once we find them, but I'll do my best to try."

"Okay, at least we've got the ball rolling. Jason and Mike should be in Almaty now with Kamarov's guy. I'll let you know the results of the 'conversation' they have with the NSC chief," Schumacher said.

"Sounds good. I'll be in touch if we get anything at our end," Whit answered as he cut the call.

***

"Sokolov, the guard will be here soon. Are you ready?" Petronovich asked.

"I'll do my part. Make sure you act deathly ill, or, better yet, dead," Sokolov replied.

The men waited for another hour before they heard the car pull up outside. Minutes later, the heavy steel door squeaked open, shedding light in the hall before being slammed shut and locked.

"Guard, guard!" Sokolov shouted in Russian.

"What do you want, prisoner?" asked the guard as he set the pot of broth and jug of water on the ground.

"The new man who was brought in yesterday is sick. He's been groaning and carrying on all day, up until about two hours ago. I think he might be dead. There's been no noise from his cell," Sokolov explained.

The guard listened to Sokolov and then walked over to Petronovich's cell.

"Prisoner, get up!" he called in a stern voice as he peered

through the slot in the door. Petronovich didn't move.

He called out again, "Prisoner, I said get up."

There was still no movement. At this point, the guard was tentative. He reached for his keys, then stopped, as if trying to decide what to do.

Sokolov called out again, trying to push him into acting. "Guard, you can't let him die! Do something."

The guard looked back toward Sokolov's cell, then pulled the keys from his belt and fumbled for the skeleton key that would open the cell door. He inserted the key into the lock hole, but, before turning and unlocking the door, the guard looked through the slot one more time. There was still no movement. He unlocked the door and stepped in. The distance from the guard to the cot where Petronovich was lying, with his back to the door, was only a couple of feet. With cat-like reflexes, using his martial arts skills, Vladi swung his right leg up in a sweeping motion, connecting the heel of his foot with the guard's jaw, which cracked instantly. He dropped to the ground, out cold, as Petronovich swung his body around, off the cot into a defensive stance, ready to continue the fight. It wasn't necessary as the guard wasn't moving. Petronovich left him on the cold floor as he stepped by him. The keys were still in the door as Petronovich closed and locked it.

"Petronovich, hurry," Sokolov whispered.

Without saying a word, Vladi walked to Sokolov's cell and let him out. He was surprised to see a wiry man, maybe 5'10'. He'd lost more like fifty pounds or more, instead of the twenty that Sokolov had suggested the day before. Petronovich unlocked the other three cells, swinging the doors wide open. He looked in each. Skeletons of men looked back from their cots, unable to move. The men looked like the pictures of people from the

German concentration camps. They were extremely malnourished and gaunt, with almost lifeless eyes.

"We can't take them, Petronovich," Said Sokolov as he looked inside the cells.

"We can't leave them. They'll die," Vladi replied.

"The best thing we can do for them is to survive and bring back help. You and I both know it! Look at them, Petronovich! They can't even stand! Lock their cell doors so the guards that come back don't think they tried to escape. Maybe they won't be beaten."

Petronovich did as suggested, telling each man, he would be back with help. "Okay, let's get out of here."

Vladi ushered Sokolov out first, then pulled the door shut. He left it unlocked. After taking what looked like the key to the guard's car, he dropped the ring of keys in the dirt.

"Get in," said Petronovich as he sat behind the wheel of the old Toyota.

***

The hotel lounge was softly lit with dark wood paneling. Volkov had a corner table. He'd ordered a Grey Goose, rocks, and was sipping it when the McClintock brothers walked in. Jason looked at Mike. "I've got the drinks, what do you want?"

"How about a Moscow Mule, given where we are?"

"You got it."

"How was that shower, Mike?" Volkov asked with a smile.

"Great! Now it's time for a much-needed drink," Mike said as he took a seat in the warm, leather, high-backed chair.

Jason came back with the drinks, handing Mike his, while he sipped his Glenfiddich scotch. As he sat, he looked at Volkov,

"So, what's the plan, Volkov?"

"Before we talk business, it is a Russian custom for the host to offer a toast to his guests. Let me begin there. It is my prayer that we find Vladi quickly, in good health, so we can get out of this Godforsaken country."

"I'll drink to that," Mike said. "Now, what do you have in mind with this NSC guy?"

"He's low-life scum, though not as bad as the Deputy Director Sergey Naryshkin. His name is Dimitri Lebedev. Kamarov gave me his home address. He's not married, so it would only make sense to meet him at his house. That way, we can have a private chat."

"When do we do this?" Mike asked.

"We don't. I will handle this on my own. I will most likely need your assistance when Lebedev gives me the prison address," Volkov explained.

"Volkov, we didn't fly for two days only to sit on our hands. Let us help you," Jason responded.

"I appreciate your need to help. The problem is that we are in a foreign country. Sure, Kazakhstan used to be part of the Soviet Union, but it is now a sovereign nation. If something went wrong, we would be in serious trouble and you could be incarcerated for years. I'm willing to take that risk once we are in Russia, but not here. The SVR director, not his deputy, may be more inclined to be lenient with us should we get caught. I frankly don't know what Kamarov was thinking in having you join me here."

"When do you plan on paying this guy a visit?" Mike asked.

"Tonight! But not until after we have a few drinks and a hearty meal. *Na Zdorovie!*" Volkov said as he raised his glass, smiling at the two brothers, looking forward to his meeting later in the evening.

Mike and Jason looked at each other, unsure as to how the evening was shaping up, wondering if Volkov would be able to get the job done. Slowly, they raised their glasses toward Volkov.

***

Petronovich stopped at the gate. The highway sign in front of him indicated that Chusovoy was to the right ten km or six miles. Turning left, going west was the town of Perm, forty-five miles. "We need to go west. The guards most likely live in Chusovoy," Petronovich said, almost to himself.

"We've got to get out of Russia, that's what we need to do. Do you know how far the border is from here?" Sokolov asked.

"No. I think Perm is east of Moscow, but I'm not sure how far. And I know Moscow is a long drive to the western border. Our best bet is to head for Latvia or Estonia if we can. Before that happens, we need to get rid of this car," Petronovich said.

"If we have a drive ahead of us like you're suggesting, how do we pay for gas, without cash or credit cards?" Sokolov asked.

"That's a problem. Also, the way you look will draw attention. Crap, you haven't had a change of clothes or a shower in three months! To be honest, you smell ripe," said Petronovich as he glanced at Sokolov while rolling down the car window. "If we had a phone, I could call Ivan Kamarov and see if he could help."

"You know Kamarov?" Sokolov asked.

"You know him?" asked Petronovich as he looked at Sokolov.

"Yes, one of the first assignments I had after graduating from the academy was with him. He's a good guy. Is he still SVR?"

"He's at the embassy in Washington, D.C.," said Petronovich. "Let's dump the car in Perm and see if we can borrow a phone."

"Sounds good to me, the sooner the better," replied Sokolov.

***

With dinner finished, Mike and Jason nursed their third drink, while Volkov finished the last of his fifth vodka. He set the glass on the table, not looking the least bit phased.

"It's time to go to work, gentlemen. I shouldn't be any more than a couple hours, say midnight, one at the latest. When I get back, I'll call." He stood and smiled. "This should be fun."

"Don't enjoy it too much, Volkov. Get the information and get out," said Mike.

Volkov smiled and walked away without saying another word.

"He seems to be a bit cocky," Jason said, as he watched him walk out of the restaurant.

"Vladi said he may have saved his life down in the Maldives. He must be good at what he does. Kamarov said the same thing," Mike replied.

"Maybe so, I just hope he gets the information, so we can get out of here," Jason responded. "We might as well get a little shut-eye. If we can fly out tonight, I'd like to."

Mike stood, placing cash for dinner and drinks on the table. "Next time, it's on Volkov. Let's go."

***

Almaty was the largest city in Kazakhstan, with a population of over two million. Dimitri Lebedev lived in the suburbs, about thirty minutes from the Holiday Inn. Volkov drove the speed limit and followed the GPS instructions without any issues. As he neared the address of the single-family home, Volkov slowed and stopped several houses away. It was a little after eleven p.m. and what looked to be a bedroom light could be seen in the back of the house. Volkov waited for it to switch off, then after ten minutes, got out and moved through the shadows toward the house. He circled around back, toward the door. Using his lock picks, Volkov unlocked the bolt.

Lebedev heard the movement on the porch through the bedroom window that was open. He grabbed the handgun on the bedstand and moved quickly to the kitchen. He stood next to the door so that when it opened, he would be behind it. The soft sound of the lock being picked was distinct. Lebedev was ready with his gun raised.

Volkov stepped quietly across the threshold as he eased open the door. Relieved that there was no alarm, he took a second step across the room with his Glock up and ready. It was then that he felt the cold steel against the back of his head.

"Drop the weapon, now!" said Lebedev. "Get on the ground."

Doing as he was told, Volkov dropped to his knees. His arms were outstretched as he slowly bent and placed the Glock on the linoleum.

"Lie on your stomach, arms out to your sides, palms up. What do you want?" asked Lebedev as he kicked Volkov's handgun across the room.

Volkov followed the instructions. "I'm SVR," he replied, facing the floor.

"What would the SVR want with me?" Lebedev asked.

"You've traveled a long way, there must be a good reason. Let's have it."

Volkov remained mute.

Lebedev said, "If that's how you want to play, fine."

Lebedev used the voice commands on his cell and phoned the precinct. The operator answered. Lebedev ordered back up to his home address. Then, looking at the intruder on the floor, he said, "We'll continue this conversation downtown, where I'm certain we will get the answers I'm looking for."

***

Petronovich parked the car in a crowded lot near the Perm train station.

"Stay here. Let me see if I can borrow a phone from someone," said Petronovich as he glanced back while opening the car door.

"I'm not going anywhere," replied Sokolov.

Petronovich walked across the lot. As he did, he noticed an older couple that had parked. They were getting luggage out of the trunk when he approached.

"Excuse me?" said Petronovich as he walked up.

"Yes?" said the man as he slammed the trunk shut and stared at Petronovich's disheveled appearance.

"Could I ask a huge favor? I was mugged and have lost my wallet and phone. Could I borrow your phone?"

"Did you report this to the police?" asked the man, not believing the story.

"I haven't yet, but I will. I wanted to call my wife first," said Petronovich.

"So, it's a local call. What is your wife's number, I'll dial," replied the elderly man.

"It's out of country, sorry," Petronovich said.

"What country?"

"United States. Please, sir, it's important," Petronovich pleaded.

The old guy put his phone in his pocket, looked at his wife and said, "Let's go," as they started walking, not looking back.

Petronovich watched them, then realized they were heading directly toward a police officer standing by the main terminal door. He quickly turned and jogged toward Sokolov and the parked car.

"What's going on?" asked Sokolov as he opened his door.

"Get out and follow me," Petronovich said as he looked across the lot and saw three police officers coming his way. The train station was busy, mostly commercial traffic. Perm was a hub for the Ural region, with major metallurgical, chemical and agricultural enterprises producing products that were eventually shipped by train. There were probably twenty tracks or more that could be seen in the distance beyond the fence that bordered the parking lot. Many had trains on them, with most going west, but some headed east.

"We've got to hide in one of those box cars," said Petronovich as he pointed.

Sokolov was in no position to run.

"How do we get over the fence?" he asked, following Petronovich.

Vladi jumped on the hood of a car and propelled himself to the top of the chain link barrier. Sokolov grunted as he pulled himself onto the car's hood. Reaching up toward Petronovich, he said, "I'm not sure I can do this."

Vladi ignored him and with the strength of two men, pulled

Sokolov up and over the fence. He dropped down the other side and both men hobbled between trains, out of the sight of the police who were at the barrier. Petronovich picked a train heading in the right direction and found an open box car. He hopped up, then reached down and pulled Sokolov inside. Both men fell backward, away from the opening. With so many trains to check, Vladi was certain the police would not follow. They made themselves comfortable and waited for the journey to begin.

***

Jason sat on the bed with his back against the headboard. Once Mike's head hit the pillow, he was asleep. Before doing so, he had said, "Wake me when you hear from Volkov."

Midnight approached and passed, as did one a.m. After two, Jason reached across to the other bed and shook Mike. "Mike, wake up."

"Is he back?" Mike mumbled.

"That's the problem, he's not, and it's after two," Jason said.

Hearing that, Mike was wide awake. "Crap!"

"I'm calling Kamarov. It's four in the afternoon in New York," Jason said as he dialed.

Kamarov saw the number and picked up. "What's going on, Jason, did you get the prison location?"

"Volkov left about four hours ago. He hasn't returned Ivan. He said he'd be no later than one, and it's almost two thirty here. What do suggest we do?"

There was silence at the other end. Finally, Kamarov responded, "He must have been compromised. He should have returned by now. I think you should catch the next plane to Moscow. If he's interrogated, he could disclose where you are staying and identify you both as accomplices. He wouldn't do this willingly, but, as you know, we have ways of extracting information. When you reach Moscow, stay at the Radisson Blu Hotel at the Sheremetyevo Airport. I'll be in touch. Don't wait. Pack and go now."

***

Two NSC agents handcuffed and escorted Volkov to the waiting car in front of Lebedev's home. Lebedev followed in his car as they headed to the station. The agents led Volkov into a stark room with a metal table and chairs. The agents sat Volkov down and stood behind him as Lebedev took a seat across from him.

"Now, SVR agent, whoever you are. We can do this the easy way, or as you know, from your experience, if, in fact you are SVR, the hard way. What is your name?" Lebedev asked, looking directly at Volkov.

Volkov stared back at Lebedev with a blank look on his face. "I'm SVR."

Lebedev shook his head. "One last time, what is your name?"

Volkov smiled. "Rumpelstiltskin."

"That's it! Bring him next door and strap him on the table," Lebedev said to the agents standing behind Volkov.

The agents lifted him in one swift movement, a man on either side and almost carried Volkov through the side door. Inside was a broad platform, angled at thirty degrees, with straps for both arms and legs. They uncuffed Volkov and placed his head toward the bottom, feet at the top on the platform. Volkov did not struggle as they strapped him tightly to the board.

Lebedev walked in.

58

"One last time before we begin. What is your name?"

"Baba Yaga," said Volkov, referencing the famous witch of the east, well known in Russia.

"Enough!" Lebedev said, "Get the water cannister."

Chapter 6

The sun had set. Petronovich and Sokolov were dozing when the train lurched and began to slowly move forward. Petronovich rose to his feet, shuffled to the side of the open door and watched as the train moved through the industrial area in the center of Perm. He looked back at Sokolov.

"We're finally on our way. I would think our next stop is Moscow."

"Thank God. I can't wait to get past Moscow and out of this godforsaken country," Sokolov replied.

***

Jason and Mike were on the hotel shuttle, headed for the airport, twenty minutes after Jason's conversation with Kamarov. It was three-thirty a.m. when they entered the almost vacant terminal. Mike had booked a five a.m. flight on Aeroflot to Moscow. They went through security, then found a coffee vendor and a place to sit.

"I don't know Jason. I have a bad feeling about this whole thing. How are we going to find Petronovich without Volkov? We are totally in the dark. Hell, we could be in danger and who knows what happened to Volkov? Did Kamarov allude to what he had in mind once we reach Moscow?" asked Mike as he sipped the steaming coffee.

"He just said that he'd contact us once we got there," Jason replied. "I don't want to abandon Vladi, but I sure as hell don't want to spend time in a Kazak or Russian prison. Maybe we should call it, and head home?"

"Let's get out of Kazakhstan and then see what Kamarov has to say before deciding if we leave," Mike said, as he watched two police officers walk past, checking out the patrons.

After they passed, Jason said, "For a minute, I thought they might be looking for us."

"If Kamarov is right, and they torture Volkov, we will definitely be in jeopardy. Our names will be revealed, as will Kamarov's, and the fact that we are looking for Petronovich and the other prisoners," said Mike.

"That might not be a bad thing, as long as we are outside of Kazakhstan," Jason said.

"Why is that?" Mike asked.

"Remember, this is a rogue group. What they have done is not sanctioned by the Russian government. They will be on the defensive," said Jason as he thought through the logic almost to himself.

"They will be defensive. So, how do they cover their tracks? I'll answer that for you. They eliminate the evidence and deny any involvement in the crime they committed. This could make the situation more dyer for Vladi and the others, shit!" exclaimed Mike.

"You're saying they would kill the prisoners and dispose of the bodies?"

"It's the only thing they can do to cover themselves and not be prosecuted. No evidence, no crime," Mike said.

Jason looked at the time. "We've got forty-five minutes before we board. I'll be breathing much easier when we are wheels up and out of this place."

"You and me both," said Mike as he finished his coffee.

***

One of the agents placed a light cloth over Volkov's face while the other poured water over it from a large watering can. Volkov squirmed, thrashing his head back and forth. The water filled his mouth and nostrils, as well as the sinus cavities in his head. Even though he could breathe, because his head was lower than his lungs, his brain was experiencing the drowning sensation. Most people couldn't take more than fifteen seconds of this torture.

After ten seconds, Lebedev said, "Stop."

The agents removed the cloth as Volkov turned his head and coughed out water. Lebedev waited a minute then said, "What is your name?"

"I told you." Volkov coughed even harder, trying to talk. "Rumpelstiltskin."

"Again!" said Lebedev, looking at the agents.

They poured the water over Volkov's face once more, only this time, going for fifteen seconds. He thrashed his head back and forth, trying to avoid the water. The act was futile, as the water entered and filled the spaces in his head.

"Stop," said Lebedev.

Once again, Volkov gagged, coughed and spat liquid out of his mouth.

Lebedev asked, "What is your name?"

Still coughing and gagging, Volkov panted, "Vasily Volkov."

"Very good. Vasily Volkov, why were you in my house? What were your intentions?" Lebedev asked. Sensing that Vasily would not cooperate, he continued, "If you do not answer, I will run the water for twenty seconds or more. Your mind may not be able to take it. If you are SVR as you say, you know people can, and do, die from this treatment. Answer the question, Vasily Volkov."

Volkov continued to cough and gag, but spoke in between bouts. "We wanted information on the location of Vladimir Petronovich and the other four prisoners."

Lebedev was stunned. "Who's we? Give me the names of the others. I know one person who is surely involved and that is Ivan Kamarov. He asked me recently about Petronovich and the prison location. Am I right?"

"Yes. The others are Americans. They are brothers. Jason and Mike McClintock."

"Is Kamarov here with the Americans? Where are they now?" asked Lebedev.

"Kamarov is in the U.S. The brothers are staying at the Holiday Inn at the airport," replied Volkov, still coughing. "They have done nothing wrong."

"Oh, but they have, Volkov. You have implicated them. They are here in Almaty, working with you," Lebedev replied. Looking at the guards, he continued, "Take him to the cell and lock him up. We are going to the Holiday Inn, immediately!"

***

Petronovich and Sokolov drifted asleep to the sound of the train's wheels clanging in a rhythmic fashion on the tracks. Vladi woke when he sensed the speed of the train beginning to slow. Looking out the wide opening of the boxcar door from the far side, he could see the dawn light turning into day. He guessed the time to be around seven a.m.

Looking at Sokolov, he said, "We're coming into a large city.

My guess is Moscow."

Sokolov yawned, stood, stretched, and walked to the opening. Peering out, he said, "I think you're right."

Petronovich kept watching as the train moved slower, into what appeared to be a rail yard. There were probably twenty to thirty tracks, parallel to each other with trains waiting to have cargo either loaded or unloaded. As the train inched forward, Petronovich turned toward Sokolov.

"It looks like this is the end of the line. We're going to need to find a train ready to go west."

"How do you plan on doing that?" Sokolov asked.

"You're going to wait here, while I check this place out. By the looks of it, the train is parked, waiting to unload. Somebody's in charge of the loading and unloading process. That's the person I need to have a talk with," Petronovich explained.

"You plan on walking up and just asking for the next train west, looking the way you do?" Sokolov responded.

"I'll find a railroad security person and borrow their uniform. Then I'll have the chat," said Petronovich. "It shouldn't be too difficult. Sit back and relax, until I come for you."

Sokolov watched as Petronovich hopped out of the boxcar to the ground.

***

The car turned into the Perm-36 complex and drove slowly toward the back. After parking, the guard reached for his keychain. The man responsible for the evening meal hadn't returned the key, so he had to use a spare. As the guard walked toward the heavy door with the broth and water, he noticed the keyring in the dirt. *That's odd,* he thought as he picked it up. It was then that he realized the door was slightly ajar and heard the loud holler of, "Help! Get me out!"

The guard dropped the two containers, pulled the heavy door open and walked in. It was then that he noticed the empty cell. Moving to the back where Petronovich was supposed to be incarcerated, he found his colleague. "What happened?"

"Just get me the hell out! I was jumped," said the man as the cell door was unlocked. "Call Naryshkin!" he ordered. "My phone is in the car."

"There is no car, they must have taken it," said the guard.

"*Der'mo!*" (shit) said the man.

***

The flight to Moscow was direct and took a little over two hours. Jason and Mike made their way through customs without incident. It was seven thirty when they exited the terminal and hailed a cab. They hadn't slept all night, so they were anxious to get to the hotel. Climbing into the taxi, Jason said, "Radisson Blu, please."

Ten minutes later, they were at the registration desk, checking in. Just as they had finished the paperwork, the clerk said, "I almost forgot. We have a message for you, Mr. McClintock," as she handed Jason the envelope.

"Must be from Kamarov," Mike said.

"Probably, we'll open it when we get to the room," Jason said, as he thanked the clerk for the letter and room key.

The view of the city from their tenth-floor room was stunning. Mike threw his bag on the bed and sat next to it. "Open the envelope, Jason," he said.

Jason sat in the chair next to the table and opened it.

"It's from Kamarov," Jason said as he read the note. "He's flying in today, arriving about one p.m. He said he'd meet us here."

"Looks like we're staying in Russia at least a little while. I don't know about you, but I'm ready for a nap," Mike said as he kicked off his shoes.

"Me too," Jason said as he leaned back in the chair and closed his eyes.

***

Lebedev's car pulled up to the Holiday Inn. He walked briskly to the registration desk and flashed his NSC I.D.

"What room are Jason and Mike McClintock in?"

"Let me check, sir," answered the clerk as she tapped the keyboard. Looking up, she said, "They checked out two hours ago."

Lebedev was furious. He walked out to his car and phoned airport security, requesting an alert be issued for the two men.

"The names are Jason and Mike McClintock. Check to see if they are scheduled to fly this morning," Lebedev commanded.

"I'm checking right now. Give me a moment," said the security officer at the desk.

Lebedev paced next to the car as he waited for an answer. The officer came back online and said, "Looks like they are on an Aeroflot flight to Moscow. The plane left thirty minutes ago."

Lebedev dropped the line and dialed Naryshkin. It was seven-thirty a.m. in Moscow when the phone rang.

"Dimitri, what's wrong? You never call."

"Our operation with Petronovich and the four others has been compromised. My home was broken into last night by a man claiming to be an SVR Agent. His name is Vasily Volkov. Check your database and confirm that for me."

"I'm not in the office. When I get there, I will. Did he specifically say he was looking for the prisoners?"

"Let's just say, he didn't readily volunteer. After a little urging, using a certain water technique, he gave up the information. But it gets worse, Sergey. I believe the CIA is working with Volkov, probably trying to get their five assets back. There are two Americans we need to be concerned with. The names are Jason and Mike McClintock. They are in the air now, on their way to Moscow. Perhaps you can intercept them?" Lebedev asked.

"Possibly. How did all this begin? Where did Volkov get instruction to pursue the prisoners?" Naryshkin asked.

"Ivan Kamarov called me several days ago, asking about Petronovich and where the prisoners were being held. I said they were under your control and that he didn't need the information. I'm certain he sent Volkov," Lebedev explained.

"Let me confirm if Volkov is SVR. If he is, he will join the others at Perm-36. In the meantime, I am going to need to permanently quell Kamarov's curiosity. He crossed the line," said Naryshkin. "I'll also check on the Americans flying in this morning from Almaty. When I get confirmation on Volkov, I'll call. If he is SVR, you'll need to fly him to Perm immediately."

***

Petronovich crouched as he moved between trains, looking for the security personnel that would almost certainly be present. He needed to find a target approximately his size before he was spotted. Making a mental note of the location of the train before he left, he moved further away. As he crossed between two more trains, in the distance, he saw a security officer. He was moving down the line of cars, looking for train hoppers. Vladi moved to the other side of the adjacent train, out of sight. He watched as the officer moved along. Petronovich anticipated the man looking in the next open boxcar. As the officer approached the car, Vladi scurried underneath the train coming out the other side behind the officer as he peered inside. Petronovich moved quickly behind him and applied a sleeper choke hold, using both of his arms to cut circulation in the neck to the man's brain. The officer dropped limply within two seconds. Petronovich hoisted him into the open box car and stripped him of his clothes. The uniform was snug but it still fit Vladi. Petronovich tore his own shirt into long strips and used the pieces to bind the man's arms and legs. He then used a strip to gag him, so he couldn't call out.

Feeling as though he looked the part, Petronovich now acted by checking the remaining boxcars. As he came to the end of the train, he noticed what looked to be a control tower situated in the middle of the yard. In fact, that's what it was. The tower had a perfect view of all activity. The personnel inside coordinated the loading and offloading of every train in the facility. They would have the schedules and know which trains were moving soon, and, more importantly, where. Petronovich headed in that direction.

A guard stood outside the main entrance to the tower.

Petronovich approached him with a smile. "I'm sorry to have to ask, my friend, but I've misplaced the roster of today's train activity. I've been given the job of checking for train hoppers immediately before trains are scheduled to leave the yard. Do you think you could get a roster from the Yardmaster?"

The guard chuckled. "Sure. Let me see what I can do," he

said as he turned towards the door. "I'll be just a minute."

Petronovich waited, trying not to be conspicuous as he paced around the tower structure. The guard emerged after ten minutes.

"Here you go, I made a copy," he said, handing over the single sheet of paper.

Petronovich thanked him and walked back toward the train he and Sokolov had ridden in on. He spotted the boxcar, but before boarding, he looked back and forth to be certain nobody was watching.

"Did you get it?" Sokolov asked.

Petronovich smiled and held up the piece of paper. Sitting next to Sokolov, he said, "Let's have a look."

***

Naryshkin was at his computer when the cell buzzed. Not recognizing the number, he answered, "Naryshkin." The deputy director listened as he was told about the agent being overpowered and Petronovich and Sokolov escaping. He was livid. "Make certain the other prisoners are secure."

While he was on the phone with Lebedev, Naryshkin's secretary came in. He motioned her to sit. After the call ended, he asked, "What do you have, Anna?"

"The Americans arrived this morning, as you suggested. According to the immigration card they completed, they are staying at the airport Radisson Blu," Anna said. "Their length of stay is one week. I ran a background check. One of the brothers is retired FBI. The other is a geologist. The FBI agent lives in Santa Ynez, California and owns a vineyard. He's married with two kids. The geologist isn't married. He lives in Montana. They could be CIA assets."

"Thank you, Anna, that's what I needed," said Naryshkin. "That will be all."

After she closed the door, Naryshkin continued in the SVR database, typing, then entering the last name, Volkov. Vasily Volkov's picture popped up, with a brief description and background data. His assignment history followed, ending with his latest being a desk job in the same building Naryshkin was located. He picked up the phone and dialed Lebedev.

Lebedev answered with, "Is he SVR?"

"He is," Naryshkin responded.

"Did you locate the Americans?" asked Lebedev.

"Yes. They are staying at the airport Radisson. We ran a background check and they could be CIA. I will arrest them in the next hour or so. Meet me in Perm. I'll arrive by five with the McClintocks," said Naryshkin.

"I'll be there with Volkov," said Lebedev.

***

Kamarov's flight landed at Moscow's Sheremetyevo International a little before noon. Having a diplomatic passport, he passed through customs quickly. Inside the main terminal, Kamarov found a pay phone and dialed the Radisson Blu, asking for McClintock's room.

The hotel phone rang and woke both men immediately.

Mike answered, "Hello?"

Not knowing Mike, Kamarov said, "I'd like to speak with Jason."

Without saying a word, Mike looked at Jason, held up the phone, and said, "It's for you."

Jason took the phone. "This is Jason."

"Kamarov here. When you completed your immigration card, did you say you were staying at the Radisson?"

"Yes," answered Jason.

"I was afraid of that. I'm leaving the airport now. I have a rental car reserved so I should be in front of the hotel in less than half an hour. Be outside with your bags. You are both in danger," said Kamarov.

"What do you mean in danger?" Jason asked.

"Jason, you must assume that Volkov revealed your names to Lebedev and that, now, Naryshkin knows. He will quickly confirm that you entered Russia and assume you are looking for the prisoners. As far as he's concerned, you both are CIA. We don't have time to waste, be outside and ready to go. Oh, one more thing, do not check out."

***

Petronovich and Sokolov scanned the roster. One train stood out almost immediately, the Latvian Railway. "Look at this one. The train is on track fourteen, three away from us, scheduled to leave at eleven forty-five this morning. Their first stop is Zilupe, Latvia! That's our train, Sokolov. Let's get over there," said Petronovich as he folded the paper and stuffed it in his pocket.

"Make sure the way is clear before I come down," said Sokolov as Vladi jumped from the car.

Looking around, Petronovich motioned Sokolov to jump. "Let's go. You can do this."

Sokolov jumped, doing a tuck and roll to break his fall. "I'll follow you."

Vladi moved low, underneath the train next to them, with Sokolov following.

"Wait here," said Petronovich as he went out the other side, making sure they were clear of any security.

"We're good, follow me," said Vladi as he moved once again to the next train over. With only one more train to go, the one they were under began to move. Petronovich looked at Sokolov.

"Lie flat until it's moved along, then take cover quickly beneath the next train. I'm going for it," Vladi said timing his move between the wheels as the train began to pick up speed. He sprinted out from underneath, with the heel of his shoe being clipped by the heavy metal wheel just as he cleared the space. He dove for the next train, praying he wasn't seen. From his vantage point, he watched Sokolov lie low and still. Knowing he would be exposed once the train had moved away, Petronovich prepared to help. As the train cleared, Sokolov surprised even himself with the speed with which he moved toward Vladi.

Gasping for breath, he said, "How much more?"

"The other side of this train is the one we want. We'll go together and get in the first open car. If anyone sees us, they'll think you are a train hopper I've found," Vladi said. "Are you ready?"

"Lead the way, let's finish this," Sokolov replied.

***

After getting the McClintocks room number, Naryshkin and four agents went to the tenth floor. Just as Naryshkin was about to knock, the door opened. Jason and Mike stood in the doorway with their bags in hand. The agents behind Naryshkin had their guns pointed at the McClintocks. Mike and Jason slowly placed the luggage on the ground and raised their hands.

"Step outside, gentlemen, turn toward the wall," said

Naryshkin as he backed up and the agents moved forward.

Taking the men into custody, the McClintocks were handcuffed.

Naryshkin looked at the two bags, speaking to one of the agents. "Throw those back in the room. They won't be needing them."

Kamarov pulled his Toyota into the registration parking area in front of the hotel, but off to the side. A black SUV took the space directly in front of the main entrance. Kamarov watched helplessly as Jason and Mike were escorted out of the hotel, into the waiting car.

The SUV drove slowly out of the parking area, turning onto the main road leading to the airport. Kamarov followed at a distance and looked on as the car turned into the gated area for private aircraft. He parked by the fence and watched as the SUV came to a stop next to a small jet with government markings. The pilots, in uniform, were standing outside the plane at the bottom of the stairs. Four agents lead Jason and Mike up the stairs and into the aircraft, followed by Naryshkin. Ten minutes later, the jet was taxiing from the private terminal toward the runway.

Kamarov shook his head in dismay as he watched the small jet take off from Moscow International. *Fifteen minutes too late,* he thought as the plane soared into the sky. *Now what?*

***

Lebedev's jet had started the descent into Perm. They were twenty minutes out. Volkov was cuffed, sitting next to a window, with an NSC agent in the aisle seat next to him. One additional agent was sat directly behind Volkov for added security. Lebedev watched the three from the other side of the plane, one row back.

He couldn't help but feel the unauthorized operation they had initiated was beginning to spiral out of control.

***

Naryshkin's plane touched down at four forty-five, just as the black SUV pulled up. SVR agents opened the backseat doors and ushered the three frail men out and up the stairs to the plane. The men were barely able to make it, taking one step at a time and waiting a moment, breathing heavily, before taking the next. Naryshkin stood outside the vehicle, scanning the horizon. In the distance, he could barely see the glint of sunlight reflecting off the metal of an incoming plane. He looked at the time on his phone. It was four fifty-five.

The SVR unit in Perm was aware that Perm-36 was partially opened. A small, select number knew of the prisoners and had the responsibility to feed and check on them daily. This group of three also boarded the aircraft. They had not been given the details of the detainees and, more importantly, knew not to ask.

The loud screech of tires connecting to the concrete runway could be heard through the roar of the jet's engines as the pilot of the aircraft selected reverse thrust. The plane continued down the runway, decelerating in the landing rollout. Soon enough, it was parked adjacent to the government jet from Moscow.

The cabin door opened with stairs folding out. The NSC agent escorted Volkov down, passing the prisoner off to the waiting SVR agent. The agent took Volkov by the arm and walked him toward the government plane. Lebedev followed down the stairs with Naryshkin waiting at the bottom.

"Walk with me," Naryshkin said to Lebedev, as they strolled away from the vehicles, out of earshot of the other men.

Lebedev followed. "Why is Volkov boarding your plane?"

"I have my reasons, which I will explain in a minute," said Naryshkin.

"I'm not comfortable with what is happening. Our operation is probably compromised now that we know that Kamarov has betrayed us. The escape of Petronovich and Sokolov compounds our problems exponentially. Have you made any progress in silencing Kamarov?"

"He has left his post at the Embassy in D.C. Flight records indicate he arrived in Moscow early today. I have people looking for him as we speak. As for Petronovich and the other one, we do not have any leads. They could be anywhere."

"You've made my point, Sergey. There are too many loose ends," Lebedev said.

"That's why we are making extreme changes. Are you aware of the Solovetsky Islands?" Naryshkin asked.

"That's the location of the Solovetsky Monastery. It's up north, on an island in the White Sea," Lebedev responded.

"Precisely. In 1929, the monastery was taken over by the Russian government and converted into what many believe to be the first Gulag. After the fall of the Soviet Union, the prison closed, and the Orthodox Church reclaimed it. The complex is huge. At one time it housed fifty thousand prisoners. For a fee, I have negotiated control of a very small section. Our prisoners are being transported there today," Naryshkin explained. "They will be confined there until I decide what to do with them. That is unless they do something stupid. The place is so remote that escape is not an option. If they try, they will be killed. Killing prisoners is nothing new to that prison."

"How many guards will you keep there?"

"Three, maybe four," Naryshkin said. "There's no need for

more."

"I hope you know what you are doing," responded Lebedev.

***

Petronovich looked both ways, then emerged from underneath the train with Sokolov following. The train in front of them was transporting lumber on mostly flat cars and other commodities in boxcars. Petronovich could see several boxcars down the line with open doors. "Let's go that way," said Petronovich as he pointed.

Once inside, Vladi closed the boxcar door, making it inconvenient for security to open and check for train hoppers. They had forty-five minutes before the scheduled departure.

"What are our plans once we reach Zilupe?" Sokolov asked as they sat in the dark corner.

"I'll find a phone and call the McClintock's. They're friends of mine and will help us. I'll also phone Kamarov. I can't believe he knows what the SVR is doing at Perm-36. If he knew, he would have put a stop to it. One way, or another, we need help freeing the guys imprisoned there."

"I can't wait to get out of Russia, so I can call my wife," Sokolov responded as he reminisced.

"That's the third call we'll make," Vladi said as the high-pitched screech of metal on metal sounded with the train's wheels beginning to turn. "I think we're safe; might as well relax a bit. Once we get out of town, I'll crack the door for fresh air."

***

Kamarov was at a loss. He thought, *First, Petronovich, then*

76

Volkov and now the McClintock brothers, all taken into custody by Naryshkin. I can't go to senior management in the SVR and risk being taken in. Maybe I can get Schumacher to help. He owes me.

With his mind made up, Kamarov decided he needed to be on the next flight to Los Angeles. It was time to pay a visit to the L.A. FBI field office, and Schumacher, the agent in charge.

Chapter 7

Naryshkin's jet landed on Solovki Island at the small airport, only a quarter mile from the Solovki Monastery gates. The plane taxied, parking in front of the one-room office building near the center of the runway. Next to the building sat two 1950s era, VW buses. They were brought to the airstrip by monks to transport Naryshkin, his guards and prisoners to their confined quarters within the monastery grounds.

The aircraft's cabin door opened, and stairs unfolded. Naryshkin was first through the jet door. Two monks stepped out of the office to meet him. One monk walked forward, offered his hand to Naryshkin, and said, as he motioned toward the vehicles, "Welcome, I have arranged transportation for your party."

"I see that, thank you," Naryshkin replied as he watched the guards escort the first handcuffed prisoners down.

"Load them quickly," said Naryshkin, as the guard ushered the three frail men to the first bus. It took a noticeably long time to get each situated inside the van. Once they were secure, Volkov, Jason and Mike were allowed down. One guard led the group, while a second followed.

Halfway down the stairs, Jason looked across the field, in the distance at the monastery.

"Look at that place," Jason said, speaking to both Volkov and Mike.

"The walls must be twenty to thirty feet high," replied Mike.

"Cut the talk!" commanded the guard. "Move!"

Jason and the others were placed in the second van with the guards and Naryshkin filling the remaining spaces. The monks started the engines, steering the vans down a dirt road toward the monastery. As they approached, the gates began to move outward, with two monks pushing the heavy wood barriers open enough for the cars to pass. Once inside, they used a perimeter road to the left, driving next to the high stone walls, built in the early 1600s. They were between twenty-five and thirty-five feet high, and an astonishing thirteen to nineteen feet thick.

Mike shook his head. "This place is a fortress."

Nobody responded. The three frail men sat with their chins resting on their chests, almost as though half dead. Volkov, Jason and Mike took in the enormity of the ancient fort. The entire area was probably one square mile if you had to guess. The vans finally parked in front of what looked like a vacant church.

"This is what we have set aside for you," said the monk, looking at Naryshkin. "This is the Uspensky Cathedral, built in the 1500s. It has a walled yard in the back as well as a common living area with bunks for your guests which have been fitted with strong deadbolts for their security. We also have living quarters for your men. As agreed, we will provide limited food for your guests, twice a day and a substantial meal for your men at dinner. Come, let me show you the way."

The monk unlocked and opened the massive cathedral door, holding it as the prisoners were allowed in. The place was empty and looked as if it had been for over one hundred years.

"Their quarters are in the back. Take the last door to the right. It is unlocked," said the monk.

The guards took Jason, Mike and Volkov first, followed by the other three failing men. The agent opened the door to a room with fifteen-foot ceilings. It had no windows or bathroom, only five sets of bunk beds, three on one side of the room and two on the other. After the men entered, the monk followed and watched as the men were uncuffed.

"The side door you see, on the left, leads to a courtyard and outbuilding. The courtyard walls are thirty feet high, so the door is unlocked, allowing your 'guests' the ability to go out and relieve themselves as needed," said the monk, speaking to the Naryshkin and the guards.

"Are there facilities inside for my men?" Naryshkin asked, knowing he would have major problems if his men had to live in primitive conditions.

"Yes, as you will soon see, they will have the modern conveniences. Not to worry," replied the monk, leaving the room. "Lock the door behind you and I will show you the rest."

The last agent did as he was told and followed the group.

After seeing the staff quarters, Naryshkin was pleased.

"This will work fine," he said to the monk.

"Good. Then you accept the accommodations. My brothers have placed your men's luggage in their quarters. I would think it's about time to drive you back to your plane. That is unless you'd like to spend the night?" asked the monk, speaking to Naryshkin.

"No, that will be fine, I must go," Naryshkin replied, relieved to be leaving the island.

***

It was early morning when the train from Moscow crossed the Russian border into the town of Zilupe, Latvia. Petronovich peered out the boxcar door as the train approached the small town.

"This should be a short stop. This town is very small," said Petronovich as he looked over at Sokolov.

"If I remember your schedule, the final stop on this line is Riga. That's the country's capital," said Sokolov.

"Right. I thought we might jump the train here, but I think our best bet is the large city. We need to get to a U.S. Embassy, and they must have one there," Petronovich continued.

"I agree, but I sure am hungry, Petronovich," Sokolov explained.

"Me too, but we've gone this far. We can wait for another two to three hours," Petronovich said.

"At least we're out of Russia. I thank God for that," said Sokolov.

"You and me both," agreed Petronovich as the train came to a stop.

Sokolov looked out the door. "You weren't kidding when you said this place was small. I'll bet the town doesn't have more than one main street."

Twenty minutes after stopping, the train began to move.

"According to the schedule, there are no other stops between Zilupe and Riga," said Petronovich as he looked at the roster he'd been given in Moscow.

The two and a half hour ride from Zilupe to Riga went by quickly as Petronovich and Sokolov anticipated their arrival. They were a little anxious about how they might be received at the Embassy, but not really concerned. Once the CIA was contacted, and their identity verified, they'd be treated like royalty.

***

It was a short ride to the airport. Before returning the rental, Kamarov checked his travel app for the next flight to Los Angeles. The Lufthansa counter wasn't that busy as he approached. The ticket agent input Kamarov's data to complete the transaction. As he did, Kamarov noticed a distinct change in the agent's demeanor. He knew something wasn't right, he had to leave.

In a separate office located in the security section of the airport, an SVR agent noticed the red flag come up on his monitor. He called to a supervisor, "We have a hit on a priority target issued by Deputy Naryshkin."

"Who and where?" asked the supervisor.

"It's Ivan Kamarov. He just booked the next Lufthansa flight out, flying to Los Angeles."

"Notify the team. We'll take him before he boards. I'll call Naryshkin and let him know we've got Kamarov," said the supervisor.

***

After the guard locked the door, the men from Perm-36 shuffled over to the three bunks against the wall and each claimed a lower berth. Jason walked over to them and asked, "Have you seen Vladimir Petronovich?"

Two men stared blankly at Jason, acting as though they didn't understand the question. The third man, lying flat on his backed stared at the bunk above his head and whispered, "There were two others. I don't know their names. I think they escaped three days ago."

"Did they mention where they were going?" Jason asked.

The man simply shook his head, no. The short conversation

82

seemed to exhaust him. Jason motioned for Mike and Volkov to follow him out the side door to the courtyard.

Once outside, Jason asked, "Either of you have any ideas?"

"None," Mike said. "Given the length of our flight and the angle of the sun when we landed, I'd say we are about as far north in Russia as you can get. The size of this compound is immense."

"Since it's run by monks, it must be a monastery," Volkov added. "I've heard of a famous monastery, in the north. It is said to have been the first Gulag. They called the place the Solovki Monastery. I'm certain that's where we are."

Jason looked around the courtyard. "There's no way we're scaling these walls."

"No," Volkov replied. "I think the only way out is through the guards and the same way we came in."

"They have the guns; in case you've forgotten. Maybe we can turn one of the monks. They're supposed to be men of God," Mike suggested.

"Men of God that have a financial interest in keeping us here," Jason replied.

Volkov looked over at the two bunks on the far wall and started walking.

Jason followed and said, "Don't even think of taking one of the lower beds, Volkov, Mike and I own them."

Volkov hopped to the top of one and replied, "No worries Jason, I'm fine up here."

***

When the train finally came to a stop inside the Riga railyard, Petronovich jumped from the boxcar. He looked back as Sokolov sat on the lip of the door and eased his way down. Looking at

Petronovich, he said, "The tuck and roll last time was too much."

Vladi chuckled. "The shape you're in, I was surprised you didn't break something. Come on, let's get out of here."

Petronovich lead the way, not caring if they were spotted by security. They both stood out; Vladi wearing the Moscow railyard security uniform, and Sokolov looking like the prisoner he'd been, smelling just as bad as he looked. After weaving their way around trains and across tracks, they made their way to a gate. Petronovich checked it, and, as he thought it would be, it was locked. They followed the fence away from the station until it stopped abruptly, allowing the two men to exit the property.

"Not much security here," said Vladi as they walked around and back towards the station parking lot. "We need the location of the embassy. Let's see if we can find a public phone with a directory."

"That's fine, but we have no money to call. The last time we asked for help, it didn't work out so well," Sokolov replied.

"We're going to find an unlocked car in the lot and hotwire it. It's been a while since I've done it, but it's not that difficult," said Petronovich.

When they reached the parking lot, Petronovich said, "You hang back here. I'm going over to the station entrance. There should be a public phone there."

"I'll be here, make it quick," Sokolov replied.

Petronovich looked around the outside of the building without success. Inside the terminal, he was equally unsuccessful. He spotted a police officer and decided to approach him. Speaking in Russian he said, "Excuse me, officer. Can you direct me to a public phone?"

The police officer looked at Petronovich with suspicion, then replied, "There are none. They discontinued service years ago.

What do you need?"

"I'm looking for the address of the U.S. Embassy," Petronovich explained.

"Come with me," said the officer as he walked toward an office off to the side. He opened the door for Petronovich. "Come in."

The officer went to the desk drawer and pulled out what looked to be a phone book. After ruffling through the pages, he sighed, "Ahh." The officer wrote the address and phone number on a slip of paper and handed it to Petronovich. "Here's what you are looking for."

After thanking the officer, Petronovich headed back to the lot. In the distance, he could see Sokolov moving from car to car, obviously looking for one that was unlocked. He finally stopped next to an old VW bug. Seeing Vladi approach, he said, "It's unlocked."

Petronovich didn't hesitate. He opened the door, bent down, pulled the wires from the ignition and began to sort them by color. There were two red wires, one from the battery and the other leading to the starter. He carefully connected the two red power wires and set them aside. He then pulled the two brown wires from the ignition. Touching the two exposed wires together should allow electrical current to the ignition and start the car.

"Here's the moment of truth," said Petronovich as he lightly touched the wires together causing the engine to turn over. Once started, he looked at Sokolov. "We're good to go, get in."

***

A plane had arrived at the next gate over, with passengers streaming out, moving down the concourse. Kamarov blended in and moved with them. Coming in the opposite direction, he noticed four men moving quickly toward his Lufthansa gate. Kamarov knew they were SVR agents. He took the escalator down to the baggage claim area and went immediately out the door, toward a waiting line of cabs. Kamarov jumped in the back seat of the next available car.

"Driver, take me to the closest off-site car rental agency," Kamarov said.

"That will be Enterprise, about a mile and a half from here," responded the driver.

The SVR agents reached the gate, spread out and searched for Kamarov. Realizing he wasn't in the waiting area, they checked the closest restroom, shops and restaurants.

The lead agent called his superior. "We've lost him."

***

The monks, seeing how emaciated three of the inmates were, elected to provide rice and beans instead of the broth requested by Naryshkin. They brought two large pots, along with six tin plates, to the guards that evening. Jason was sitting on his bunk when the sound of the keys could be heard unlocking the deadbolt. As the door swung open, a guard with an AK-47 stepped through the opening. A second followed, setting the two pots and plates on the floor in the middle of the bare room.

Volkov jumped off the bunk and spoke to the guards. "You two are SVR, right?"

"Stay back," said the guard with the AK-47.

"I am as well! You know that what Naryshkin is doing is illegal?" asked Volkov as he walked forward. "Help us and we will see that you are treated right. As far as you were concerned,

86

you were simply following the deputy director's orders. I get it, help us, please."

"If you are SVR, you must have done something serious to be sent here," said the guard after he placed the food on the floor.

"My only crime was in trying to get evidence to bring charges against Naryshkin while trying to find the location of the three men over there on the bunks," Volkov replied as he pointed across the room.

"Eat your meal, and shut up," replied the guard as he stood up and backed toward the door and his partner with the weapon.

"Where are our utensils?" Jason asked looking at the plates and food.

"Use your hands. You're lucky to have what the monks brought. You were supposed to have been given broth," said the guard as he shut and locked the heavy wooden door.

***

Surprisingly, there were no marine guards at the entrance to the embassy parking lot as Petronovich turned in and parked. A marine was standing guard at the entrance to the main door. As Petronovich and Sokolov approached, the guard took a special interest, especially in Sokolov, given his appearance. Vladi didn't hesitate, he walked straight toward the man. In a non-threatening manner, he said quietly, "We are CIA officers that have just escaped from captivity in Russia. Can you bring us in and verify our identity?"

"Yes, sir, follow me," replied the marine as he led them inside to a private waiting room with a table and chairs. "Have a seat while I call for assistance. Would you like bottled water or coffee?"

Sokolov replied, "Water would be great."

"Make that two," said Petronovich as he took a seat at the table.

Five minutes later, a young man, probably mid-thirties, walked in. He handed a bottle of water to Sokolov and Petronovich and then sat across from them. "I'm FSS Jenkins. I know what you told the marine. Let's start with your names, then you can tell me how I can help you."

When Jenkins introduced himself, Petronovich knew he was talking to the right guy. In U.S. embassies worldwide, CIA officers typically had titles of Foreign Service Reserve (FSR), which is among the highest ranking, or Foreign Service Staff (FSS). State Department employees were considered Foreign Service Officers (FSO). Petronovich and Sokolov both gave their names and then Sokolov told his story. He started with how and where he was apprehended and ended with his meeting Petronovich at Perm-36.

Petronovich continued, explaining his visit to Almaty, Kazakhstan, and subsequent abduction. He ended with their escape and arrival this morning in Riga. He continued, "If you will call Langley, they will confirm our disappearance and we can continue the conversation regarding the others in captivity."

"There are more?" asked Jenkins.

"Three more that I'm aware of," replied Sokolov. "They were at Perm-36, two to three months before me. They're in very bad shape. The Russians had us on a starvation diet. I look great compared to them."

Jenkins filled two pages of his legal pad taking notes and asking questions where warranted. He looked up from the pad and stood.

"Give me a few minutes to make some calls. If you need

anything, use the phone on the wall and ask for me. My office staff will pick up." Jenkins motioned to the side door. "The restroom is over there."

***

Kamarov checked his maps app before leaving the car rental lot. He needed to get out of Moscow. The drive from Moscow to Zelenograd was a little over twenty-nine miles. He could be there in thirty minutes. After leaving the city limits, Kamarov decided to phone Schumacher. It was three p.m. and, with Moscow being ten hours ahead, that would be five a.m. in Los Angeles. He spoke into his cell. "Siri, phone Jack Schumacher, on speaker."

The phone was picked up after the third ring. Not recognizing the number, Schumacher answered, "Schumacher."

"Agent Schumacher, this is Ivan Kamarov. I'm sorry to be calling so early, but I need your help," said Kamarov.

"Did Jason and Mike make it to Almaty?" Schumacher asked.

"They did, but we have a problem. I believe my agent, Volkov, was compromised and taken into custody in Almaty. He intended to interview Lebedev alone. Jason phoned me when Volkov didn't return to the hotel. At that point, I told Jason and Mike to fly to Moscow, where I planned to meet them. I arrived at their hotel as they were being escorted out of the lobby in handcuffs. I followed their car to the airport and watched as a jet flew them away. I believe they are being taken to the prison where the others are being held."

"I could assist if we knew where they were being taken, but we don't. Where do we start, Kamarov? This is your country and your rogue SVR agent," Schumacher said, clearly upset.

"I don't know. Can you speak with your counterpart at the CIA and see if he has any leads?" Kamarov asked.

"I guess that's a place to start. I have your number. As soon as I have any information, I'll call," Schumacher said as he dropped the call and dialed Whittington.

***

The oldest monk approached the SVR guard. "I am here to collect the pots and plates."

"What do you have in your hands?" asked the SVR agent, noticing cloths and a bucket of water.

"Three of your 'guests' seem to be in a very bad way. I have a little medical training. May I check on them? They are worth nothing to you dead," said the monk, trying to reason.

"I could care less if they are dead or alive. If you want to waste your time, go ahead," replied the guard as he walked with the monk to the door and let him in with the prisoners.

The pots were in the middle of the floor with the plates stacked next to them. The door creaked open as the monk was let inside. He bowed to the men in the room, then shuffled toward the three bunks against the far wall. The door slammed shut behind him as he made his way. Jason, Mike and Vasily watched as the monk tended to the other three men. He didn't say a word as he wiped them down, doing his best to clean them with the water. When he was finished, he looked at Jason and said, "I will try to come back soon with supplements for these men. They are severely malnourished."

"That would be appreciated," responded Jason. "Can I ask you a question before you go?"

"Certainly, my son."

90

"Where are we?" Jason asked.

"You are in the Solovki Monastery," said the monk. "There are ten of us here, trying to restore it. Housing you gives us a little extra money for the task. I don't know what you did to deserve this, nor do I care. It is not my business. But I won't have you starve either."

"We have done nothing wrong, my friend. Can you help us?" whispered Jason as Mike and Volkov looked on.

The monk stared at Jason for what seemed like the longest time, then said, "I will pray for all of you, my son." He juggled the bucket, pots and plates, then pounded on the door, "Guard!"

***

Jenkins walked back in and sat across from Petronovich. Sokolov was pacing the room and he took a seat as well.

"I was in touch with Langley, and your story checks out," Jenkins said. "You are going to be debriefed tomorrow. In fact, Petronovich, your superior from Los Angeles will be here."

"Whittington is flying over?" Vladi asked.

"He'll be here late morning. In the meantime, I have two rooms reserved for you at the Hilton Garden Inn, down the street. I know you'll want to get cleaned up. I had my assistant go and buy you clothes and toiletries. I guessed your sizes and I hope I'm close. You'll have an open tab at the hotel, so use it for food and drinks. They have an excellent steak house I'm sure you'll enjoy," Jenkins explained.

"Can we use the phone there as well? I need to call my wife," Sokolov asked.

"Unlimited. We're glad you made it out. Tomorrow may be a long day, so make the best of this afternoon and tonight. Let's get you over there," Jenkins said as he stood and held the door open for the men.

***

Whittington ended his call with Langley just as Schumacher phoned.

"Jack, I just got off with Langley. Petronovich escaped with a second man! He is at the U.S. Embassy in Latvia."

"Did he mention the location of the prison?" Schumacher asked.

"He did to embassy staff, but I didn't get the details. I'm flying over this afternoon and will be there tomorrow to debrief them," said Whit. "We don't normally do this, but it is a Federal matter. Do you want to ride along?"

"I'll be ready, what time?" answered Schumacher.

"Meet me at the Burbank FBO, four p.m. That will put us into Riga at noon tomorrow," Whit said. "See you there."

Schumacher dropped the line and dialed Kamarov. Seeing the number, Kamarov answered, "Agent Schumacher, that was quick."

"The CIA have Petronovich and one of the other men. They are at the U.S. Embassy in Latvia. We are flying over this afternoon to debrief them," Schumacher said, "You might as well stay put until we get a handle on the prison location. Once we do, I'll call so we can coordinate the recovery."

"Very good news! I'll find a place to stay until I hear from you," Kamarov replied.

***

Several hours after the morning meal, the prisoners heard the clanging of keys and the heavy squeak as the door opened. The old monk entered with hand towels and a bucket of water. He paused at the door, bowed and then shuffled once again across the floor to the three emaciated men. Without saying a word, he pulled a plastic bag from beneath the cloths and laid it on the bed. He had vitamin supplements for everyone. He looked over at Mike and Jason. "Will one of you pass these around?"

Mike walked over, took the baggie and handed one pill to each man. Afterwards, he set the baggie next to the monk. "Thank you, father."

The monk looked up and smiled. "You are welcome, my son, if I could do more, I would."

Mike knelt next to the monk and watched as he wiped down one of the men with the wet rag. "Is there a way for you to contact the American Embassy in Finland? They are very close. If you could let someone know we are here, we would be forever in your debt," Mike said.

The monk didn't turn his attention away from the man he was washing, but he did respond. "We have no telephones in the monastery. If we wished to use one, we would need to borrow one in town. That would be too dangerous for us and for you."

"Father, you have been very helpful. We appreciate what you have done for us with the additional food and supplements. Please take time to think of a way you might be able to notify our people in Finland," Mike pleaded.

The monk rose from the bed after having finished washing the men.

"I will pray for all of you," he said as he gathered the plates and pots and shuffled to the prison door.

***

Sokolov dropped his clothes at the door and headed immediately to the shower. The moment he'd been dreaming about for the last month and a half finally arrived as he looked up into the spray of steaming hot water. The months of accumulated filth swept down the drain, as he reveled in the cleansing experience.

Jenkins knocked on Sokolov's door. Hearing the water in the shower, he used his own key to open the door and set the clothes and toiletries that had been purchased for him on the bed.

Petronovich was dialing Jason when he heard the knock at his door. Setting the phone down, he walked across the room and answered it. "I thought you might enjoy having these," Jenkins said as he handed the large sack to Vladi. "I'll have a car pick you and Sokolov up at ten a.m. No need to be in at the crack of dawn, see you tomorrow."

"Thanks, Jenkins, I really appreciate this," Petronovich responded.

Vladi went back to the phone and dialed Jason's number. It went right to voicemail. He then phoned Mike, getting the same result. *What the fuck?* he thought as he dialed Julie.

Julie answered with, "Vladi! What in God's name happened to you?"

"It's a long story, Julie. I tried calling Mike and Jason but got only voicemails. Are they with you? You're still on the cruise, aren't you?" Vladi asked.

"Your friend Kamarov phoned Jason on the second day of our trip. He was concerned about you and asked for their help. They flew to Almaty three days ago from Mazatlan. We haven't heard from them since their arrival. We're worried," Julie replied.

"I'm sorry Kamarov got them involved. I'll try him and see

if he can shed any light on what has happened. As soon as I hear anything, I'll call," said Petronovich as he disconnected.

Vladi looked around the room and noticed the minibar. He opened it and took two small bottles of vodka and poured them into a glass that sat on the tray next to the ice bucket. After taking a long drink, he exhaled and dialed Kamarov.

Recognizing the number, Kamarov answered, "Vladi, thank God you're safe! Schumacher told me you were at the embassy in Riga!"

"Ivan, why did you get the McClintocks involved in this? They are not trained or prepared for what we do in any way!" said Petronovich. "Where are they?"

"I was wrong to have involved them. I thought they would be safe with Volkov. I sent him to Almaty to look for you."

"Once again, where are they?" Petronovich demanded.

"I'm assuming Volkov was arrested by the NSC. After he failed to return to his hotel, Jason called me. I told him that he and Mike should fly immediately to Moscow. I flew in to meet them, arriving at their hotel in time to see them being escorted out in cuffs. I think they've been taken to the place you escaped from."

"Lebedev and Naryshkin are behind this. I was taken to Perm-36, outside Perm. There is a section that is open and being used by the SVR," said Petronovich. "You said you spoke with Schumacher?"

"Yes, he said he was flying into Riga and would be there tomorrow," said Kamarov.

"He must be coming with Whittington, he's CIA. I'll phone you after I meet with them and we'll decide what to do. The drive from Moscow to Perm is long. If you are in Moscow, I'd head to Perm as soon as possible," said Vladi.

"I just checked into a hotel outside Moscow. But you're right, if I leave now, I could be in Perm to meet your group if they decide to fly in. Call as soon as you know something, we need to get the McClintocks and Volkov to safety."

Petronovich placed the phone in the cradle and slugged back the remainder of his drink. He looked forward to the shower.

***

Whittington stood at the bottom of the stairs, talking with the pilot as Schumacher walked out of the FBO lounge. The cabin steward took Schumacher's carryon and stowed it in the back of the plane while the men fueling the aircraft unhooked the hoses and wound them back onto the truck.

"Looks like we're almost ready to go," said the pilot as he completed the walk around of the C-37A, which was the government equivalent of the Gulfstream V. "You might as well board."

Schumacher followed Whittington up the stairs into the posh interior of the business jet. After being seated in the double-wide leather chairs, the cabin steward approached. "Can I get you gentlemen a drink?"

Whit didn't hesitate. "Thank you, yes, I'd like a double Makers, rocks, please."

Schumacher followed. "How about a Tito's vodka neat, thanks."

"Do we have a stop on the east coast before we cross the pond?" asked Schumacher.

"I asked the captain that very question. He said the range on this bird is six thousand, five hundred miles and that flying direct, we'd have five hundred miles to spare. So, it's a direct flight,"

Whit explained.

The cabin steward brought the drinks with a small bowl of mixed nuts and said, "Make sure you're buckled, we're ready to go."

The plane began to taxi toward the end of the runway. After receiving clearance from the tower, the pilot powered up the engines and released the brakes. The light jet hurled down the runway, flinging effortlessly into the sky. Whit looked at Schumacher and raised his glass. "Here's to a successful trip."

***

That night, one of the younger monks brought the prisoners the evening meal. He was allowed into the room by an SVR agent. The guard waited while the monk set the pots and tin plates in the middle of the floor. Without saying a word, he left the room, with the guard locking the door behind him.

As had been the pattern, Jason took one plate and added a portion of beans and rice, handing it to Mike to take to one of the men lying on the beds. Volkov took the second plate and Mike gave a plate to the third man. Jason waited for Mike and Volkov to get their portion, before taking the last. Using his hands to get the remnants of the beans, after finishing the rice, he felt the long, metal object at the bottom of the pot. He lifted the skeleton key out of the beans and whispered, "Son of a bitch!" After showing Mike and Volkov what he'd found, he quickly slid it into his shoe.

Jason brought his plate across the room and sat by Mike and Volkov.

"This is a game changer," said Jason as he ate the small portion on his plate.

"Yes and no," said Volkov. "We're on an island. So, we

escape from here, then what? We can't count on the islanders helping us."

"I think you might be underestimating the island people, Volkov. I'm not so sure they are fans of the Russians after they confiscated the monastery and used it as a gulag for so many years," Mike responded.

"Since the monks placed the key in the food, it seems they might be willing to help," Jason said. "The next time the old guy comes in, we'll ask if he could assist us in getting off the island. If he says yes, then we can begin to put a plan together to escape. Until that time, we need to stick it out."

"Agreed. But one thing is certain. The three over there are staying," Mike whispered as he nodded across the room.

"Maybe we can come up with a story that the guards will buy," Jason suggested.

"What are you thinking?" Volkov asked.

"Those guys are really sick; you can't argue that. If we can get the monks to suggest they need hospital care, maybe the guards will go along. Knowing they are in good hands will make me feel better about leaving them," Jason said.

"Okay, we'll work on the monks helping us as well as getting the others medical attention. That's where we start," Mike said, putting a cap on the quiet conversation.

***

There was a tap at Naryshkin's door.

"Enter."

His assistant came in holding a piece of paper.

"What do you have?"

"Enterprise, near the airport, rented a car to Kamarov this

afternoon," said the agent, handing the paper which verified the rental.

Naryshkin took the paper, scanned the information and said, "He's leaving Moscow, but where's he going?"

"Maybe to Perm?" offered the agent.

Naryshkin thought for a minute. "If Petronovich has contacted Kamarov, that could very well be his destination," said Naryshkin. "Notify all hotels to be on alert for Kamarov, Petronovich and the other one, what was his name?"

"Sokolov, sir."

"Yes, Sokolov," replied Naryshkin. "We already have airports around the country on watch for Kamarov; add Petronovich and Sokolov to the list. Include their photographs. That will be all."

"Yes, sir," said the agent as he left the office.

***

After his shower, Petronovich thought he'd get Sokolov and head to the restaurant for dinner and drinks. He walked across the hall and tapped on Sokolov's door. There was no answer. He lightly tapped again, waiting for a response. When the door didn't open, Vladi went back to his room and thought, *Maybe a power nap is a good idea,* as he slipped out of his shoes and laid back on the bed.

Two hours later, Petronovich woke with a start at the knocking of the door. He was disoriented and had to take a minute to remember where he was. Vladi went to the door and opened it.

"You must have passed out after the shower, like me," Sokolov said, standing in the doorway, looking like a completely different person.

"Who the hell are you? And what have you done to Alexander Sokolov!" Petronovich exclaimed, "Come in. Man, you clean up well."

"It's amazing what a shower and shave will do to one's appearance," Sokolov smiled.

"And smell," Vladi added. "I don't know about you, but I'm famished."

"That steakhouse restaurant Jenkins mentioned is sounding pretty good," Sokolov added.

The dining room was small but well-appointed with white tablecloths and centerpiece candles. The men were taken to a corner table where the waiter handed them menus and took drink orders. After deciding on an entrée, Sokolov looked up, "I have to thank you, Petronovich, I could have never gotten out of there without your help."

"I'm glad we were as lucky as we were. We have a problem. I spoke to Kamarov this afternoon. He sent three men to search for us, starting in Kazakhstan. All are believed to have been taken to Perm-36 by the SVR. After the debrief tomorrow, I'm going back in after them. They are my friends," Petronovich said as the drinks were delivered.

"I'd like to help, but I," Sokolov was stopped by Petronovich.

"You're in no condition to go, Sokolov. I'm certain Whittington will have assets in the country, he can tap into for assistance," Petronovich explained.

"Who's Whittington?" Sokolov asked.

"I work for him out of the Los Angeles office. He and the FBI Special Agent in Charge of L.A., are flying in for the debrief."

"I sure as hell hope you can get them all out safely," said

100

Sokolov.

"That's the plan," responded Petronovich raising his glass, "Here's to freedom."

"To freedom!" said Sokolov as he drained his drink. "I could eat half a cow right now."

***

The lights in the cabin had been dimmed for the last six hours.

The cabin steward gently shook Whittington. "Sir, I have the bathroom prepared for you in case you'd like to freshen up."

"Great, I'll do that," replied Whittington as Schumacher stirred. "You want to go first, Jack?"

"No, I'm good. I'll grab some coffee," said Schumacher as the steward went back to the galley for a pot.

It was mid-morning as the jet approached the continent. The view out the cabin window was stunning. Both men watched as land could be seen in the distance.

"It shouldn't be too much longer," Schumacher said almost to himself.

The cabin steward overheard the conversation and came back.

"The captain said we're about forty-five minutes out," he said as he topped off the coffee.

"I'm anxious to hear what Petronovich has to say. It's going to be a little dicey going into Russia to get our men," Whittington said. "Langley strongly intimated it would be our collective asses if we screwed up and created an international incident."

"If we did, it wouldn't be because it wasn't warranted. Those assholes started this, and we'll finish it one way or another," Schumacher replied.

"Strap in, gentlemen, we'll be landing shortly," said the steward as he collected the coffee cups and prepared the galley.

The C-37A floated gently down toward the runway. A brief, but soft, screech could be heard as the tires connected with the pavement. The jet completed the rollout and taxied toward the airport FBO, where a black SUV waited.

***

The old monk entered once again to retrieve the morning plates and pots. He carried a bucket of water and cloths across the room to the frail men. The guard, before locking the door, said, "Let me know when you're ready to come out."

"Yes, my son," said the monk without looking back. He reached the bunks, pulled out the baggie and motioned Mike to get it.

"Thank you, father," Mike said as he passed out a vitamin supplement to each of the men in the room. He set the plastic bag next to the monk. "Father, thank you for the key. These three men are seriously ill and need medical care. If we can escape, they will not be physically able to make it out with us," Mike whispered.

"It appears that they are now running fevers," the monk said as he dabbed cold water on the forehead of one of the men.

"Can you possibly convince the guards that they should be taken to a hospital?" Mike asked.

"I doubt I would be able to do that. You understand, the SVR do not care whether you or these men, as sick as they are, live or die. Let me finish up here and we will talk tomorrow," said the monk, dismissing Mike. After a half hour, he stood and shuffled to the plates and pots.

102

Jason followed the cleric, bent and handed him the pots, then asked, "Father, if we are able to escape, is there a way we can get off the island by boat?"

"There may be, but I must think about it. We can talk more tomorrow. If these men get worse, call the guards and send for me," replied the monk as he moved toward the door. "Guards!"

***

Petronovich was dressed and ready, sitting at the small table when the hotel phone rang. He picked it up. "Hello?"

"I'll be there in ten minutes, can you and Sokolov be outside?" asked Jenkins.

"We'll be ready," replied Vladi. He grabbed the windbreaker he had been given and went across the hall for Sokolov.

Jenkins was waiting in his car in front of the lobby when the men walked out.

"How was your night?" he asked as they got in, Petronovich taking the front seat.

"Great. The steakhouse was as good as you suggested," said Sokolov.

"After dinner, I was out like a light. I don't know about you, Sokolov, but I haven't slept as good in years," Petronovich said as he looked at Jenkins. "When will Whittington get in?"

"They should be in about noon. The debrief will take some time. I'd plan on all afternoon, if not into the evening," said Jenkins, as he turned into the embassy parking lot.

Petronovich and Sokolov followed Jenkins into the embassy, past security, to the back and the FSS offices. He opened the door to the conference room and said, "Make yourself comfortable, I'll have water and coffee brought in."

The conference table sat fourteen people. Petronovich and Sokolov selected chairs across from each other in the middle.

Sokolov fidgeted. "I can't wait for this to be finished. I'll be catching the next available flight out of Riga."

"I hope Whittington has activated the assets he has in the country to help us with this op," Petronovich said as he topped off his coffee.

Forty minutes later, the conference room door opened with Whittington and Schumacher entering, followed by Jenkins.

Petronovich stood and walked over to meet them. "Whit, it's good to see you. You too, Jack," he said as he shook their hands.

Jenkins introduced Sokolov and then everyone took a seat.

Jenkins placed a recording device on the table. He pressed record and then gave the date, time, place and all those in attendance.

After five hours of recapping what had transpired over the last two months for Sokolov, and five days for Petronovich, Whittington brought the debrief to a close. "Gentlemen, that should do it. We have six men unaccounted for and need to initiate a rescue mission inside Russian territory. We'll work on that tonight. In the meantime, I can have the Gulfstream take you back to the states this evening," Whit said.

"The only place I'm going is back to Perm-36," said Petronovich. "Sokolov can take the plane back."

"You're up to this, Vladi?" Whit asked.

"Three of my closest friends are captive because of me. I'm getting them out, with or without your help. Naryshkin and Lebedev are going to pay."

Chapter 8

Jason, Mike and Volkov were in the courtyard when the old monk was let into the large cell with the bucket of water and clean cloths. They approached the old man as he began to cool down the frail prisoners. Without looking up, he spoke: "I talked to the senior guard. I asked him to move these men to the infirmary in town. Without any hesitation, he said absolutely not."

Jason sighed. "After you finish, can we talk outside? We'll wait for you there."

"I'll come out before I go," replied the monk.

Half an hour later, the monk joined the three men. Just as Jason began to talk, the door to the large room opened with two armed guards entering. They saw the four outside and immediately called out, "Friar, you are not to talk with these men. Get your pots and plates and leave! From now on, you will not be caring for this scum and you are no longer allowed in here. One of the other brothers can bring the food."

Without saying a word, the monk turned and walked inside.

The guards held the door for him as he left the room.

"I can tell you three are thinking of something. We'll be paying closer attention to your actions going forward," said the guard.

Jason finally spoke. "These men will die if you don't get them the care they need."

"If they die, so be it. There will be fewer mouths feed," replied the guard as he shut and locked the door.

"Now what?" asked Mike. "Seems like we are on our own."

"We still have the key," said Volkov. "There can't be more than four guards and there are three of us."

"Yes, but they have had the same SVR training as you, Volkov, and they have the guns," Mike said.

"I'm concerned about those three in there," said Jason as he motioned toward the courtyard door.

"I'm afraid we won't be let alone with the monks any longer," said Volkov.

"I think you're right," agreed Jason as he began to walk the courtyard perimeter, thinking of their limited options.

***

Petronovich, Schumacher and Jenkins sat at the conference table with Whittington at the head. It was nine p.m. and Sokolov had already been in the air for two hours on his way back home. Two coffee pots and sack lunches with sandwich wrappers from the food that had been brought in were spread out on the table before the group as they finalized their plan.

"Okay, I think we are all in agreement. It's too dangerous from both a political and physical standpoint for a large contingent going in. It will be Petronovich and Kamarov. Vladi will fly into Perm and meet up with Kamarov. We will supply both of you with new passports and credit cards. They will be ready in the morning for you to catch your commercial flight to Perm," said Whit as he looked at Vladi. "We will give as much support as we can from here. I think we need to get Kamarov on the line."

Jenkins placed a Polycom Sound Station in the center of the table while Petronovich dialed. Kamarov picked up, not recognizing the number. "Kamarov."

"Ivan, this is Vladi. I'm at the embassy in Riga, you are on speaker. With me are Whit Whittington, CIA, Los Angeles, Jack Schumacher, FBI also Los Angeles and FSS Jenkins, embassy staff," said Petronovich.

"Hello, gentlemen," said Kamarov.

"Mr. Kamarov, this is Whittington. I understand you are on your way to Perm?"

"I am. I'm a few hours out," Kamarov replied.

"Good. You can pick Petronovich up at the airport in Perm in the morning. His flight arrives at ten forty. We will have an American passport and credit card for you both under different names should you need identification. The last thing we need is for either of you to be flagged. Now, you and Vladi will start by approaching Perm-36. I can't believe the prisoners will be there, knowing Petronovich and Sokolov escaped, but we need to eliminate the option. After that, I think you will be paying a visit to either Naryshkin or Lebedev," Whit said. "It's your call. I want to know the status of Perm-36. I will expect a call soon after you make that determination."

Petronovich added, "Naryshkin will be more difficult to isolate. At this point, I'd prefer we fly to Almaty."

"Understood. But this is fluid, you may change your mind," said Whittington. "Once you have the prisoners, we can assist with the exfil, but no more boots on the ground in Russia until that objective is accomplished, understood?"

"I understand. I'm grateful for the assistance you are providing," Kamarov replied. "Vladi, text me your flight information and I'll see you tomorrow."

"Do either of you have any questions?" asked Whittington.

"I'm good," replied Kamarov.

"It's a go," said Petronovich.

"Anything to add?" asked Whittington as he looked at Schumacher and Jenkins, who both shook their heads no. "All right then, let's hit it. Good luck, gentlemen."

Jenkins reached across the table and clicked the speaker off.

***

Even though the cell they were confined in was damp and chilly, the three men lying on the bunks were perspiring and almost delirious. They could no longer verbally communicate, if anything only a simple nod, or shake of the head. Mike motioned Jason and Volkov outside to the courtyard.

"If we don't do something soon, those men inside are going to die," whispered Mike.

"I agree," said Volkov, "We have the key, we need to use it."

"The men inside will die if they don't get medical help, I know that. According to the old monk, that's not happening. But if we screw this up, we could end up dead as well and for what? We don't know the monastery grounds and we can't count on the monks for help. The minute the guards find us missing, this island will be crawling with SVR agents from Moscow. I don't know, give me the night to think about it," said Jason.

***

The Aeroflot flight to Perm was on time, leaving Riga International at five past five a.m. With a time change of two hours, they were scheduled to land at eleven fifty-six a.m. Petronovich had texted Kamarov the flight times the previous night.

108

As agreed, Kamarov waited off airport property for Petronovich to text once he was off the plane and outside the terminal. Having received the message, Kamarov pulled away from the curb and drove the short distance to the airport. He pulled in front of the Aeroflot baggage claim just as Petronovich exited the building. Getting his attention, Kamarov double-tapped the car horn. Petronovich recognized Kamarov and waved as he strode toward the vehicle.

"It's good to see you, Ivan," said Vladi as he threw his bag in the backseat and got in front.

"This whole thing is a cluster fuck, Vladi. I'm sorry it's come to this. You have every right to be pissed at me for getting the McClintocks involved. I made a serious mistake," explained Kamarov looking forward as he drove out of the airport property.

"Ivan, hindsight is, and always will be, twenty-twenty. If your plan had worked and Volkov received the information about our location, it might not have come to this. But shit happens. It's behind us, so let's move forward. How far to Perm-36?" asked Petronovich.

" Forty-five miles. We should be there in about an hour, with traffic," replied Kamarov.

"What about weapons?" asked Petronovich. "I don't want to be throwing stones."

"In the glove box, you'll find a Makarov nine mm, with three extra magazines. You should know that weapon like the back of your hand," said Kamarov.

"Standard issue KGB," said Petronovich. "If the prisoners are not at the Gulag, we'll need to either drive back to Moscow or fly to Almaty. We can't take the weapons in the air, and I don't want to confront Naryshkin just yet in Moscow."

"No need to speculate. We'll know soon enough if we have

to make that decision," said Kamarov as he drove out of the city.

A half hour into the trip, Petronovich recognized the road. He had driven it from the Gulag into Perm only days before.

"Perm-36 is maybe ten miles up the road on the right. When we pull in, you will need to drive toward the back of the facility. That's where we were held," Petronovich explained.

Historic signs on the side of the road indicated Perm-36 was two kilometers away.

"Here we go," said Kamarov as he turned onto the property, only to find the main gate to the facility locked.

Petronovich took the handgun out of the glove box and chambered a round.

"Wait here," he said, looking around. The Gulag was surrounded by fields and no cars were coming either way. Vladi walked quickly up to the gate, pointed and fired one round into the padlock, snapping it open. He took the lock off and swung the gate open, motioning Kamarov through, then closing it behind him.

"There goes the element of surprise," said Kamarov as Vladi got back in the car.

"Doesn't matter, they're not here," responded Petronovich. "Drive to the back and park. I'll show you."

***

The young monk placed the pots of food and plates in the middle of the floor. Jason wanted to speak with him but couldn't with two armed guards watching. The monk smiled at the men then turned toward the door and left without saying a word. After the door was locked Jason began the ritual of handing out the food for the frail men, then themselves.

"I wish we could find a way to get them to eat," said Jason, motioning to the men just lying there with the plates in front of them.

"At this point, I think the only nourishment they can handle is through an I.V.," replied Volkov. "Getting them to even sip water has been almost futile today."

"Okay. We can't wait. Tonight, about two, we'll try to get out of here. I don't like winging it, but it's the best we can do. If we can get into town, with Volkov's Russian language ability, maybe we can get someone to help us," explained Jason. "Are we in agreement?"

"I've been ready ever since we were given the key," said Mike.

"I'm in," added Volkov.

"Okay, try to get a little sleep. Once we're out of here we're going to need it," said Jason.

***

Kamarov turned in toward the last building in the back, parking in front of the door.

"This is the place?" he asked.

"This is it, let's go," said Petronovich as he exited the car with his gun raised.

"I thought you said nobody was here," said Kamarov as he raised his weapon and followed.

"Doesn't hurt to be safe," said Petronovich as he approached the door.

Vladi turned the handle, hoping it was unlocked. It was. He opened the door, stepped inside and turned on the light with the switch next to the door. The light hanging in the long hallway illuminated the empty cells on both sides as he walked toward the back. Motioning to the last cell on the right, he said, "This is where I was held. The place is vacant, as expected. Let's go, it's getting late, I need to call Whittington."

"There are plenty of hotels in Perm. Let's pick one, then call Whittington and discuss with him what our next move should be," Kamarov replied.

The Four Elements Hotel in Perm was only five miles from the airport. It was five fifteen p.m. and three front desk clerks were registering guests. Most of the patrons were businessmen and women. The registration desk manager stood in the background, watching the team do business. When Petronovich and Kamarov stepped forward, the manager took immediate notice. Two hours earlier, the hotel had received a lookout alert from the SVR. The two men identified in the alert looked like the two stepping up to register. Petronovich and Kamarov checked in using the forged passports and credit cards issued by the CIA.

After the men completed the paperwork and left registration, the manager came up from behind. "Let me see the registration for the last two men."

The clerk tapped the keys and moved the monitor for the manager to see. The names didn't match the alert. He took a piece of paper and wrote the two names they had registered under, then walked back to his office. He pulled the alert up on his computer. The names Petronovich and Kamarov were not a match. The pictures, though, were spot on. He dialed the SVR office in Perm.

After they received their room assignments and keys, Petronovich and Kamarov promised to meet thirty minutes later in Kamarov's room to make the call to Whittington.

***

112

Naryshkin took the call after being told it was the SVR office in Perm. He listened as the agent in charge relayed the information received from the Four Elements Hotel. The Perm office had a small staff, but large enough to handle the arrest of Petronovich and Kamarov.

"Go immediately to the hotel and take them into custody," said Naryshkin. "Petronovich got away once and it better not happen again. Understood?"

"Yes, sir, we'll have them within the hour," replied the agent.

"Call me when you do." Naryshkin cut the connection, then sat back and thought, *This was a stroke of luck.*

The agent in charge assembled his men outside the hotel. He left two men at the main entrance and another two in the rear, next to the employee entrance. After getting the emergency key from the front desk, the agent in charge, as well as three others, took the elevator to the fifth floor where Petronovich and Kamarov were located. Petronovich's room was near the elevator while Kamarov's was four doors down. Leaving one agent at the elevator, they approached Vladi's room. After knocking several times, they used the emergency key to gain access. The room was empty.

***

Nobody slept, as much as they tried. Finally, Jason rose from the bunk, with Mike and Volkov following.

"We've got to make this quick and quiet," whispered Jason with the key in hand as he approached the locked door.

He put the skeleton key in the lock and gently turned it, hoping not to make much noise. They heard the distinct click of the lock as it disengaged. Knowing that the door squeaked, Jason turned the handle and opened it slowly, inch by inch. The squeak was there, but less so, given that he had moved it so slowly. When it was wide enough to squeeze through, he stopped and motioned Mike and Volkov through as he followed. They were once again in the main portion of the cathedral with the large doors to the entrance at the end to the left. The guard's quarters were somewhere off to the right.

Jason reached the oversized wooden doors and pushed the old metal handle down to open them. As he did, there was a loud clang as the ancient locking mechanism lifted from its resting place and allowed the door to swing free.

"That does it," whispered Mike as they heard movement somewhere inside. "Let's get the hell out of here."

Jason led the way to the left, staying in the shadows. As they rounded the corner of the cathedral, exterior flood lights came on, turning the perimeter from night to the light of day. They continued moving forward, distancing themselves from the cathedral lights and the men that were sure to follow.

***

Kamarov and Petronovich finished the brief call with Whittington, deciding they would fly to Almaty, using any means necessary to get Lebedev to give the location of the prisoners. Whittington gave them permission to use excessive force if needed.

"I believe it's time for a drink," Petronovich said as he stood up from the hotel room's small corner table. He took the handgun from the table and placed it underneath his shirt, in the small of his back. Kamarov did the same.

"Let's go. The bar and restaurant are on the top floor," replied Kamarov as he opened the hotel room door and started out.

They heard commotion emanating from Vladi's room and quickly walked the other way. The agent by the elevators spotted the men, calling out, "Stop!" and started running toward them.

"Get to the stairs!" whispered Petronovich as he sprinted down the long hallway with Kamarov close behind.

They reached the end of the hall and shoved the door to the stairwell open, taking the stairs down two at a time. The clatter of footsteps could be heard following behind. When they reached the first floor, Petronovich opened the door to the hotel lobby and slammed it shut, while at the same time motioning for Kamarov to go down one more level to the basement. His hope was to make the men following believe they had left the stairs and were somewhere on the main floor. Reaching the basement, Petronovich and Kamarov ducked underneath the stairwell and waited in the dark. They heard the door one floor above open and close. Then, there was silence.

***

By the time the McClintocks and Volkov made it outside, the SVR agents could not determine which way the prisoners had gone. The floodlight illuminated the immediate area, but not beyond a twenty-yard perimeter. The agent in charge sent one man to the right while he and the third man went left. The monastery grounds were immense, like a small town. Through the ages, four cathedrals were built by monks on the property, not to mention a refectory, bell tower, watermill and eight guard towers. *The prisoners must have had help,* thought the agent in charge. "Follow me! We're going to the dormitory."

The monk's quarters were half a mile across the compound.

The agents sprinted in the dark, trying to keep their bearing while looking for the escapees. Reaching the old dorm building, he pounded on the locked door, repeatedly until the door opened. The old monk stood silently before them.

"How did the prisoners escape, old man?" asked the agent as he shook the monk by his shoulders and shoved him against the interior wall.

"I do not understand, what has happened?" asked the old monk.

The SVR agent, out of frustration, hit the gray-bearded monk in the face, breaking the man's nose and sending him to the floor.

"I saw you speaking with them in the courtyard. You helped them, somehow. You will pay dearly for what you've done, old man. Get me keys to one of your vehicles!"

The monk rose slowly from the floor, blood dripping from his nose and disappeared through the door. A few minutes later, he returned, handing the keys to the agent.

"The car is in the garage, next door."

The two agents left the building without saying another word.

***

There were seven gates spaced along the perimeter of the high monastery walls. Jason led Mike and Volkov through the shadows, skirting around buildings while following the wall for the next possible opening. At thirty feet high and fifteen feet thick, the walls couldn't be climbed. In the distance, Jason could see a small portion of the wall texture change from stone to wood.

"This is it, let's go," he said, crossing the dirt road from the shadows of a building.

Volkov reached the massive gate first, lifting the iron bar which secured it. He swung the gate open enough for the three men to squeeze through, then closed it, so it appeared to be locked.

"Where to?" Volkov asked.

"Let's follow the bay toward town," Mike replied. "See the lights in the distance?"

"Looks like a mile, two at most," said Jason, moving off the road to the water's edge.

"We'd better find a way off this island soon. It won't be long before a large contingent of SVR agents arrive," Volkov said as they moved quickly, but close to the ground, hoping to diminish their silhouettes.

"We should find a place to hole up before the sun comes up," Jason said as they moved along.

"There's what looks like an old, abandoned boathouse up ahead. Let's check it out," Mike replied leading the way.

To reach the boathouse, the three had to maneuver onto a dock that looked to be at least fifty years old and ready to fall into the water. Planks were brittle and some were nonexistent as they stepped cautiously toward the boathouse door, twenty yards away. The door looked as though it was ready to come off its hinges as Mike turned the knob and opened it. Inside was a slip, barely covered from the elements by what could loosely be called a roof. Off to the side was a storage room with an open door. Peering inside, Mike noticed several mice scurrying for safety in corners and behind debris which must have been as old as the boathouse itself.

"Well, this place hasn't had any love and attention in

decades," Jason commented.

"That's precisely why this might be the perfect spot to hang out until we decide how to get out of here," said Volkov as he kicked aside debris and sat against the wall.

"I think you're right," Jason said. "Why don't you two get a nap? I'll take the first watch."

Volkov was already snoring softly, with his chin resting on his chest.

"Get me up in an hour, Jason. I'll spell you so you can rest," said Mike, finding a spot to sit.

"You got it," said Jason as he moved out of the storage room and positioned himself near the boathouse door, with an unobstructed view of the dock and shoreline.

***

Petronovich looked at Kamarov and whispered, "What do you think?"

"We can't stay here, but I don't know where we would be safe. The documents given to us by your CIA are flawless," replied Kamarov.

"Our personal pictures gave us away. That means every major hotel between Perm and Moscow probably has them," said Petronovich. "I think we'd be safe at a small mom-and-pop motel anywhere in the country. That leaves us with what to do next. Driving to Kazakhstan is too far. What about our bags in the room?"

"I agree, Lebedev can't be our next move. We have our ID and money, let's leave the bags and find a way out of here," Kamarov said.

Petronovich thought for a minute, then said, "We can't fly

118

commercial. But Whittington may be able to help us out in that department."

"You're talking about a private aircraft?"

"Precisely, but let's get away from here first," Petronovich replied as he moved out from under the stairwell. "There's probably an employee entrance somewhere on the first floor. But they also must have a loading dock for food and hotel supplies, most likely on this level. Let's see if we can find it."

**

The SVR agents slowly circled the perimeter of the grounds in the monk's old vehicle, looking for any signs of the prisoners. Finally, the agent in charge said, "They must have left the monastery. Let's head for town."

Outside the monastery walls, the agents followed the dirt road past old, abandoned boats which looked to have been grounded on shore for years, as well as an old dock and boathouse which appeared to be ready to fall into the bay. The drive to town was no more than three minutes. The town of Solovetsky was small, with a population of no more than one thousand. The men drove down the short main street, then turned around and made another sweep back. Realizing they were unlikely to find the prisoners without help, they turned toward the main monastery gate.

"I need to call Naryshkin. This won't be pleasant," said the agent.

**

Jason watched as the car left the monastery grounds and drove slowly past the dock into town. Ten minutes later, the car drove back toward the monastery, passing through the main gate. It had been over an hour when Jason woke Mike.

"Mike, I'm ready for a break," whispered Jason.

Mike stirred, and rose from the floor. "Anything going on?"

"The guards drove by a little over half an hour ago. They're back inside the compound now. Give me thirty minutes for a power nap, then we need to move," said Jason, stifling a yawn as he took Mike's place on the floor and looked on as his brother took over watch at the boat house door.

After twenty-seven minutes, Jason opened his eyes. It took him a second to remember where he was, but then he whispered, "Volkov, let's go."

The men left the storage room and met Mike at the boat house door.

Mike looked up. "Any suggestions?"

"We have about an hour before sunrise. Let's check out the marina. Maybe we can get someone to help us," said Jason.

"It won't be long, and this place will be overrun with SVR agents," Volkov added.

"Okay, follow me," said Mike as he crept out the door across the rickety dock to the shore.

As they approached the small marina, they could see activity coming from one small vessel. A light illuminated the exterior of the boat while a single fisherman appeared to be prepping for a day at sea.

"Let me handle this," said Volkov as he walked out of the shadows toward the moored boat.

The fisherman looked up, startled as Volkov approached. He grabbed an iron bar, held it by his side and asked, "What do you want?"

"I'm sorry to have frightened you, sir. I need help. I just escaped from the monastery. The SVR had me and my friends captive."

"The monastery hasn't been a prison since the war. What are you talking about?"

"The monks are being paid by the SVR to rent a small section and use it as a prison. We need help off the island. Can you help me? Us?"

"How many people?" asked the fisherman, "As you can see, my boat is small."

"Me and two others."

"I'm going to Belomorsk for supplies this morning. If you want to ride with me, you can, but I'm leaving now."

"Thank you, sir," said Volkov as he whistled softly and motioned for Jason and Mike.

***

Kamarov followed Petronovich out of the basement stairwell, into the long, narrow corridor. Heavy doors were marked with plaques identifying equipment on the other side including the boiler room, electrical distribution, cable distribution and the low hum of the HVAC room. At the end were two double doors, one of which Petronovich opened carefully. Peering inside, he noticed the pallets along the wall wrapped in cellophane, containing supplies needed by the hotel. Off to the side was a huge roll-up door used to off-load material from delivery trucks. The room was vacant. Kamarov followed Petronovich as they walked across the expansive room toward a side door.

"Here's our exit," said Petronovich.

"Watch for SVR covering the door," whispered Kamarov as

he stood back while Petronovich cracked it open slowly.

Petronovich stepped out, looking both ways. "We're clear."

"The parking lot is around the side. Let's find our car and get the hell out of here," said Kamarov as they quickened their pace to a fast walk.

***

Naryshkin had arrived at the office early. His cell rang as he sat at his desk, reviewing reports left for him the previous day. Looking, but not recognizing the number, he answered, "Naryshkin." His face began to turn red as his blood pressure skyrocketed while listening to the agent in charge at the monastery on the other end of the line.

"Eliminate the remaining three and dispose of the bodies! I'll have additional men there this morning to assist in the search. In the meantime, secure all transportation off the island, including private aircraft and boats! Nothing leaves. Your heads are going to roll if these prisoners are not apprehended!"

Naryshkin cut the line and sat back. He made the call to the Perm SVR office and mobilized ten agents. They would arrive at the Solovki Island airport that morning. He then dialed Lebedev.

"Sergey, why are you calling? Is everything okay?" Lebedev asked, knowing there must be an issue since Naryshkin never phoned.

"Volkov and the McClintock brothers have escaped from the monastery."

"We were on a knife's edge when Petronovich and Kamarov escaped from Perm. Now this! What kind of imbeciles do you have watching them? I've had enough! I will not be brought down by your seemingly apparent incompetence."

122

"What does that mean, Lebedev? If you say anything, you will bring the axe down on your own neck as well," replied Naryshkin.

"You're on your own. I'm out," Lebedev said as he disconnected the call and thought about what he might do to distance himself from the debacle.

Staring at the blank screen on his phone, Naryshkin placed it on the desk and tapped his keyboard. After entering two separate security codes, he accessed the screen with a short list of names. The name of the file was 'Wetwork.' The list of names included all of the SVR assassins in his immediate area.

Recognizing the first name on the list, Naryshkin dialed. He was furious at Petronovich and the Americans for what they were putting him through, denying the fact that he was responsible for everything that was taking place.

Chapter 9

The boat captain steered the small trawler into the three-foot swells as they crossed Onega Bay, puffing on a pipe, thoroughly enjoying the moment. Volkov stood behind the captain in the cramped wheelhouse while Mike and Jason hunkered down on the aft deck, doing their best to avoid the cold wind that blew. The captain pointed toward the land.

"That's Belomorsk in the distance. We are a half hour out."

"Is there cell reception out here?" Volkov asked while steadying himself, holding the back of the captain's chair as the small boat rolled slightly.

"Not here. Once we enter the harbor, we'll have reasonable reception, why?"

"You've been a great help to us. I was hoping you could do one more thing."

"You want to borrow my phone?"

"If we could make one call, I would make sure you were compensated for the cost of the call as well as the fuel for your boat, once we are rescued."

The old man stared straight ahead. "I'll think about it."

***

Kamarov eased the car out of the lot, not wanting to attract any attention from the men positioned outside the hotel's lobby door. They turned onto the main street, driving the speed limit through town.

"Call Whittington and see if he can give us assistance with air transportation to Almaty," suggested Kamarov.

Petronovich dialed, and Whittington picked up. "Speak to me, Petronovich."

Vladi explained what had happened and how their identities had been compromised. "The bottom line is, do you have access to air assets in-country that can get us to Kazakhstan?"

"Let me work on it. Find a place to stay that's out of the way and I'll be back to you as soon as I can."

"We'll wait for the call," said Petronovich as he disconnected and looked at Kamarov. "Might as well find a small motel on the outskirts of town."

***

The assassin was in Almaty the next day. He positioned himself across the street from the NSC office and waited. He held a modified Colt 1911, which contained a dart the width of a strand of hair and only a quarter inch long. The dart was a frozen liquid, kept cold by a battery attached to the weapon. It was strong enough to penetrate clothing and would leave only a slight red mark the size of a mosquito sting. In fact, most people believed it to be a bug bite when hit. The dart contained a shellfish toxin at its center. After penetrating the body, it would melt, releasing the toxin and causing the heart to stop, mimicking a heart attack. Few coroners knew the dart existed and what to look for. It was the perfect weapon for 'Wetwork.'

Lebedev drove through the gate and parked inside the secure area. The assassin took note of his car and waited for Lebedev to leave. He was prepared to stay for hours if need be. Late

125

afternoon, the assassin looked up from his iPhone and watched as Lebedev left the building for his car. The assassin followed him for several miles before turning into a grocery store parking lot. He waited as Lebedev found a space and then parked one row over with an unobstructed line of fire to the driver's side of the car. The assassin prepared the weapon, certain the laser sight was up and operational. Lebedev returned to his car with a bag of groceries. He placed them in the back seat and then turned toward the car's front door. Before he opened it, he felt a slight sting on his upper left chest. Instinctively, he reached for the spot and rubbed it while opening the door. Once inside, he became light-headed, perspiring and began gasping for breath. Lebedev clutched his chest with both hands as his heart stopped. He slumped to the passenger side of the car and died.

The assassin walked casually past the car, glancing inside to be certain the target was eliminated. Confirming the kill, he smiled, walked back to his car and headed for the airport and the trip back to Moscow.

***

As they entered the Belomorsk harbor, the old captain reached for his cell phone on the dash above the wheel. He handed it to Volkov.

"Make the call short. I don't have many funds to pay for a long-distance call should I not be reimbursed."

"Thank you, sir," said Volkov as he took the phone, then hesitated, "Sir, we work for the U.S. Government. If I can keep this phone, we will have a new fishing boat purchased for you."

The old man looked into Volkov's eyes for a minute, then said, "With all new rigging?"

126

"Yes."

"Deal, I believe you. Keep the phone," said the old man as he wrote down his name and address on a slip of paper and handed it to Volkov.

Volkov walked out of the wheelhouse and showed Mike and Jason the phone. "I'm calling Kamarov."

Kamarov was driving when his cell rang. He didn't recognize the number but knew it was Russian. "I wonder who this is?"

"Better answer," said Petronovich.

"Hello?" said Kamarov tentatively.

"Ivan, this is Vasily!"

"Volkov, where are you?" asked Kamarov as he pulled to the side of the road and parked.

Volkov kept the explanation short. "Jason, Mike and I escaped from the Solovki Monastery. We caught a ride off the island and are just entering the marina at Belomorsk. Can you coordinate an extraction?"

"Belomorsk? That's on the White Sea, correct?"

"Yes."

"I'll make a call to Whit. Are there others still in custody?" asked Kamarov.

"Three are being held in the monastery, by the SVR. I don't know if they'll make it. They are in bad shape."

"As soon as I have instructions from Whittington, I'll phone this number. Stay put in Belomorsk."

"No problem. I bought the phone from the fisherman giving us a ride," explained Volkov. "We owe him a new boat."

"That's an expensive phone, but okay, I'll call as soon as I have instructions for you. I'm glad you're safe," Kamarov replied, cutting the connection. Looking at Petronovich, he continued, "Better call Whittington back."

***

The SVR agents from Perm arrived at the Solovki airport at noon. Four vehicles were waiting to be used in the search. The search shouldn't take that long. The island was only sixteen miles long and ten miles wide with mostly open terrain except for the small town where the search would be concentrated. The men broke up into teams of four. One vehicle was dispatched to circle the island's outlying area. The other three made an extensive search of the small town, including all shops and the inhabitants' homes. The search was tedious, with no stone left unturned. The men were nowhere to be found. As the sun was setting, one of the teams noticed a small vessel motoring into port.

"Let's see where he's been," suggested one of the agents.

They waited as the old man tied off at the dock before jumping aboard and searching the small boat.

"What were you doing on the water?" asked the agent.

"Fishing," replied the old man as he lifted the lid to the hold, revealing the fresh fish. He had fished on the way back from Belomorsk, failing to mention the stop.

Without a word, the agents jumped off the boat and drove back to the rally point in the center of town. Men milled about the four vehicles as the agent in charge made the call back to Perm, explaining the lack of success.

After listening to the report, the senior agent in Perm dialed Naryshkin and gave him the news. Without saying a word, Naryshkin cut the call. He left the office for home, where he grabbed his go-bag, multiple fake passports and cash. It would take no more than a few hours before the events in Perm and the

128

Solovki island reached Moscow. He needed to be far away from the repercussions that would be directed his way once the government found his actions could have compromised the relationship with the U.S., as tenuous as it is.

***

Petronovich called Whittington and relayed the good news about the McClintock brothers and Volkov. Whittington hesitated, then said, "Let me see how we can get them out. I'll call you back."

Whittington called Jenkins into his temporary office at the embassy in Riga and explained the situation. "The bottom line is that we need to get you to Belomorsk and bring in the McClintock brothers and Volkov. Research the quickest way to do it and get back to me. I need you out of here asap. I'll work on extracting the remaining men from the monastery."

Jenkins went back to his office. It didn't take him long to realize that Belomorsk was in the middle of nowhere and that the trip would take hours. He would need to fly from Riga to Kuusamo, Finland, rent a car and drive seven hours to Belomorsk. He made the reservations, then went back to Whittington's office, tapping on the door.

"Enter, Jenkins, what have you got?" asked Whit.

Jenkins explained the trip details, "The next flight out is at five p.m. It's going to take me ten hours to reach Belomorsk, including flight and driving time. I can be there at ten a.m. tomorrow. Have them meet me at the Pogibshim Memorial Park in the center of town, near the statue with the red star. I'll have Finnish passports fabricated and with me when I go."

"Good work, Jenkins. Bring them home!"

***

Before Whittington phoned Petronovich, he arranged for private transportation from Moscow to Almaty. He then called Petronovich and gave the time and place where Volkov and the McClintocks should meet Jenkins. He followed with, "Have Kamarov call Volkov back now. You two be at the Moscow FBO tomorrow morning at six. Ask for Alexei Morozov. He's the pilot that will fly you."

"Can he be trusted?"

"He's reliable and has worked for us in the past. You can trust him. He's being paid to wait for you. The mission, now that we know where the others are being held, is to terminate the subject with extreme prejudice. Understood?"

"I'll enjoy this job," said Petronovich, not mincing words.

***

The elegant, five-bedroom villa sat on the Black Sea coast in the central district of Sochi near the Caucasus Mountains. Sochi was a mid-sized city with a population of under half a million. The climate was subtropical, offering hot summers and mild winters, but access to winter sports in the nearby mountains. It hosted the 2014 winter Olympic games. Naryshkin purchased the villa years ago, under a different name, for two purposes; a place to retire and, if need be, a place to hide. The flight from Moscow was two and a half hours. Naryshkin had given the caretakers, a middle-aged couple, notice of his arrival. The home was open, bright and vibrant with fresh-cut flowers in every room. He never tired of the magnificent foyer with a stunning staircase which greeted him as he crossed through the massive double doors. In fact, this was a big part of the reason he purchased the property. The ornate pool and spa in the back, as well as proximity to the beach, had sealed the deal. Whether on vacation or in hiding, he could relax in seclusion, but absolute luxury.

Naryshkin threw his bag on the bed, changed into his swimsuit and headed for the pool. On the way, he grabbed a bottle of Ciroc X Vodka, his favorite, and a bucket of ice. Sitting on a chaise lounge under an umbrella, he poured the clear liquid and held the glass to his nose. There was a refreshing hint of citrus and honey, smooth and dry to the taste. At $220 per liter, it should be better than good. He had destroyed his iPhone and Notepad, replacing them both with new devices that he now logged onto. Thinking about how everything had unraveled, he was more than furious with Petronovich and the Americans. In time, he swore to himself, he would exact revenge.

***

It was mid-day when the G-280 landed in Almaty. Kamarov was anxious to get the job done and leave Kazakhstan without attracting attention. They needed to find Lebedev's location. Assuming he was at the NSC headquarters, Kamarov dialed the office to confirm. The telephone rang and was picked up by the receptionist.

"NSC Almaty, how may I direct your call?"

"I would like to speak with Agent Lebedev," responded Kamarov.

"I'm sorry sir, he is no longer with us."

"He's left the NSC?"

"No, sir. He's dead, heart attack yesterday," replied the secretary without emotion.

Kamarov dropped the line and looked at Petronovich. "Back on the plane. Lebedev was taken out."

"I would bet good money Naryshkin's behind it," said Petronovich.

"I wouldn't take that bet. Better call Whittington and find out where he wants us to fly. I'd like to get the hell out of Kazakhstan and Russia."

Both men walked back up into the plane, taking their seats. Petronovich dialed Whittington while the pilot and co-pilot serviced the jet, having the fuel topped off.

The conversation was short. Petronovich listened and replied, "Got it. See you soon." He looked at Kamarov. "Volkov and the McClintocks are being picked up in Belomorsk by Jenkins. Whit has a team lined up to rescue the men at the monastery. He wants us to fly to Riga from here. He said he would text the pilot orders."

The small Gulfstream sped down the runway and lifted gracefully into the air. Petronovich and Kamarov settled back for the five and a half hour's flight, with an arrival time being close to nine p.m.

***

Jason and Mike sat on the bench in the Pogibshim Memorial park, in view of the statue of the red star. Volkov, not wanting to bring attention to the three men, strolled the perimeter of the grounds, keeping the McClintock brothers in sight. They had arrived twenty minutes prior to the time arranged by Jenkins.

Jenkins left the car at the other side of the park and approached the statue from the back, behind the McClintocks' bench. Volkov noticed the man approaching and walked cautiously toward him, ready to intercede should a confrontation occur. The man had his hands in his coat pockets which caused Volkov to be even more concerned, thinking he might be concealing a weapon. About ten feet from the McClintocks, the man withdrew his hands, causing Volkov's adrenalin to spike, preparing to take down the assailant. Instead of a weapon, he held what looked to be passports. Jason turned and rose from the bench when he heard the footsteps. Jenkins stretched his hand toward Jason, handing him a passport.

"I think you'll want to have this, Jason."

Jason smiled, taking the passport. "It's nice to meet you Jenkins."

Volkov walked up. "You had me going for a second. I thought you might be SVR."

"I know. I saw you watching, and I didn't want to spook you, so I took my hands out of my pockets with the passports. Here's yours, Vasily. And you must be Mike," said Jenkins, handing the last one to him.

Mike looked at the passport. "Finnish. Looks authentic. I think we should continue this dialogue once we are on the road. Where's your car?"

"This way, gentlemen. With any luck, we will be in Riga this evening before midnight."

***

Whittington, Schumacher, Petronovich and Kamarov sat in the conference room, waiting for Jenkin's arrival. Their luggage was placed by the door in the corner. They were prepared to leave immediately. Petronovich looked over at Whit.

"So, what exactly did your men find when they entered the monastery?"

"The SVR were nowhere in sight and the monks disavowed any involvement with prisoners being held on monastery

133

grounds. It was as if the three men vanished."

"Why don't we approach Naryshkin?" Petronovich asked, not willing to let the other captives down.

"Our sources have tried to isolate him, but he can't be found. He's gone to ground."

"He is the only one who knows what happened to those men," replied Petronovich as the conference door opened, with Jason, Mike and Volkov stepping inside, followed by Jenkins.

After a round of celebratory drinks, Whit looked at his watch.

"I think we should wind this up and get to the airport. I'm sure you guys are anxious to see your families."

Volkov hesitated as did Kamarov, and Whittington noticed.

"Vasily, we have a place for you in the CIA if you're interested. I'm not sure staying in Russia would be in the best interest of your health, or longevity. Kamarov, I don't think you are safe in Russia either. We have a place for you as well."

Without any hesitation, Volkov answered, "I'm in if the arrangement is similar to the one given Petronovich."

"It is. It will be the same for both of you. There will be work for you to do, but on a sporadic basis. You will work for me out of southern California. You both will fit in nicely there. Volkov, given your tan and blonde hair, the beach lifestyle is made for you," said Whit, shaking Volkov's hand. He then looked at Kamarov and smiled. "Ivan, maybe not so much," he said as he shook his hand. "Welcome to the agency, gentlemen."

"You both can stay with me in Dana Point until you get settled," offered Petronovich as he grabbed his carry-on.

"Jenkins, can you give us a ride to the plane?" Whit asked.

Chapter 10

It had been six months since Jason, Mike and Petronovich had returned to the United States. Mike was busy tending the vineyard, mostly trimming vines and fertilizing in anticipation of the buds that would soon grow into Syrah grape clusters which eventually produced a fantastic wine. With the school year winding down and only a few days left, Julie, along with Zach and Sam, were looking forward to summer. They all swore that it would be years before they took another cruise. After the harvest this year, they were thinking a 'glamping' trip might be in order, up north in the Lake Tahoe area. That would be September.

Jason was back in Montana with Brenda. He worked the mine while Brenda continued to paint. Rosie, Jason's retriever, was at his side from morning until night, inside the mine. The vein of gold he struck had the potential to produce in the tens of millions of dollars.

Vladimir Petronovich enjoyed the simplicity of his beach-style life in Dana Point. Doheny Beach, made famous by the Beach Boys' song, 'Surfin Safari' was directly across Highway 1 from his house, a double-wide mobile home. Make no mistake, this was no ordinary 'trailer park.' His home would probably sell for close to $1,000,000 on the market, though that thought had never crossed Petronovich's mind. Petronovich had initially been busy helping Vasily Volkov and his friend Kamarov find homes to buy and adjust to life in the United States, but more specifically, Southern California.

Volkov did find a home on the beach in Carlsbad, a city just north of San Diego. After arriving in the U.S., he went through an intensive indoctrination in CIA protocol. Whittington, with Petronovich's help, guided Volkov through the process. With his previous SVR training, Volkov was already up to speed in the tradecraft. He just needed to become familiar with agency procedures. It did not take long for him to assimilate and become comfortable with the organization.

Kamarov was a treasure trove of information, given his previous senior position in the SVR. He had spent the last six months mostly away from California in Langley, Virginia. He offered the CIA as much information as he could, exposing secrets they could only dream of uncovering. For his help, Kamarov was given a home in Palm Desert, a pension, and retirement. His days of service had ended, and he looked forward to some golf and exploring the United States.

Naryshkin remained at his estate in Sochi, on the Black Sea. He felt like a caged animal as he paced the grounds. The only contact outside the villa was his weekly call to his mother in Moscow. He phoned every Sunday at precisely ten past five p.m., always using a burner phone. His rumination of the events that caused his 'lockdown' was so extreme that it was hard for him to think of anything else. He was obsessed with exacting revenge on the McClintock brothers, as well as the traitors Petronovich, Kamarov and Volkov for having placed him in such a situation.

***

He sat in his office staring at his laptop and the iPhone next to it. Naryshkin had avoided contact with everyone. His mother and the few friends he had were unaware of his location and he had planned to keep it that way. He could not stand the solitude and, more importantly, the inaction. His hatred for the Americans and the three traitors was too over-powering. There was one person in the SVR he could trust. It was Mikhail Kozlov. He and Mikhail had gone through SVR training and, like Naryshkin, Kozlov had risen in the SVR ranks, though not as high. Kozlov still had access to sensitive information that Naryshkin needed. It was early evening when he picked up the phone and dialed.

Kozlov looked at his phone as the call rang through. Not recognizing the number, he hesitated, but answered, "Hello?"

"Mikhail, it's me," said Naryshkin.

"Sergey, my God! What have you done? You are a wanted man!"

"Listen to me, Mikhail. What I did, I did for Mother Russia. I am not a traitor. My only goal was to punish those who betrayed our country."

"I understand, but you almost caused a major international incident," replied Kozlov.

"I need your help, Mikhail," said Naryshkin, ignoring the last statement.

"I won't sacrifice myself, Sergey."

"Just two things. It should be easy, a couple of calls at most. We have moles in the CIA and FBI, correct?"

"Yes."

"Have the CIA asset find contact information and addresses for Vasiliy Volkov, Ivan Kamarov, Vladimir Petronovich, as well as Mike and Jason McClintock in the States. Can you do it?" Naryshkin asked.

There was silence for a few moments, then, "I will help you this one time, no more. I'll call this number when I have the information."

"Thank you, Mikhail."

Naryshkin terminated the call and sat back in his chair, smiling for the first time in months. He walked over to the bar, poured three fingers of Ciroc X into a tumbler, and then took an Arturo Fuente Hemingway from the humidor and sat back down. It is *time for a small celebration,* he thought as he lit the cigar and sipped his vodka.

***

Volkov's home sat directly on the beach in Carlsbad with an Ocean Street address. He was only two blocks away from Carlsbad Village and the hip restaurant and bar scene. From the back patio of his home, he had direct access to the beach and the volleyball tournaments that occurred every afternoon in the three sand courts just yards away from his patio lounge chairs and gate. It didn't take long for the young girls to notice the long blonde hair and tan, typical for many south coast surfers. What surprised them was his Russian accent. Volkov, being athletic and physically young, took to the game of volleyball and was soon a regular participant in the afternoon matches. His home became the after-match hangout for a select few, mostly women. He was enjoying this new life and culture in southern California.

Volkov sat back on the lounge chair under the umbrella, looking out toward the ocean as small waves rolled slowly toward shore. The volleyball match was over and happy hour had begun. Tina, a tan, long-legged brunette, came out of the house with a pitcher of margaritas and two glasses. She poured two glasses and set the pitcher on the table between the two chairs.

"This never gets old," Volkov commented as he clicked

Tina's glass. "*Na Zdorovie.*"

"Cheers," Tina replied. "Vasily, you've never mentioned what you do. How do you spend your time during the day?"

"Unlike you, my school days are over. I think I might look at getting a job at a dive shop. I used to do that."

"Are you certified?"

"Certified crazy? Possibly, but certified scuba, yes. I owned a dive shop once upon a time in the Maldives."

"The Maldives? I've heard of that. Where is it located?" asked Tina innocently.

"A long way from here. It seems like another life," explained Volkov. "Let's change the subject. How were your classes today?"

"We've got three more weeks, then finals. I'll be happy to get the year over and begin grad school. I'm thinking of becoming a family therapist."

Volkov was about to respond when his phone buzzed. "Hello?"

***

It was early morning. Naryshkin was watching the news on television when he received the call. Recognizing Kozlov's number, he answered the phone with, "What do you have for me, Mikhail?" Naryshkin listened, writing down the information that was conveyed.

"That's it, Sergey. Don't call me again."

The call lasted no more than a minute. Kozlov ended it without waiting for a reply.

Naryshkin looked at the time. With the difference being ten

hours, he calculated that, in southern California, the time would be six p.m. He decided not to wait and dialed the number given to him by Kozlov, using a burner phone. The phone rang and was picked up by Volkov.

Naryshkin listened to the voice at the other end. It was Volkov. Mikhail had provided the correct information. He noted that Volkov was in the San Diego area.

Tina watched as Volkov listened for a response. There was none. He terminated the call without saying another word.

"Is everything okay?" she asked.

Volkov set his drink on the table and got up from the chair and walked toward the patio gate, looking toward the ocean.

"Probably just a prank call, Tina," Volkov said a little disturbed. He let it go. "Now how about another margarita?"

***

The home that Kamarov purchased was off Monterey street in Palm Desert. It was in a well-kept, older neighborhood. The home's curb appeal was deceiving, looking small in front, when, in fact, the home was large with most of the living area located in the back. The pool, spa and covered gazebo with fireplace and television were where Kamarov lived most of the time.

Kamarov was under the gazebo with the overhead fan rotating at a moderate speed, watching the evening news, when his phone rang. He recognized the number and answered.

"Vasily, my friend, how's the beach and all of those young college girls you hang out with?"

Volkov ignored the question and asked, "Ivan, have you had any strange calls lately?"

"By strange, what are you referring to? I get the normal

140

solicitations, that I ignore."

"I guess I may be reading into things. Can I drive out to see you this weekend? A break from the coast might be what I need."

"By all means. Pack your bag and come for a visit in the desert. We'll barbeque steaks, the way Americans do, but drink vodka our way! I'll see you in a couple of days," Kamarov replied with a smile on his face, looking forward to seeing his friend. *I wonder what's bothering him? He seemed flustered.*

***

As was his habit, before leaving the house, Volkov clipped two pieces of string and placed one in the top corner of the closed back door, between the door and jamb, as well as one in the corner of the front door. If anyone entered the house through either door while he was away, the string would drop to the ground and he would know the house had been penetrated. Satisfied that everything was in position, he walked to the carport, and his BMW X5. He was anxious to see Kamarov.

Kamarov could sense that something was wrong. The evening air was warm, close to eighty degrees with no breeze.

They sat under the gazebo with a soft light glowing, while the interior pool lights glimmered off the walls of the house. The bottle of Grey Goose sat between them. Volkov seemed to down his first drink in two or three large sips. He set his tumbler on the table. While Kamarov refilled it without saying a word, Volkov began by reminiscing. They had gone through so much in the previous six, now almost seven, months. He concluded, "We have one loose end that bothers me."

Looking up, Kamarov asked, "Why would Naryshkin bother you? He is nowhere to be seen."

"He's out there, I can feel it. He wants retribution, nothing more. I believe without a doubt, he will try and come after us all."

Kamarov sat for a moment, sipping his drink, thinking.

"Well, I believe your imagination is getting the better of you. Naryshkin wouldn't be that stupid to try taking out three former SVR agents and one retired FBI agent in a foreign country."

"You're making my point! I don't believe he's thinking rationally. Naryshkin is a narcissistic psychopath. He lost his position of power in the SVR and has gone underground because of us! He's got to be furious, wherever he is. I can't explain it, Ivan, but I have a bad feeling about this."

"I think what you need is another drink, then a two-inch ribeye steak! After that, a good night's sleep. Tomorrow will be better than tonight, you'll see, my friend," Kamarov said reassuringly.

***

Naryshkin waited outside his home with his carry-on sitting on the ground next to his feet. He checked the Uber app, noting his ride was only a quarter mile away. The red Mercedes GLA SUV pulled up to the curb with the young female driver jumping out to get Naryshkin's bag, placing it in the back. Naryshkin took a seat in front, waiting for the driver.

She returned to the driver's side and put the car in gear. "It's a nice day to fly. Where are you going?"

"Out of the country," Naryshkin replied, not wanting to engage in the light banter.

She wouldn't take the hint. "Fun, where to?"

"Los Angeles."

"That's quite a trip. How long does it take? Fifteen, sixteen hours?"

"Closer to twenty-one. It's going to be a long day. If you don't mind, I have emails I need to read," said Naryshkin as he logged into his phone and began scanning nothing in particular.

The ride took twenty minutes with the driver coming to a stop in front of Turkish Airlines. She handed Naryshkin his bag and with a smile said, "Enjoy your flight."

Naryshkin took his bag, and turned toward the terminal doors, ignoring her comment.

***

Volkov woke to the smell of coffee and bacon. He heard Kamarov moving about in the kitchen, obviously preparing breakfast. He had slept a solid seven uninterrupted hours, which was good for him. He would normally wake at about one a.m. with his mind racing for an hour or two, before nodding off again for a couple more hours. He walked down the hall to the kitchen.

Kamarov looked up. "The Keurig is ready to go, just press start. How'd you sleep?"

"Great! I think what you said last night is probably right. I'm being paranoid," Volkov said as the machine finished brewing the coffee. "What are your plans for the day?"

"I might do a round of golf over at the Marriott on Country Club. Do you want to join me?"

"Thanks, no. I should head back home. I've decided to look for a job at a dive shop. I love the water and sitting around the house playing volleyball in the afternoon isn't cutting it. I'm too young not to be busy."

"I get that. Waiting on Whittington to call can be boring. According to Petronovich, you can go months before you hear anything. And then the assignment is something mundane and may last only a week. I've got breakfast almost ready. You can eat, then get out of here," Kamarov said as he fried the eggs, over easy, and simmered the bacon.

***

Naryshkin settled back in the seat. As soon as he sat down, the flight attendant was at his side, asking for his drink order. On a flight lasting longer than five hours, first class was the only way to travel. He had one stop during the trip, Istanbul. He could have gone west with a layover in Moscow, but he was intent on avoiding that city at all costs. The flight to Istanbul was seven hours with two hours to wait before the final fourteen-hour leg to LAX. Naryshkin took out his iPhone and scanned the addresses of the four men. Up until seven months ago, Kamarov had been chief of station at the Russian embassy in Washington D.C. He had willfully betrayed Naryshkin and for that, he would be the first to die. The driving time from LAX to Palm Desert would be a little over two hours. *After Kamarov, Volkov will be next, followed by Petronovich. The McClintock brothers will be last,* thought Naryshkin as he smiled and sipped his vodka.

***

It was after eight in the evening when Kamarov clicked off the television, sitting above the outdoor fireplace in the gazebo.

At a dry eighty-five degrees, the fireplace remained off, but during the chilly winter months, it provided the warmth and ambiance of the high-desert lifestyle. He stood, stretched, and yawned. *This has been a nice, relaxing day,* he thought as he

144

turned off the fan and walked down the steps past the hot tub and pool, toward the house. After locking the back door and turning off the outdoor lights, he set the alarm and headed for the back bedroom. As he pulled the covers back to the bed, he glanced at the sliding door and, through the closed drapes, he noticed a dim glow of light attached to the fan above the outdoor fireplace. *I thought I turned that off.* Kamarov slid on his shorts, walked down the hall to the back door, where he turned off the alarm and stepped outside. As he walked up the steps past the hot tub on his right, he noticed the individual sitting in the furthest chair back in the shadows.

"Have a seat Ivan," Naryshkin whispered, motioning to a chair with the handgun he was holding.

"What do you want, Naryshkin?" Kamarov answered as he eased into a chair, watching the weapon, with attached suppressor, follow him as he sat.

"I've been looking forward to this conversation. Why did you have to get involved when we apprehended Petronovich? He was a traitor, plain and simple. You should have let it go. Instead, you had to get yourself and Volkov involved."

"You're a sick son of a bitch, Naryshkin."

"I may be, but I'm holding the gun."

"If you plan to use it, do it now!" replied Kamarov as he stood, turning toward the house. "I'm going to bed."

"Good night, Ivan," said Naryshkin as he fired two barely audible shots into Kamarov's back and one to the head, watching him tumble forward from the raised living area into the spa below.

Naryshkin slowly rose from the chair and walked to the back door passing the spa, with a plume of red surrounding the body which was face down in the water. He entered the kitchen, hoping for something to eat from the evening dinner. He had watched Kamarov grill and was rewarded with half of a rib-eye steak in a freezer bag in the fridge. After consuming the steak and a bottle of wine, he opted for the guest room and a good night's sleep before leaving for Carlsbad in the morning.

***

After the visit with Kamarov in Palm Desert, Volkov was energized and put his concerns about Naryshkin into the recesses of his mind. His goal now was to find a job in a local dive shop which would allow him to do the things he loved to do, which were teaching scuba courses and helping people enjoy the wonders of life that exists below the surface of the ocean. As an NDL, Divemaster, (the Russian equivalent to a PADI Divemaster), he had all the necessary qualifications. If a dive shop happened to need an experienced diver, they'd be lucky to have him, or so he thought. After calling on seven dive shops from Oceanside to San Diego, he was beginning to think his skill set wasn't that special. He had learned that Southern California had more talented and experienced divers than he had previously thought. It seemed that his timing for a job was off. He left his name and number with each store, should an opening occur.

The sweet smell of the ocean air, along with the sound of seagulls squawking as they flew by, added to the beauty as sailboats slowly drifted out of their mooring into the bay, heading for open water. Volkov sipped his coffee and watched the scene from his patio, almost mesmerized. The vibration of his phone startled him for a brief second. He looked at the number, it was a local call. "Hello?"

"Is this Vasily?"

"Yes, how can I help you?" asked Volkov, believing it was a solicitor.

"Vasily, this is Maggie from South Coast Scuba. We talked yesterday morning. The reason for my call is that, late yesterday afternoon, my head instructor informed me that he had a family emergency back east and would need to take an extended leave of absence. Your dropping by the shop seemed to be fortuitous. Would you be interested in taking on the Dive Master position for our store?" Maggie asked.

"Sure, I'd love the position. When would you like me to start Maggie?"

"We actually have a class at eleven this morning. You will be the instructor. Can you do it?"

"Yes, let me get squared away here and I'll be there in about an hour if that works?" Volkov asked.

"It works, you're a lifesaver, Vasily, thanks so much! See you soon," Maggie replied as she cut the call.

Chapter 11

Petronovich sat on his front porch, staring across Highway 1 at Doheny Beach. It was early evening, the sun about two hours from setting. He nursed his Grey Goose and simply felt off. *Something's wrong,* he thought. He picked up his phone and dialed Mike's cell. Mike picked up after the second ring while out in the vineyard.

"Vladi, how you doing, buddy? I've been thinking about you and the guys. Are they situated yet?"

"They are. Kamarov is in Palm Desert and Volkov has a place on the beach in Carslbad, perfect for him. How are you, Julie and the kids doing? Is everything okay up there in God's country?"

"We're all fine. The kids get out of school next week. I'm thinking of sending Julie and them up to see Jason and Brenda for a week. After all we've been through, the fresh mountain air might be a good change. The busy season is coming soon, and I won't be going anywhere until after the harvest. If you're bored, maybe you could come up and give me a hand," Mike suggested, half serious.

"When you begin the harvest, I promise to be there to help. I'll let you go, I just wanted to touch base," Petronovich said, happy that everyone was safe.

"Take care, Vladi, talk to you soon," replied Mike as he disconnected and headed toward the house to clean up.

Petronovich took a long sip of his drink and then dialed

Jason. Jason was sitting on his porch with Rosie by his side. He'd had a long, but productive, day at the mine and was nursing a glass of Glenfiddich when the phone vibrated. He noticed it was Petronovich, then answered, "Vladi, good to hear from you, everything okay?"

"Just checking in, how are you and Brenda?"

"Good. Brenda's at an art show in Phoenix for a few days, so Rosie and I are roughing it. When do you plan on coming up to Montana? Summer is the best time of year. We could probably get some fishing in at Georgetown Lake or, better yet, the Big Hole river."

"Jason, I've never fished a day in my life," Vladi responded.

"Then, it's about time, what do you say?" asked Jason prodding.

"I'll be honest, Jason. You know that I have a certain intuition. When my gut tells me something is off, it normally is, right?"

Jason hesitated, "Yes, it happened once in Uruguay and the other time, more recently, in Mexico. What's going on? Are you getting that feeling?"

"It's happening again. I can't explain it, but wish I could," Vladi answered softly. "I'm glad you and Brenda are safe. I'm going to check on Kamarov and Volkov. If something comes up, I'll call. See you, Jason," said Petronovich as he dropped the line, with his gut churning more than ever.

Jason looked at the phone. *Crap! I hope he's wrong.*

Volkov had completed his first class and had then begun to orient himself with the dive shop, making certain the new and the used rental equipment were in order and properly cared for. It was five p.m. when Maggie handed Vasily keys to the store.

"It's official, close up shop at six and I'll see you in the

149

morning, Vasily."

"Thanks for everything, Maggie," Volkov replied as he continued working on the inventory. It was six thirty when Volkov looked at the time. *Time to wrap things up,* he thought.

He locked the store doors and headed for home. The short drive along the beach was relaxing with the sun still ninety minutes from setting. It was the best time of the day as far as Volkov was concerned. He planned to be in his swimsuit, with a drink, on the patio within thirty minutes. After parking in the carport, he walked to the front door, and automatically looked up, spotting the string. It was still in place. He unlocked the door, grabbed the string and headed for the bedroom to change.

On the patio, with a Dragoon IPA in hand, he watched the waves rolling slowly toward the shore. The volleyball game had ended over an hour ago and the few people on the beach were strolling along, one couple with their dog on a leash. Volkov's phone buzzed, it was Petronovich. "Vladi, how's it going?"

Petronovich didn't mince his words. "Vasily, have you talked with Kamarov recently?"

"I was at his place two days ago, why?"

"I called him just now and there was no answer," said Petronovich.

"He might not have his phone near him, or he didn't hear it. I wouldn't be concerned."

"You're probably right. I'll call again in a bit," replied Petronovich. "How are you doing?"

"Great!" Vasily explained the new job and the excitement he felt getting back into the workforce. After ten minutes, the conversation slowed.

"I'll talk to you soon, Vasily," said Petronovich as the call terminated.

Petronovich waited until eight p.m. then dialed Kamarov once again. The result was the same, ringing, then voicemail. This time he didn't leave a message. Petronovich was determined to phone once more in the morning. If there was no answer, he would drive to Palm Desert to check on his friend.

***

Volkov was out the door by seven thirty. Starbucks was on the way. He picked up a regular coffee, Grande for himself and he guessed Maggie might like the Grande White Chocolate Mocha with an extra shot of espresso. His fingers were crossed on this one. Either he had her pegged, or his intuition was off by a long shot. He had no idea that he had missed Naryshkin by only ten minutes.

***

Naryshkin parked a block away. Seeing that the carport was empty, he assumed that Volkov was gone. He looked out of place in a dark suit. Having no tie helped a little but not much to anyone paying attention. As luck would have it, the street was empty. He walked to the front door and used his lock pick to unlock it. With his weapon ready, holding it concealed in his coat pocket, he slowly and quietly opened the door, stepping in quickly while closing it at the same time. He paused, looking around. The home was small but well kept, with everything in place. Nothing seemed to be out of order. *Typical for a type-A personality,* thought Naryshkin. It didn't take more than five minutes to clear the house and make certain that Volkov was gone. Now, the hard part: waiting.

***

The driving time from Dana Point to Palm Desert was normally about two hours and twenty minutes. It took Petronovich exactly two hours to reach Kamarov's home. After parking in the driveway, he checked his Glock 17, with a suppressor. It was racked and ready. He approached the house, rang the doorbell and waited. After thirty seconds, he tried the handle. The door was unlocked.

He stepped through the threshold and called out, "Ivan!"

There was no response.

He started at the left side of the house and, what he assumed, was the master bedroom. The light was on, and the bedding unruffled. He then moved to the other side of the house and what appeared to be the guest wing. The bed had been slept in with no attempt to make it, which was unusual for Kamarov, as fastidious as he was. The kitchen had a plate in the sink and an empty bottle of wine with stemware on the counter, once again unlike Kamarov. Petronovich glanced outside and noticed the gazebo light and fan were on. He stepped out back and proceeded up the stairs to the outdoor living area until he was stopped in his tracks.

Kamarov's body was face down in the spa, bloated and floating.

"Oh, Ivan, my friend," he whispered.

***

Maggie was at the counter, checking the class schedule, as well as equipment rentals reserved for the day, when Volkov walked in.

"I stopped for coffee and bought you one. I hope it's a good choice," said Vasily as he handed the Starbucks cup to Maggie.

After sipping the drink, Maggie replied, "Thanks! This is one of the two that I normally buy!"

I've still got it, thought Volkov, smiling. "What's on schedule for today?"

Maggie proceeded to go through the schedule and ended with, "It's going to be a long one. But better to be busy and have a job than sitting on our hands."

***

Petronovich signed into his phone, went to his contacts and dialed Whittington. After several minutes on hold, Whit answered.

"What's up Petronovich?"

"I'm at Kamarov's home in Palm Desert. He's been eliminated. Looks to be a professional hit. We're going to need a clean-up team and forensics ASAP."

"Crap! Secure the site, Vladi, I don't want law enforcement involved. I'll have help there within the hour," responded Whit. "Are there any signs that this could have been a random burglary gone bad?"

Petronovich hesitated, looked around, and responded, "Negative. This was professional. It may be related to Russia and what we were involved with a few months ago."

"I sure as hell hope not. That would mean our entire team is in danger. After forensics completes their work, I'll contact you. In the meantime, I think you should notify Volkov and the McClintock brothers."

"I'll take care of that now," said Petronovich as he walked

up the steps to the gazebo and took a seat.

***

Volkov was checking the regulator and diving tank for a customer. After he finished, he handed the rental equipment over.

"You should be good to go. Have fun, be safe, see you in a few hours." His phone buzzed as the customer went out the door. Seeing that it was Petronovich, he answered, "Were you able to contact Kamarov?"

"I have some bad news. I'm at his place now. He was killed," Petronovich responded. "It looks to be professional, Vasily. We could all be in danger, so watch your back. As soon as I know more, I'll call. Are you armed?"

"Always. I will wait to hear from you. This is devastating news," said Volkov as he hung up and felt the Glock 26 in the small of his back. Maggie had gone for the day and he had thirty minutes before closing the shop. Now, he waited for two customers to return the diving equipment they'd rented. After cleaning and disinfecting everything, he would be able to go home. He was anxious about what he might find.

***

The volleyball game was coming to an end on the beach outside Volkov's home. The usual participants were playing, including Tina. She had glanced over at Vasily's place during the match and thought she had seen movement inside. After the game was over, she walked toward the short gate, when one of her teammates called out, "Tina, are you joining us?"

"I'll be a second, I'm going to see if Vasily is home," she

replied. "I'll be right there, go ahead." Tina opened the gate and walked toward the sliding door. She tapped lightly, thinking she saw movement, then peered in, cupping her hand above her eye to cut the glare and tapped once more, smiling at the guy sitting in the corner, offering a friendly wave. The man approached the sliding door and opened it.

"I'm sorry, I thought you were Vasily," Tina explained.

"No, I'm Vasily's uncle from Russia, and you are?" asked Naryshkin as he opened the door wider, "Please come in."

Tina stepped inside. "My name's Tina, I'm a friend. I'm sure Vasily will be home soon. He gets off about now. I know where he keeps his liquor. Would you like a margarita while you wait, I'd be happy to make it?"

"That would be great, I am a bit parched," Naryshkin replied.

"Margaritas coming right up, I'll make a pitcher," Tina replied as she bounded toward the kitchen and liquor cabinet. She pulled down the Don Julio tequila, Cointreau, Triple Sec and, out of the fridge, the lime juice. Using the shot glass, she concentrated as she mixed the ingredients in a pitcher.

Naryshkin walked up behind her. "That's quite a production, looks good."

"If you like tequila, you're going to love these," she replied as she continued mixing. Naryshkin closed the distance between her, wrapping his right arm tightly around her neck while using his left hand to violently twist her head until he heard the distinct snap. She dropped, lifeless. The assassin carried her into Volkov's bedroom placing her on the bed. He then walked back into the kitchen, shut off the lights and returned to his chair in the corner to wait.

***

As promised, two solid panel vans backed into Kamarov's driveway, pulling as close to the garage door as possible. After the garage door was raised, the vans' back doors would be opened and provide an obstructed view for any curious neighbors. The team, dressed in coveralls, several carrying cleaning equipment, went in the front door and immediately got to work. The forensic team easily gathered the data needed given the wine bottle, glass, plate, and utensils left behind in the kitchen by the killer.

Kamarov was carried out to one of the waiting vans through the garage in a body bag. It took the team of six a little over two hours to get the data and clean the home. When they were finished, there was no indication that a crime had been committed, even down to draining and scrubbing the spa. A pool cleaning company had already been hired to fill the spa and bring the chemicals back to normal the next day. Petronovich waited until everyone was done, before he followed them out, making certain the home was secure once again. He had two more calls to make and planned on doing that on the drive back to Dana Point.

Jason answered the phone immediately. He listened to Petronovich as he explained what had happened to Kamarov.

After Petronovich finished, Jason waited a few seconds, processing the potential meaning and implication of the hit. "So, where does that leave us, Vladi?"

"We cannot definitively say that the murder is probably related to Russia. Forensics has plenty of prints and DNA. We'll put the results through the national and international data banks and see if we get a hit. In the meantime, we all need to be alert. If anything out of the ordinary occurs, don't dismiss it. Be extra vigilant. I'll be in touch. Can you pass this on to Mike? I'm really concerned about the family. I think it might be wise for Mike to hire private security until we get this squared away. You might consider it as well, Jason."

"No, I'm good. I'll call Mike right now and pass along the suggestion of security. Thanks, Vladi."

***

Volkov parked a block away from his house. He moved slowly toward the home, staying as close to his neighbor's property as possible. The ability of anyone inside his residence seeing his approach at such an extreme angle was minimal. He reached the corner of his house, ducked below the front window, and walked low to the front door. The string was on the cement, directly below the door handle. He crept back to the corner and moved toward the back of the house. Without exposing his position, he glanced around the corner to the patio and sliding door. Once again, the string was gone. It was obvious that someone was inside. *The question now is how do I avoid an ambush and getting dead? Focus, Vasily! Remember your training,* he thought. He needed a distraction. Looking around, he noticed the next-door neighbor's kid, Tommy, playing in the back with a buddy. Volkov looked down at the planter along the side of his house and pried away a loose brick. He shuffled quickly next door.

"Tommy, come here."

Tommy and his buddy were probably fifteen years old or so. He had his driver's learner permit, so that was a good guess. Volkov fished two twenty-dollar bills from his wallet.

"Hi Vasily," responded Tommy.

"Would you and your buddy like to earn an easy $20 each?" asked Volkov.

"Sure, what do we have to do?" asked the kid.

"Real simple. Take this brick. Go to the front of my house and throw it through the dining room window."

"You're kidding, right?"

"Nope. Dead serious, but you need to do it right now. After the brick goes through the window, run like hell. Can you do it?" asked Vasily, offering Tommy the brick and cash.

Tommy took the two bills, handed one to his friend, then the brick. "Consider it done. I sure would like to know what you're smoking."

"Through the window. Don't miss," Volkov replied.

The two teenagers went to the front of the house, quietly counted one, two, three and hurled the brick, which hit the center pane, smashing through the plate glass window, shattering a vase with flowers sitting on the dinette table. As soon as the brick took to flight, the boys were gone.

***

Naryshkin jumped out of his chair and bolted toward the kitchen. As he did, the minute Volkov heard the shatter, he sprinted to the sliding door with his gun raised. Naryshkin saw Volkov out of the corner of his eye. He swung his weapon up and around sending a nine mm hollow point at Volkov.

Sensing the action, Volkov dove left, crashing into an armchair, toppling it over while returning fire with his Glock 26, nine mm. The bullet went high. With nowhere to go and in tight quarters, Naryshkin lunged at Volkov, getting off one shot that hit Vasily's gun, flinging it out of his hand across the room.

At half Naryshkin's age, Volkov had the advantage of youth. Unfortunately, Naryshkin had the weapon.

Vasily grabbed a lamp from the corner table and swung it as Naryshkin fired another round. The lamp hit Naryshkin's gun arm, sending the weapon flying toward the kitchen. Naryshkin's shot was off target but still managed to graze Volkov's shoulder.

Volkov dropped to the ground, his shooting arm rendered useless, while Naryshkin dove for his gun. Vasily crawled toward his Glock, picked it up with his other hand and turned to shoot.

Naryshkin was one second quicker, firing one quick round which landed center-mass.

The fight was over.

Naryshkin ran through the sliding door, past several homes and toward the marina where he disappeared. The confrontation was violent and quick, taking no more than thirty to forty seconds at most.

Chapter 12

Petronovich waited until six before calling to check on Volkov. The call rang and then went to voicemail. Petronovich waited another thirty minutes and dialed, with the same result. He then phoned Whittington.

"What do you have, Petronovich?" asked Whit.

"You better send a team to Volkov's place. He's not answering his phone and I've got a bad feeling about this. I'll be heading that way now, but your boys should get there first."

"I'll make the call. I sure as hell hope it's not what you think," replied Whittington as he hung up and dialed.

When Petronovich pulled up in front of Volkov's home, he found the white solid panel van backed as close to the front door as possible. The team had erected a plastic tarp-like privacy barrier to keep prying eyes from seeing what might be brought inside the home or out.

Petronovich came around the corner at the back of the house and stopped. His jaw dropped as he noticed the volume of blood on the floor. One of the 'technicians' motioned him toward the scene.

"I'm sorry for the loss of your friend, we moved him to the van. There's a second body in the bedroom, a young girl. Probably at the wrong place, wrong time."

"Any weapons found?" asked Petronovich as he ignored the news of the second body.

"One, a Glock 26."

"Vasily owned a 26, probably his."

"We have plenty of prints. If the killer is the same guy that hit Kamarov, we should have a match. We've already notified Whittington and he is pissed."

Petronovich nodded, turned away from the carnage and went back to his car. The thirty minute drive home was a fog. He couldn't even remember making the trip. As he pulled into the driveway, he came out of it.

***

Petronovich was about finished with his second drink and was preparing to call the McClintock brothers by conference call. He had decided it best to have everyone on the line when he told the brothers what had happened. As he was dialing, Petronovich's phone buzzed. He looked at it and thought, *It's Whittington.*

"Hello?"

"Vladi, we are looking at the safe-house option. Given the number of lives involved, we may need two locations, though we'd prefer one. We need to act quickly. As soon as I've sourced the best option, I'll let you know. I don't need to tell you, but I will anyway, watch your six. Can you call the McClintocks and explain what we are doing?

"I was about to call when you phoned. I'll contact them right now," Petronovich replied.

"One more thing before you go, I've requested that each of your properties have law enforcement on the premises until we can get everyone safely tucked away."

"I won't be needing that. But it's a good idea for the McClintocks," answered Petronovich.

"It is already done, Vladi, not an option," replied Whit as he

161

cut the line.

***

Petronovich texted Jason, asking if he was available for a conference call. Jason typed back immediately, 'Yes.' Vladi then texted the same message to Mike, receiving a similar response. *I guess we're ready,* he thought. *I'll phone Jason first, then get Mike on the line.* Vladi dialed the phone with the speaker on.

Jason answered, "Hello?"

"Hang on, Jason, let me get Mike on the line," said Petronovich as he dialed Mike.

When Mike answered, Petronovich told him to hold, while he brought everyone together.

"Jason and Mike, can you hear me?" asked Petronovich.

"Yup," Jason replied.

"Loud and clear," said Mike. "Are you the reason I have a Santa Barbara County Sheriff that just pulled into my property? I was about to ask him why he was here when you called."

"That's part of the reason for the call. I have some bad news," said Petronovich, looking up at the ceiling and taking a deep breath to control his emotions.

Petronovich relayed what had happened to Volkov. "The bottom line is that we have no confirmation that Naryshkin killed Kamarov or Vasily. Whit is assuming the worst and will most likely bring all of us into protective custody, in other words, to a safe house. This will happen in the next twelve to twenty-four hours. I would start packing now for an extended period. The CIA can't mandate that you comply, but they can strongly suggest you do. Jason, you have Brenda to consider and Mike, your family is most important. I have no family, besides the two of you. I'm

162

opting out. I plan to find and kill whoever is responsible."

"Any idea where we will go?" Jason asked, almost in shock.

"Most likely western U.S. It wouldn't make sense to send us east," Petronovich responded.

"I'm with you, Vladi. Brenda can go, but I can't sit and wait."

"That makes two of us. I'm in too. Knowing Julie and the kids are safe is my only concern. I've got a vineyard manager who can take over the chores until we get back," Mike explained. "I'll get Julie going with the packing and pull the kids out of school."

"Before you commit to coming with me, I think you should talk to Brenda and Julie. They might have a different opinion," Petronovich suggested.

"Vladi, I think you know Julie and Brenda by now. They are both strong-willed women and will go along with whatever we believe is best for the families," replied Mike.

Vladi paused for a second. "Okay, it's settled. I'll call Whit back and tell him to find a place that will house Brenda, Julie and the kids. I'll also tell him that we are volunteering for the task force. I suspect he won't take that well and I'll tell him if he won't take us in, we can go alone. At which point, he will accede."

"It's settled, we'll be waiting for your call. Once we have Brenda and Mike's family secured, where do you want to meet?" Jason asked.

Mike jumped in. "Here at the vineyard. We have the space and given the land surrounding the house, it's safer than a highly populated area."

"I agree," said Petronovich. "We'll start there and see how Whit wants to handle this. I'm sure that he'll bring Schumacher on board since this is FBI territory, not CIA."

"I guarantee he will do that," said Mike, being retired FBI.

"Okay, anything else? If not, I'll call Whit and let you know about the safe house when I get more information. In the meantime, remain vigilant. Jason, you and Brenda should probably catch the next flight out to Santa Barbara. Talk to you soon," said Petronovich as he was about to end the call.

"One more thing, Vladi. We are really sorry about Vasily, he was a good man," said Jason sincerely.

***

Naryshkin jogged past the homes on the beach, then slowed to a walk once he reached the marina. He circled back toward his car which was parked several blocks from Volkov's house. Certain he was not being followed, Naryshkin made the final turn to the parked car. He got in and drove slowly down the street, past Volkov's home. A white van was now parked in front with some activity going on inside. He continued past, trying to determine his next step.

At this point, all potential targets have probably been notified of the danger they are in. But who is the most vulnerable? Mike McClintock and his family. Let's see how far away his vineyard is on maps, thought Naryshkin.

***

Whittington dropped the call, getting nowhere with his SVR counterpart in Moscow, explaining he had reason to believe the SVR had rogue agents in the U.S. committing murder. He answered the other line waiting. "Whittington."

"Whit, this is Jack Schumacher. I understand we have a

problem."

Whittington explained what had happened to Kamarov and Volkov, ending with, "Bottom line, Jack, we need a safe house for the McClintock spouses and kids. We must have room for four and it needs to be now. Whoever is out there is dangerous and these families are exposed."

"I have some immediate options. Let me make a few calls and we can probably have them moved by the morning," Schumacher replied. "Let them know to be ready by first light. I'll have transportation at the vineyard. Have the Russians committed to helping us since this appears to be a rogue SVR agent we are dealing with?"

"No, I just got off a call with them and they won't even acknowledge that there is an issue. They said we were trying to stir the pot and cause international problems. It's pointless to pursue, we're on our own. I'll tell the McClintocks to be ready. Thanks, Jack."

**

It was eight thirty in the evening when the Uber dropped Jason and Brenda off at the vineyard. Petronovich had driven north that afternoon. The house would be full, but they were safe in numbers, especially with a second county sheriff parked on the premises. Jason tapped lightly on the front door, knowing Zach and Sam would probably be in bed. Mike answered, speaking quietly, "Come in, let me take your bags," after first giving them hugs.

Under different circumstances, the gathering would have been a festive event. Given what they were dealing with, it was somewhat somber. After getting drinks all around, Jason looked

165

at Mike and asked, "Any idea where the girls and kids will be taken?"

"Schumacher called this afternoon. It looks like they are going to Arizona," Mike replied.

"Phoenix area?" asked Petronovich.

"No, a suburb of Tucson. Vail is the name of the town. Jack said the house is in a gated community. The Bureau owns the home across the street. There will be twenty-four-hour surveillance. The home even has a pool."

"If you have to be tucked away, that doesn't sound half bad," Jason replied.

"I wish we weren't dealing with any of this," commented Julie. "I'm actually sick of all this."

"The sooner we get this behind us, the better off we'll be," said Jason. "Once again, Vladi, we're sorry about Kamarov and Vasily, they were both good men."

There was silence in the room.

Petronovich finally responded with, "Yes, they were. Tomorrow is going to be a long day. I suggest we turn in and get some sleep. Sunrise is about five thirty and we must be ready to go."

***

Naryshkin passed through Santa Barbara. He turned off the freeway onto Highway 154, also known as the San Marcos Pass. This two-lane road took him over the Santa Ynez Mountains and into the Santa Ynez Valley, known as the Santa Barbara wine country. His maps app told him the McClintock vineyard was thirty-five minutes away. It was nine p.m. when he drove slowly past the small vineyard. The house and exterior lights were

166

illuminated, revealing two Santa Barbara County Sheriff vehicles and one unmarked sedan, probably FBI on the premises.

***

Schumacher was true to his word. A dark-colored van with tinted windows and two unmarked vehicles, also tinted, were sitting in the driveway when Mike woke everyone up. He noticed the men in suits talking with the deputy sheriffs outside their car. He poked his head out the front door and said, "I've got coffee inside for anyone that would like a cup."

One of the FBI agents responded, "We stopped before we pulled in. But these two," he added, motioning to the deputies, "They might want one."

"Two coffees coming right up. Everyone is packed and getting dressed. We'll be out with the bags in about ten. The coffee will be just a couple of minutes," Mike answered.

The kids looked tired as they stepped down the stairs toward the car. Sam held her stuffed bear, yawning as she walked, almost half asleep. An agent opened the van's sliding door and she climbed in followed by Zach. Julie and Brenda gave hugs to their men, admonishing them to be safe. The doors closed, with the first unmarked car leading the way down the drive, followed by the van with the second unmarked car taking up the rear. There was no way anyone would try anything with that much firepower in the vehicles.

Jason looked at the three guys standing next to him. "Let's go inside and decide a course of action. We might want to get Whit on the phone as well."

"I think that's a good idea, but caffeine first," responded Petronovich.

***

The drive was long, with the kids getting antsy. The agent in the passenger seat noticed this as they passed the northern suburb of Marana.

"We are only about a half hour away. With the weather as warm as it is, I'll bet your mom might let you take a swim in the pool. Isn't that right, Mom?" asked the agent, looking back at Julie.

Julie smiled. "Sure, I think that's a great idea. Is the pool heated?"

"Most pools in southern Arizona aren't heated. They heat up quickly with the warm weather. Given the number of one hundred degree days they've had recently, I'd bet the pool temp is well over eighty degrees."

Highway 10 was busy going through Tucson. After twenty minutes, they took the off-ramp to Vail.

"We're five minutes from the house," said the agent as the van turned onto a private road, passing the clubhouse, and approaching a closed gate.

The driver rolled down the window. "What was that code?"

"The pound symbol, then three, zero, six. A great high-powered caliber," said the responding agent with a chuckle.

The gate opened and the three vehicles moved slowly into the gated community. The homes were immaculate, with a low water, desert landscape.

"Welcome to Vail."

The van pulled into the drive, with the two unmarked cars parked on the street with the agents standing next to their cars.

The van's driver got out and unlocked the front door. Once

168

it was opened, the other agent ushered Julie, Brenda and the kids into the home. As they stepped through the front door, the first thing they noticed was the pool in the back with water flowing over the rock waterfall into the pool.

"This is nice," commented Julie.

"Wait until you see the house and the rest of the outdoor living area. The patio even has a television and misters," said the agent, excited for them to see.

The bags were brought in and placed in each of the four bedrooms. As the agents were about to leave one said, "The fridge is stocked. If there is anything you need, call me, here's my card." He handed it to Julie. "The bureau owns the home directly across the street. This house will be watched twenty-four seven, you have nothing to worry about. Do not go out front, ever. We will contact you several times a day and make as many trips to the store as needed to keep you happy. That said, I think it's pool time for everyone. Relax, you've had a long day. There's white wine, soda and water in the fridge as well as liquor with mixes above the oven."

The agent closed the front door, waiting outside for Julie to lock it. Satisfied after hearing the deadbolt slide into place, he walked across the street to his new home.

Chapter 13

Jason, Mike and Vladi sat at the kitchen table with Vladi's phone in the center with the speaker on.

Whittington explained, "The prints at Kamarov's place are a match with those taken from Volkov's home. And, as everyone expected, the ballistics are a match as well. We've run the prints through the national database as well as Interpol's international data, striking out on both counts."

"So, where does that leave us?" Petronovich asked.

"Nowhere good. We can assume the killer is Naryshkin, but without direct evidence, we have no leverage with Moscow. We've put an all-points bulletin out across the country, including every point of entry, ports, railway stations and airports. We have a file picture, several years old that we've released as well. If he tries to leave the country, we'll get him."

"What about moving across the border by car?" Jason asked.

"That's our weak spot. He can drive into Mexico unimpeded. Canada, not quite so easy."

"So, we do nothing but wait until he attacks again," Petronovich stated, not asking.

"I'm afraid so unless you have other ideas," replied Whit.

"Does Naryshkin have any living relatives that we know of?" asked Petronovich.

"I don't know. But I'll look into it. What are you suggesting, Vladi?"

"Bring the attack to him. Threaten his family, lure him in," explained Petronovich, waiting for a response.

"Let me see what I can do. In the meantime, I'm keeping the deputies on-site, Mike. I'll be in touch as soon as I learn anything," Whit said as he finished the call.

***

Naryshkin knew he was compromised and most likely on a watch list with every law enforcement establishment in the country. Facial recognition technology was readily available in the U.S. and Canada, but probably only at the major hubs in Mexico. Naryshkin Googled cities in Baja California Sur. Only three had commercial airports; La Paz, with a population of two hundred and forty thousand, San Jose del Cabo, ninety-three thousand and Loreto with twenty thousand people. The choice was obvious, Loreto. The chance of that airport having advanced technology was slim to none. He would fly from Loreto to Mexico City. From there, he hoped to catch a flight to Sochi, avoiding Moscow.

Given the time of night, the drive through Los Angeles toward San Diego was quick. Naryshkin crossed the U.S.–Mexico border at four a.m. He calculated the drive time to Loreto to be about sixteen hours. A little longer with a two-hour break for sleep about halfway. With any luck, he would arrive in Loreto about ten that night. He passed through Rosarito as the sun began to rise in the east, reflecting off the Pacific surf to his right, with waves crashing. After passing through Ensenada, the road became barren and desolate. He anticipated nothing less for the remainder of the drive. As he drove, he reflected on what had transpired during the last four days.

I didn't get all the targets, but I was able to kill two of the three most important. Petronovich will have to wait, thought Naryshkin.

***

Whittington phoned Petronovich the next day, "We used our resources and determined that Naryshkin is an only child. His father is dead, but his mother is still alive, living in a condo in Moscow. We have her address. Her name is Natalia, same last name."

"I'm going to pay Mrs. Naryshkin a visit," said Petronovich. "There's a good chance she keeps in touch with her son."

"I thought you'd say that. I will have a new passport and credit cards ready for you at the office tomorrow. When you come, we'll brief you on her location and discuss how you plan to approach her."

"Sounds good," said Petronovich as he dropped the call. He turned and looked at Jason and Mike. Both had been listening.

Jason was the first to speak., "You're not going without me. Mike can join the family in Vail."

Mike was about to complain when Petronovich interjected.

"Mike, Jason is right. You need to be with your family. I'll call Whit back and he can talk to Schumacher about having a vehicle here to take you tomorrow. I'll also tell him to have paperwork for Jason." He looked at Jason, "You realize you're going back into the lion's den?"

"I wouldn't have it any other way," Jason replied. "I think it's time for a drink."

Mike shook his head, "I don't like it. The risk is too high."

"You're right, Mike! The risk is too high! If we don't act, we risk losing your family and Brenda, forget about us," whispered

172

Petronovich as he dialed Whittington.

***

Naryshkin reached the Loreto Airport at about ten thirty. The small parking lot was empty, and the airport effectively shut down until morning. He checked his travel app for the first flight to Mexico City. With a nine thirty a.m. Aeromexico flight booked, Naryshkin focused on flight possibilities from Mexico City that would get him close to Sochi without flying into Russia.

Trabzon, Turkey immediately came to mind. It was a city on the Black Sea with a population of about three hundred and fifty thousand. As the crow flies, Trabzon was one hundred and eighty miles from Sochi. That would mean a trip by boat.

He booked the flight from Mexico City to Trabzon with one stop in Istanbul. It would be long, but it was the safest way to go.

Naryshkin was not concerned about the last leg of the trip and having to rent a boat, at least, not yet. The first thing he had to do was get through security in Loreto. With the reservations made, he reclined his car seat and slept for six hours.

***

The three men were up and ready to go before sunrise. Sitting at the kitchen table with them were two deputy sheriffs.

"Once Mike's ride arrives and we take off, you guys are free to go. We appreciate all you've done," said Jason as he looked at the deputies and sipped his coffee.

One of the deputies responded, "It's what we do, our pleasure. We just hope the guy that killed your friends is found and dealt with in the proper manner, if you know what I mean."

173

"We'll get him," Petronovich replied, matter of fact.

They saw the lights from the kitchen window before they heard the black Suburban's heavy 6.2-liter V8 engine pull into the driveway next to the house.

"I guess this is your ride," commented the second deputy, looking at Mike.

"Looks like it. I'll get my bag and be right out," replied Mike as the men headed for the door and he turned toward the hallway and bedrooms.

There were two FBI agents in the vehicle when they pulled up and cut the engine.

"Mike will be right out," Jason said as the men exited the car and stretched.

"No problem, it feels good to stand after driving for two hours," replied the driver.

"Right, but this is just the beginning," Petronovich chimed in.

"Tell me. I figure about ten hours with one, no more than two, stops."

Jason asked, "Has the family been notified about Mike?"

"No, we thought it would be a nice surprise," said the second agent as Mike walked up to the vehicle before opening the rear gate and throwing his bag in the back.

"Okay, let's get this drive done," Mike said as he gave a quick, brief hug to Jason and Vladi. "You two be safe."

"Always," replied Petronovich as he waited for Mike to get settled in the back seat, then closed the door.

The two agents got back in the car, started the engine, and headed back up the drive past the vineyard and toward the main road. The sun began to peek over the Santa Ynez Mountains in the distance as the black Suburban tuned on to Refugio Road.

Petronovich looked at Jason. "We might as well hit the road and get this job done."

***

As expected, the Loreto Airport was small and lightly staffed. Going through security was almost a joke. It was obvious that the security personnel were bored. They glanced quickly at Naryshkin's passport and airline ticket and then motioned him through. As he passed the guard, Naryshkin looked quickly left, then right, confirming what he had expected. Surveillance was sparse to non-existent, just what you would expect from one of the smallest airports in Mexico.

He stopped at a coffee hut along the way to his gate, which was one of only three. Taking a chair along the wall, facing passengers as they milled about, most traveling also to Mexico City, he kept watch for anyone looking remotely out of place. In other words, looking for airport authority which might have been tipped off as he moved through security. After twenty minutes, seeing nothing unusual, Naryshkin began to relax. The Aeromexico flight to Mexico City would begin boarding first class shortly, with the main cabin to follow. Once they were wheels up, the trip would take a little over two hours. In Mexico City, his layover was about seven hours.

***

It was three thirty in the afternoon when they entered the town of Vail. After putting in the gate code to the private community, the metal gate swung open. The heavy black Suburban eased through, keeping the speed under twenty mph as they worked

175

their way toward the back of the development and the safe house. As they pulled into the driveway, the driver commented, "This is it, your new home for the time being."

"I guess it could be worse, but it looks pretty nice. I kind of like the desert landscape, even though I'm not fond of cactus or plants that can hurt you," Mike replied.

"I get that. I'm partial to a nice lawn and the smell of fresh cut grass, none of that here," said the driver. "Grab your bag and I'll unlock the front door."

Mike followed the agent up the walk and waited as he rang the doorbell and then unlocked and opened the door. He let Mike in and through the living room windows, he noticed the family in the back, with the kids in the pool and Julie and Brenda on lounge chairs in the lagoon or sundeck.

"Looks like they're in the pool. If you need anything, our team will be across the street. The ladies have the number. We're heading back to L.A. right now."

"Thanks for the ride," Mike said as he closed the door, setting his bag by the sofa.

As he stepped out the back door, Sam noticed him and screamed, "Dad!"

"Hi, pumpkin!"

Julie jumped from the lounge, standing under the umbrella, and said, "Mike, what are you doing? What's going on?"

Mike pulled a chair next to the lagoon and sat. "Jason and Petronovich are going after Naryshkin. There's no need for us all to go, so I'm here for now."

Julie looked at him for a moment. "I know you aren't happy with that, but we are glad you're here," she said as she sloshed over in the water and gave Mike a kiss on the cheek.

"Dad! Get your swimsuit on and come in," commented

Zack. "The water is nice."

"That's not a bad idea. I'd bet the temp out here is well over one hundred," Mike said eyeing the drinks that Julie and Brenda had.

Julie noticed. "Liquor and mixes are in the kitchen. Change your clothes, make a drink, and come out. We have about an hour before we freshen up and get dinner going."

***

Whittington had the two passports and credit cards on his desk when Petronovich and Jason walked in. From his desk, he motioned them to take a chair in front.

"I have your passports and credit cards," said Whit as he reached across and handed the items to both men. "I also have verification of employment papers, should anyone ask what your business interests are in Russia."

"And what might that be?" Petronovich asked.

Whit slid one page to each and replied, "You are sales employees of Engine Alliance, they make aero gas turbine engines."

"Never heard of them," Jason commented.

"The company was formed through a joint venture between General Electric and Pratt and Whitney. You've heard of them, I'm sure. The company has sold jet engines to a Russian airline called Transaero, headquartered in St. Petersburg, but its main hub is located in Moscow. Your cover is simply a courtesy call to make certain your clients are happy with the product. If anyone were to dig into your background further, we have you on the payroll of Engine Alliance, working out of their headquarters in Hartford, Connecticut."

"We shouldn't have any issues," said Petronovich as he took the slip of paper and scanned it.

"Okay, let's talk about Natalia Naryshkin. She lives in an exclusive condo complex in the center of Moscow. It's actually in the historical and cultural center of old Moscow in the Tverskoy District. The place is called the Tverskaya Residence. It has twelve floors, thirteen if you include one underground. Her unit is twelve-one hundred, a penthouse on the twelfth floor. I'm sure security is going to be tight. I'm also sure you'll be able to find a legitimate way in. We have a contact in Moscow contracted to assist you when you arrive. His name is Kostas Vachovska. Here is his contact information," explained Whit as he slid a thin piece of paper toward Petronovich. "Call him when you land. He will have a bag of items I think you will be happy having. I suggest you stay at the Hotel Ukraine, it's within sight of Naryshkin's condo complex. Any questions?"

"Do the items in the bag happen to be of the nine mm variety?" Petronovich replied.

"Most probably."

"Good, then we're good to go," responded Petronovich.

"Good luck, gentlemen," said Whit as he stood from his desk, indicating the meeting was over.

***

First-class passengers were in their seats when the main cabin began the boarding process. It was Sunday morning. Naryshkin almost never missed making the call to his mother, always at ten past five p.m. Moscow was eight hours ahead of Mexico City so that meant calling at ten past nine a.m., twenty minutes before takeoff. It was nine minutes after the hour when Naryshkin dialed the number. He looked at the time when the phone began ringing, it was ten past nine when she picked up.

After fifteen minutes of catching up, Naryshkin promised his mother, as he always did, that he would call next week. He hung up and settled back in his seat with a vodka tonic. He didn't care about the time, after all, it was after five p.m. in Moscow. The flight to Istanbul would be long and he hoped to sleep through a good part of it. The vodka would help.

**

Whittington sat at his desk. The intercom squawked with his secretary saying, "Sir, your two o'clock is here."

"Send him in, Stephanie."

The door opened.

Whit came from behind his desk, wrapped an arm around his shoulder and asked, "How are you feeling, Vasily? Have a seat."

Volkov smiled. "Lucky to have been wearing my gold medallion otherwise the confrontation with Naryshkin would have turned out much differently."

"I'd have to say you're right. The doctors said the metal took the brunt of the impact, deflecting the round down away from vital organs, penetrating your side and exiting cleanly out your back. Somebody was watching out for you. To keep you safe, we had to let everyone, especially Petronovich and the McClintocks believe you were killed. Jason and Vladi are on their way to Moscow right about now. Mike, his family and Brenda are at a safe house in Arizona."

"Why are they going back into Russia?"

Whit explained that they'd found Naryshkin's mother. "I felt it was important to confront her. Petronovich might be able to get

179

her to shed light on her son's location, either here or in Russia. That brings me to the reason I asked you in. Are you up for a little travel?"

Volkov smiled. "As long as I'm traveling to Mother Russia."

"You will be going to Moscow. We monitor calls in and out of the SVR headquarters building twenty-four seven. We analyzed tapes beginning two weeks prior to Kamarov's death, hoping to red flag the name Sergey Naryshkin. We had a hit one week before Kamarov was murdered. Naryshkin made a call to one Mikhail Kozlov asking for the contact information, including phone numbers and home addresses for you, Petronovich and the McClintocks."

"How could this Kozlov have that information?"

"Kozlov confirmed to Naryshkin that the SVR has assets in the agency and FBI. I want you to find Kozlov. The number phoned was not a cell, so we assume it was a dedicated office line. Here's the number." Whittington passed a slip of paper across the desk. "Use your interrogation skills to determine everything he knows about Naryshkin's whereabouts. Also, and I cannot stress this enough, it is of utmost importance that you get the name of the informant in our organization. After you're satisfied that you've learned everything, eliminate Kozlov with extreme prejudice. I have a new passport and credit card for your travel," said Whittington as he handed the documents to Volkov. "Any questions?"

"I'll get what you need. When do I leave?"

"Tonight. There's a flight at five."

***

The Aeroflot flight from Los Angeles to Moscow was eleven

hours and forty minutes. The agency had reserved two coach tickets for Vladi and Jason, which were promptly upgraded to business class by each man. They both determined there was no way they were flying that long in coach, after having flown back from Europe six months earlier in luxury on a C-37A, which was the government equivalent of the Gulfstream V, courtesy of the CIA. Petronovich took his seat next to Jason on the airliner and whispered, "We'll find a creative, but legitimate way to expense the cost of this upgrade when we get back."

The flight attendant placed a Grey Goose in front of Vladi and a Glenfiddich in front of Jason as he replied, "I don't care. The only concern I have now is finding Naryshkin and putting an end to his miserable life."

"I'll drink to that," said Petronovich as he raised his glass toward Jason.

***

After fourteen hours, Turkey was on the horizon. The aircraft was on the final descent, twenty minutes out, flying over the Black Sea and crossing through ten thousand feet.

Naryshkin stared out the window and watched as white caps rolled on the sea below, a result of the wind which was now buffeting the large airliner with the turbulence that tended to unsettle some of the inexperienced flying passengers. It was Tuesday morning in Istanbul and the pilot had promised to be at the gate by seven thirty. The Istanbul New Airport, as it was called, was new, as the name implied, having opened its doors in 2018. The airport had six runways and could accommodate five hundred aircraft at various gates and one hundred and fifty million passengers in one year. To say it was large was an understatement. Naryshkin watched below as the plane

181

transitioned from water to land. Three minutes later, he saw asphalt and white stripes from the runway, rising to meet the aircraft as wheels bit the dark surface, jumped once, and settled into the rollout with the large engines in reverse thrust.

The pilot had miscalculated. The taxiing was longer than expected and the plane arrived at the gate at seven thirty-two. Naryshkin was slightly annoyed but happy to be among the first passengers freed from the confines of the aircraft. When the plane came to a complete stop, he stood from the seat, grabbed his carry-on from the overhead compartment and waited for the cabin doors to open. The passengers in the row in front of him were first to exit. He ignored the flight attendant's comment to "Have a nice day," stepping out of the plane and onto the jetway.

He had one hour to make a connecting flight to Trabzon, Turkey, where he would hire a boat to take him across the Black Sea to Sochi.

***

Volkov landed in Moscow, rented a car, and proceeded to SVR headquarters, located in south Moscow in the Yasenevo District. He knew the area well, having worked in the complex for several years, until six months ago. He didn't know Kozlov personally but recognized the name and knew he was in the upper echelon of the organization. Out of habit, Volkov turned into the massive parking area surrounding the large Y-shaped, three-story structure, backed by a towering twenty-one-floor building which could be seen for miles. He parked in the area he had always parked, taking a space toward the back, but probably still three hundred yards from the main doors. It was four thirty in the afternoon and people were already beginning to trickle out, ending their workday. Volkov took the slip of paper from his pocket and dialed the number.

182

Kozlov was sitting at his desk when the phone rang.

"Hello?"

"Mikhail Kozlov?"

"Who's this?"

"We have a common friend, or, I should say, had."

"What are you talking about? I'm going to hang up," Kozlov said, ready to slam down the phone.

"I wouldn't do that, comrade. It would be an insult to Ivan Kamarov."

There was now silence at the end of the line.

"What do you want?"

Volkov replied, "I want to meet."

"Where, how do I recognize you?" Kozlov asked.

"I will recognize you. Be at the Grass-Hopper Craft Pub in thirty minutes. And Kozlov, don't be late," insisted Volkov in a tone seldom spoken to Mikhail Kozlov.

Kozlov was clearly upset. His hands were shaking slightly as he reached for his briefcase, stuffing the work from his desk inside. He then took a deep breath, calmed down and dialed an interoffice line. After explaining the phone call he had received, four SVR agents were tasked to accompany him to the pub. It was decided that two would be spaced inside the pub in view of Kozlov and the other two would be outside, looking for anything suspicious.

***

The Aeroflot flight to Russia touched down in Moscow at one forty p.m., ten hours ahead of the pacific time zone.

Petronovich dialed the number for Kostas Vachovska, given to him by Whittington. As if waiting by his cell, Vachovska answered after the first ring: "Hello?"

"Is this Vachovska?" Petronovich asked.

"It is. Are you the person to whom I am to deliver a package?" Vachovska asked, not wanting to use Vladi's name on an open line.

"I am. We are waiting out in front of baggage claim carousel number one."

"I will be there in five minutes. I drive a yellow Lada Priora, hard to miss," Vachovska responded.

Vachovska pulled up in front of Petronovich and McClintock, popped the trunk from inside and motioned the men in. Petronovich sat in the front passenger seat while Jason took the back.

"Thanks for the ride," said Petronovich.

"It is my pleasure. I am here to assist you in any way I can. I was instructed to reserve rooms for you at Hotel Ukraine. I would think you'd like to freshen up after the long flight. Maybe we can meet for dinner in the hotel restaurant and I can tell you what I've learned about the Tverskaya Residence?"

"That sounds good. About five?" asked Vladi. "How far is this place?"

"Not far." Looking in the rearview mirror at Jason, he said, "Under my seat is a package. When we stop at the hotel, put it into your luggage before removing your bag from the trunk."

Jason looked at the driver, bent forward and pulled the sack out from under the seat. He opened it and glanced inside. As promised, there were two handguns with four magazines.

"I've never seen a handgun like this, what is it?" asked Jason as he slipped the weapon to Petronovich in the front seat.

Petronovich took the gun, examined it, and looked at Vachovska. "Is this the new Udav?"

"You know your guns, my friend. Yes, it's the new Udav. It fires a nine by twenty-one mm cartridge and has a magazine capacity of eighteen rounds plus one in the chamber. It's similar to your American .40 caliber S&W. I think you will like it."

184

Petronovich gave the handgun back to Jason. He slid it into the sack and placed it on the seat beside him. Fifteen minutes later they pulled up in front of the Hotel Ukraine. As the men got out, Vachovska pointed, "See that tall building in the distance?"

Both looked toward the skyline in the direction Vachovska was pointing.

Jason responded, "Yes."

"That's the Tverskaya Residence. There are several places to dine in this hotel. Let's meet in the Club Restaurant. See you in a few hours."

Chapter 14

The Trabzon airport sat right next to the Black Sea, only one km, or a little over half a mile, from the marina. Naryshkin could have walked, but instead opted for the short cab ride. Five minutes after leaving the airport grounds, he was dropped off in front of the marina's harbor master's office where many fishing trawlers could be seen coming in and moving out of port.

Seagulls squawked above, following the boats as they moved through the harbor. Naryshkin took a moment and scanned the vessels which seemed to be preparing to leave. Several were loading what looked like bait for fishing as well as provisions for the small crew, no more than two or three men.

Naryshkin decided to approach the smaller of the three boats. The fishing vessel's name was *Sansli*, or *Lucky*. He walked down the floating walkway where the crew were working, and said, "Excuse me, can you tell me where I can find the captain?"

The youngest of the men looked up. "Why are you asking?"

"I have a proposition," said Naryshkin.

"Who are you?" asked the young man.

"My name is Alex Ivanov. Are you the captain?"

"I am."

"How much do you earn in a week, fishing, captain?" asked Naryshkin.

"What business is that of yours, Ivanov?"

"I will double whatever that number is for a ride to Sochi. You can still fish while you make the trip. What is the number?"

"About 14,940 TRY." (Turkish lira, or $2,000 USD).

"I'll pay you 30,000 TRY for the trip. Add the money you make fishing, that could bring you close to 45,000 TRY. What do you say?" Naryshkin asked.

The young man thought about it while his crew mates looked on. "Are you running from the law?"

"I am not. But I prefer my privacy," answered Naryshkin.

"We leave in an hour, Ivanov. You can stow your bag inside the cabin and have a seat on the bridge while we finish loading. I want half of the fee now and the rest when we arrive in Sochi."

"How long will the trip take?" asked Naryshkin.

"About four and a half hours. I can have you there in time for dinner."

"Great," said Naryshkin as he jumped aboard the small trawler, took out his wallet and handed 15,000 TRY over to the captain.

***

Kozlov was inside the pub five minutes early. The two SVR agents were seated on opposite sides of the dark pub in clear view of Kozlov, who occupied a table toward the back of the room, set against the wall. The pub was beginning to get busy with the late afternoon and early evening crowd.

Volkov was a frequent patron of this establishment not long ago. He and his friends would have had a couple of craft brews after work at least once, but more likely twice, a week. It was a good place for single professionals to mingle. As he approached the pub, he slowed looking for signs that Kozlov was being watched and protected. Volkov assumed he would be and was not let down.

The men were easily spotted. One was parked directly across the street from the main entrance to the pub, acting as though he was reading a newspaper, when, in fact, he was peering over the top, watching every car that passed. Volkov didn't slow, but mentally took note of the color, make and model of the car and its lone occupant. A second agent was spotted on the same side of the street as the pub, acting as though he was window shopping in front of a hardware supply store, which was odd and obviously out of order. He kept rolling past, moving down the street, making a right at the next corner. He came around the block and parked two blocks from the pub with a view of the two agents outside as well as the main entrance.

At five thirty, thirty minutes past the appointed time to meet, three men came out of the pub. One walked across the street and spoke to the man in the car. The agent near the supply store came up the block and said something to the other two. Of the five people in view, four were in their mid-to-late thirties and the other, his early sixties.

He had Kozlov in sight. Now he hoped to follow him.

***

The Club Restaurant was exclusively for guests staying on the tenth and eleventh floors, which was where Vochovska had reserved the rooms. The dining room was ornate, with gold trimmed beams on the ceiling displaying intricate carvings, as well as navy blue and gold window coverings, draped on either side of large picture windows which were looking out across the city of Moscow.

Vochovska sat at a corner table, nursing a Beluga vodka. He was fifteen minutes early on purpose, enjoying the quiet time at the expense of the U.S. Government. Petronovich and McClintock spotted him easily when they entered, given that there were only two tables occupied, with his being one. Most diners came in between seven and eight thirty, not five p.m., cocktail hour.

"Nice place," commented Petronovich as he approached the table.

"Have a seat, gentlemen, I trust your accommodations are acceptable?" asked Vochovska.

Jason and Vladi both sat as the waitress immediately appeared.

"They will do," responded Jason as he looked at the Russian, then the waitress. "I'll have a Glenfiddich, rocks."

"Grey Goose up," added Petronovich.

They continued with the pleasantries until the drinks arrived.

After both men had sipped their drinks, Petronovich spoke. "Tell us about Tverskaya Residence."

"It is an exclusive hotel, residential complex. The hotel is easily accessed, but the condominium, not so much. Especially the penthouse floor where the subject you wish to question resides."

Jason asked, "Do you have any ideas as to how we might get in?"

"I've given this some thought. I have a friend that owns an HVAC company, Schiberg is the name. They have a contract to service the property. I could speak with him and see if I could get one of you access to the property, acting as a company technician. He would need to be paid though."

Petronovich was silent, thinking about what Vochovska had said.

"That might work," he finally replied. "How much would we

need to pay?"

"I'm guessing 375,000 Rubles, or $5,000 USD. For this, he would provide technician clothing, equipment, a work van and necessary passes. Not to mention confidentiality."

Petronovich looked at Jason, who nodded, yes, then replied, "Set it up, Vochovska. I'd like to be paying Mrs. Naryshkin a visit tomorrow."

Vochovska raised his glass to the other two. "It shall be done. Let's order another round or two, before dinner."

***

An hour into the trip, the young captain announced to his two-man crew that it was time. Naryshkin watched with interest as the crew slowly let out the cone-shaped net from the stern's starboard and port sides, allowing the water to pull the weighted net away from the trawler toward the seabed. They were fishing for herring, sardines, and anchovies.

"How long will you keep the net out?" asked Naryshkin, speaking to the captain on the bridge.

"About an hour from Sochi, we will bring the net in. That's still considered international waters. You realize our boat will be inspected by authorities when we arrive in Sochi, including each crew members' papers and that includes you."

"I've been thinking about that. There's no way to get me to land without avoiding authorities?" asked Naryshkin.

"I thought this might be an issue. I have a friend who fishes out of Sochi. I contacted him after we got underway. He's fishing today and will not be too far from us. I asked him if he could take on a passenger; you. He agreed. The fee will be an additional 30,000 TRY for him as well as another 15,000 TRY for me as commission for brokering the deal. You will board his boat after we bring in the gill nets. His boat is registered in Russia, so you will have no issues in port. It also saves me time going all the way to Sochi. Is that acceptable?"

Naryshkin hesitated, then smiled. "You are one bright son-of-a-bitch. It's a deal."

***

Volkov watched as the two cars pulled out of the parking lot. Two men were in the first car with Kozlov following alone in a black sedan. The agents in the car across from the bar did a u-turn and followed the other two. Kozlov's vehicle was in the middle.

Volkov stayed back, behind several other vehicles, hoping not to attract attention but keeping the black sedan in view. After two miles, the cars with the agents turned right, heading back to SVR headquarters while Kozlov continued west toward the outskirts of Moscow, along the Rublyovo-Uspenskoye Highway and into, what Volkov believed, was the exclusive suburb called Rublyovka. Volkov knew that homes in this area ranged in size from miniature mansions to small palaces, valued in the hundreds of millions of USD. To put this development into perspective, at one time, Peter the Great had a home here.

Kozlov made a left turn toward the gated community.

Instead of using a button to open the gate, as many communities in the U.S. did, Kozlov had to stop and present identification at a manned guardhouse, as though he was entering a military complex.

Volkov watched this as he drove slowly past. He realized that isolating Kozlov was not going to be that easy.

***

Petronovich was wearing coveralls with the Schiberg logo on the left breast pocket. His identification hung around his neck as he parked the van a short distance from the front entrance to the building complex. He walked to the back of the van, pulled the tool belt out and strapped it on. The doorman watched as Petronovich approached. Vladi noticed this and waved as he came closer to the door.

"Good morning, sir, here to do some maintenance?" asked the uniformed attendant.

Petronovich flashed his credentials and smiled. "Time for the annual HVAC tune-up for the condos."

"I haven't seen you before, is this your first time?"

"Yes. I joined the company last week," Petronovich replied.

"Right, then. You have the correct building. The hotel is next door. Elevators are on the left as you can see. There is a door at the end of the hall on the twelfth floor which will give you access to the equipment you're looking for. You should have no trouble finding it. My name is Boris, there is a house phone in the hallway if you need anything."

"Thank you, my friend, I'm sure I'll be fine. I might be a little while," Petronovich said as he turned to the bank of elevators.

Petronovich exited the elevator. On the wall in front of him were arrows pointing left indicating units twelve-two hundred and twelve-four hundred were in that direction and arrows to the right were twelve-one hundred and twelve-three hundred. Only four units occupied the twelfth floor. He turned right to twelve-one hundred, rang the doorbell, and waited. A petite, elderly woman in her late eighties opened the door.

192

"Can I help you?"

"Mrs. Naryshkin? My name is Vladimir, I'm with Schiberg. I'm here to inspect your heating and air conditioning unit. May I come in?"

Natalia Naryshkin examined Vladi's identification, hanging from the lanyard, then stepped back allowing him access.

"How long will this take?"

Petronovich turned slightly as he stepped through the doorway, careful not to scratch the door or walls with the tools hanging from the belt.

"It shouldn't take too long."

He stopped for a moment and took in the room. The family room was bright with large picture windows looking down upon the old town and across the city of Moscow. "This is quite a view."

Natalia was pleased and crossed the room to the windows.

"Come, take a look. On a clear day, you can see the Kremlin."

Petronovich walked over and took it all in. Sensing the opportunity, he said, as if reminiscing, "I once worked for the government."

Natalia looked up at Vladi. "Oh, in what capacity?"

"This was when Gorbachev was in office. I hesitate to say, but I was with the old KGB."

"Really? My son was with the KGB, he's now SVR. He still is. Why didn't you stay?"

"I needed a change. But I must tell you, I recognized your name. Your son is Sergey, correct? He and I were in the same training class. I knew him well," explained Petronovich. "How is he doing? He's still working?"

"Yes, he is. Oh my, where are my manners?" Natalia looked

surprised and then again at his identification. "Mr. Petronovich, would you like some tea?"

Vladi didn't bother with a fake I.D. Both Mrs. Naryshkin and her son would know his identity soon enough. In fact, being truthful about his identity could move this quasi-interrogation along quicker.

"That would be nice, it's almost break time anyway. Can I set my tool belt down by the door?" asked Petronovich as he unbuckled the work belt.

"Certainly, then come sit at the dining room table while I brew the tea," said Natalia as she shuffled into the kitchen. "You must tell me all about how you know my Sergey."

***

Three hours into the trip, in the wheelhouse, the young captain pointed and spoke to Naryshkin. "On the horizon, you can just begin to see the hills of Sochi." He then turned and looked back down onto the deck at his crew. "Prepare to bring in the nets."

The two men opened the hold in preparation to receive the fish they hoped were in the nets being dragged across the ocean's floor. One man was on the port side while the other was on the starboard side of the vessel, each ready to guide the nets toward the gaping hole where the fish would be released into a tank with oxygenated salt water to keep them alive and well until they were off-loaded at the processing plant back in Trabzon. The captain called out, "Reel in the nets!"

There was a hum as the motor began to pull the heavy steel cables, winding them around a large spool on either side of the deck. The nets were several hundred feet deep and an eighth of a mile aft of the vessel. The process was slow and took close to

194

half an hour before the first glimpse of netting broke the ocean's surface. As it did, the captain's cell rang. He listened then looked west.

"I see you. After our nets are in, we'll come your way and make the exchange." After ending the call, he looked over at Naryshkin. "That was my friend. We will meet in about forty-five minutes. We are three miles from him."

"Good. I'm anxious to see your catch," Naryshkin replied without taking his eyes off the nets which were now being raised above the hold with one of the crew guiding the net full of flopping fish while the other controlled the hydraulic winch. The winch operator lowered the nets, and, as if on cue, the second crew member released the load of fish, dropping them with a splash into the hold.

"Nicely done!" hollered the captain. "Secure the nets and prepare the dinghy to transport our passenger to the other trawler."

The men strapped down the nets, and then went to the stern where the dinghy rested on a thin platform. It was used as a life raft in case of emergency, but, in this case, was perfect to transfer the passenger. The men unstrapped all but two belts which held the dinghy snug to the trawler.

"We're ready to drop the raft when you are," hollered one of the crew to the captain.

"We'll be about twenty minutes. Relax and I'll tell you when to release."

Naryshkin listened to the conversation and looked out of the wheelhouse window. The trawler from Sochi was cutting through the waves, not wasting more time than necessary so they could continue fishing. Naryshkin pulled out his wallet and counted the balance due the young captain, including the commission for brokering safe passage into Russia with his friend. He handed the money to the captain who pocketed it without counting.

"Aren't you going to count it?" Naryshkin asked.

"I will a little later. If you've shorted me, my friend from Sochi will see that you are let off his boat short of land," chuckled the captain. "Better that you move down on the deck and prepare to board the dinghy."

***

Volkov waited in his car, parked in the back of the lot that Kozlov exited the day before. He knew the color, make and model of the vehicle that Kozlov drove. At seven a.m., the cars began to trickle in. By seven forty-five, there was a constant stream of vehicles, all jockeying for a spot closest to the building's multiple entrances. At eight ten, the car he'd been waiting for arrived. Unlike others that had pulled in before eight Kozlov had an assigned space near the front.

Volkov watched as Kozlov got out of the car, looked around the expansive lot and retrieved his briefcase from the backseat. He locked the car and then walked quickly toward the main SVR Headquarters door.

The morning seemed to drag on. At about eleven a.m., Volkov took the slip of paper from his pocket and dialed the number. When the call was answered, he simply said, "You have a package for me?"

"I've been waiting for your call. Yes, I have the package, where are you?" asked Vachovska.

Volkov gave his location as well as the make and model of his rental car. "I'll be there in fifteen minutes. I drive a yellow Lada Priora."

196

As promised, Vachovska arrived on time. He parked in front of Volkov. Keeping the car running, he stepped out with a bag in hand and, without a word, handed it through the driver's side window to Volkov.

Vachovska returned quickly to his car and drove out of the lot.

After four p.m., people began to leave for the day. As the five p.m. hour approached, the crowd that had seemed to arrive at the same time that morning began to leave in unison. Volkov was attentive, watching the door that Kozlov had entered earlier. By five thirty, there were several empty parking spaces close to Kozlov's vehicle.

Volkov started his car and slowly made his way forward, carefully avoiding the rush of autos leaving the lot. Volkov selected a spot one row behind and two spaces to the left of Kozlov's car. He continued to wait and watch. Stakeouts were boring and monotonous. Given his training, Volkov was prepared to wait. He knew, at the end of the day, he would accomplish the assignment given to him. Volkov wasn't a killer, but he relished the thought of payback for what Kozlov had done to him and Kamarov, by giving Naryshkin their contact information and home addresses.

Volkov smiled when he thought about how this day would end for Kozlov. Finally, Kozlov stepped out of the building. He was hesitant, stopping to look out across the parking lot for anything out of the ordinary. Feeling a little apprehensive, he ventured toward his car.

Volkov slumped down in the seat, barely able to see Kozlov as he approached. Volkov watched as Kozlov unlocked the car doors from a distance, with the rear lights of his car flashing as he pressed the remote. Kozlov reached his car and looked inside

197

before opening either the driver's, or backseat, door. Seeing that it was clear, he opened the back door and placed his briefcase on the floor. While he did this, with cat-like reflexes, Volkov was out of his vehicle and behind Kozlov with the suppressed Udav pressed against the small of Kozlov's back.

"Get in the car slowly. We are going for a ride."

Kozlov tensed, then slowly entered the car.

"I have a Udav pointed at the base of your skull. If you make one wrong move, your brains will be splattered across your windshield. Do you understand?"

"Yes."

"Good," replied Volkov as he slipped into the back seat. "Drive to Bitsevski Park."

***

Petronovich studied the living space from the dining room table. The home was well kept, to the point that it almost seemed as though it wasn't lived in. He listened to the clatter of plates as Natalia prepared what was obviously going to be more than a simple cup of tea. As if on cue, the little old lady shuffled through the kitchen door with two plates, one with cookies, the other with a couple of croissants and jam.

Petronovich jumped to his feet and relieved Natalia of the plates. "Let me help you with that," he said. "This is too much."

"Nonsense, young man, please sit. The water is almost boiling."

Petronovich did as he was told. While he sat, he decided to be as honest with Natalia as he possibly could without revealing his true intent, which was to hunt down Naryshkin and kill him. That said, he couldn't say much.

Natalia shuffled through the swinging door, with two cups and saucers. "The tea is almost done. Please help yourself to a croissant, Mr. Petronovich."

"Please call me Vladi," Petronovich replied as he helped himself to a pastry and spoonful of strawberry jam.

While Natalia was in the kitchen, he placed a small, circular listening device underneath the table, secured by a strong adhesive.

Natalia came back through and poured the tea before sitting down next to Petronovich, who had a seat at the head of the table.

After taking a small cookie, she looked at Petronovich and asked, "Now tell me how you know my Sergey, Vladimir?" She refused to shorten his name.

"Well, as I mentioned, Sergey and I went through the Academy of Foreign Intelligence together years ago. In fact, we were in the same class. Sergey was top of the class, while I managed to squeak by, finishing the four-year curriculum near the bottom."

"I'm sure you are being modest, Vladimir. Tell me, why did you leave the KGB?"

"After the cold war ended, to be honest, I was simply tired. Those were dangerous times and more than once, I was almost sent to the grave. For my own psychological well-being, I had to leave." Petronovich at this point, was being totally honest.

"Working for an HVAC company is a far cry from the elite work you did for the KGB."

"It's mindless, which is what I prefer. I also get to have tea at times with friendly clientele that I know aren't trying to kill me. Now, enough about me. Tell me about Sergey. You said he still works for the SVR?"

"He does, but I don't get to see him very much. He's very

busy you know, being way up there in the command structure. He doesn't even tell me his title. But I do get to speak with him every week. He calls me at ten past five every Sunday evening. I so look forward to those calls."

"So, he is at SVR headquarters here in Moscow, not stationed somewhere else?"

"Yes, he has an apartment not far from work. I don't have the address," Natalia replied as she nibbled at her cookie and took a sip of tea.

"Do you have a number, so I might call him?" Petronovich asked.

"It must seem odd, but I do not. I have asked him repeatedly and he refuses to give it to me. He said, in his line of work, he changes phones often. If I need to reach him, I can call the office."

"You said he calls every Sunday. When you speak to him, tell him I said hello, would you?"

Natalia thought for a moment, then smiled. "Of course!"

"Good," said Petronovich as he rose from the table, bowed, and shook Natalia Naryshkin's hand. "Stay seated, it was nice to have met you, I'll let myself out. Thank you for the tea and pastry."

***

The captain hollered from the wheelhouse, "Lower the dinghy!"

The trawler, *Kalinovka*, was a quarter mile off the port bow.

The captain continued, "Take Mr. Ivanov over to the *Kalinovka* and assist him aboard. Good luck, Alex Ivanov, or whatever your name is."

"Thank you for your assistance, captain. I hope you have an

200

abundance of fish in your nets on your trip home." With that, Naryshkin threw his bag into the dinghy and stepped in with the help of one of the crew. After Naryshkin was seated, the small outboard engine was revved up and put into gear. The distance between the two vessels was covered in a matter of minutes.

The dinghy slowed abruptly as the small boat came along the starboard side of the trawler. A line was thrown to the Russian crew. After securing it, they helped Naryshkin up. The Russian captain didn't introduce himself. He spoke to Naryshkin simply saying, "This is a fishing vessel. We have several more hours of work before we head back to Sochi. Stay in the cabin, away from the deck. It can be dangerous out here. I'll tell you when you can come out. I'll take my fee before you go inside."

Naryshkin opened his wallet and counted the money in front of the Russian captain. Noting the amount to be accurate, the captain said, "Good, now go inside."

The crew of *Kalinovka* watched as the dinghy returned to its vessel. Both captains waved, turned their backs, and got to work once again.

Inside the cabin, Naryshkin sat at the galley table and looked at his cell. He had only one bar on the phone but tried to make a call anyway. He dialed his home in Sochi, hoping one of the caretakers would answer. They did. The conversation was short: "Have a steak and salad ready. I will be home by eight tonight. Be sure the Ciroc X is chilled." Naryshkin then, with his arms folded on the table, lowered his head down and fell asleep.

***

Kozlov headed north out of the SVR headquarters parking lot. Bitsevski Park was a dense forest in Moscow which ran 6.2 miles north to south and covered a little over eleven square miles. Two rivers, the Chertanovka and Bitsa, traversed the forest. Volkov knew the park well, having hunted small game there as a teenager years ago. The forest could be a dangerous place for those not familiar with the outdoors, simply because of the dense foliage. People often became disoriented and lost. Because of the seclusion the forest provided, it was the site of the majority of Moscow's notorious serial killer, Alexander Pichuskin's sixty-one murders. A perfect place to have an in-depth conversation with Kozlov.

"Drive around the park to the far side, I'll tell you where to turn in," Volkov said firmly.

Trickles of sweat began to form on Kozlov's face. "You are the one that phoned yesterday." It wasn't a question. "After you mentioned Kamarov, I pulled all the files that Naryshkin requested information on. I'm assuming that's why you are here. You are Vasily Volkov."

"You don't have to be a genius to have deduced that, Kozlov."

"I am certainly no genius, but at the same time, I'm not stupid. I can help you and the CIA in more ways than you know."

"Keep your mouth shut, Kozlov, and drive until I tell you where to turn," Volkov replied, thinking about the offer Kozlov was suggesting. Vasily liked things to be either black or white. Playing in the gray area was not his strong suit. He would much rather extract the name of the mole within the CIA then kill Kozlov as directed, rather than keep him as an informant, or double agent.

"You must believe me when I say that I had no idea what Naryshkin was planning with the contact information I retained for him."

Volkov watched Kozlov's eyes in the rear-view mirror when he asked, "Are you familiar with Perm-36?"

Kozlov looked back at Volkov while driving. "Everyone knows about the Perm-36 Gulag. Why do you ask?"

There seemed to be no anxiousness or anxiety in his eyes as Volkov followed with, "Are you familiar with Naryshkin's recent use of a portion of Perm-36 as a prison for a few select individuals?"

Genuine surprise lit up Kozlov's eyes when Volkov asked the question. "No. I, we, the SVR, as far as I know, have no idea what Naryshkin was or is doing at Perm-36."

Much to Volkov's dismay, he believed that Kozlov was telling the truth. The drive to Bitsevski Park from headquarters was only 3.5 miles, but to drive the perimeter to the other, more remote side took about twenty minutes.

"There is a dirt road coming up about a quarter mile on your left, take it, then drive slowly back as far as you can and park."

Kozlov turned as directed. The road was empty, with no vehicles in sight. He came to the road's end, stopped by thick underbrush, and densely packed pine trees, perfect tinder for a forest fire. With his hands on the wheel, in plain view, he said, "I am worth more to you alive than dead."

"Give me the name of the mole in our country," Volkov demanded with the Udav now firmly pressed at the base of Kozlov's head.

With his eyes closed, Kozlov nodded. "His name is Kent Foster. He works in the Russian and European Analysis Section at Langley."

"How did you get him to turn?"

"It wasn't hard. Two kids in college, credit card limits maxed out, a recent divorce and alimony through the nose. The guy was drowning. We threw him a lifeline and he didn't hesitate to latch on."

"Are there others?" Volkov asked as he recorded the conversation with the small hand-held device out of sight by his side.

"Yes."

"How many? Be specific."

"I will once you have talked with your superiors and I know we have come to an agreement."

"Kozlov, you are in no position to negotiate, and you know it."

"I beg to differ, Vasily Volkov. I think you are beginning to realize you may have hit a, how do the Americans say? Home run?" Kozlov looked in the rear-view mirror and smiled at Vasily as he lowered the weapon.

***

The vibrations from the engines slowed considerably as the captain throttled back the rpms, upon entering the port of Sochi. Naryshkin stirred as one of the crew entered the galley, "The captain asked me to tell you we have arrived, and you may come on deck."

Naryshkin rose from the table, stretched his arms above his head and grabbed his bag, "Thank you," then followed the young man outside. Being the largest resort city in Russia, the port was mostly occupied by yachts, but several trawlers were berthed at one small section away from the public and out of sight of most of the million-dollar pleasure vessels. This suited Naryshkin's goal of anonymity and his ability to blend into the crowd as he made his way off the boat and into the city where he could wave

204

a cab down for a ride home.

After tying off the lines the captain hollered from the wheelhouse, "You are free to go, Ivanov."

Naryshkin glanced at the wheelhouse, nodded at the captain then turned and jumped onto the rickety pier. He walked toward the boulevard that bordered the port, less than a quarter mile from city center. The ride to his home would take less than fifteen minutes. Naryshkin sighed with relief as the cab pulled up in front. He let himself in through the large double doors, threw his bag on the sofa and went immediately to the kitchen where the Ciroc X was being cooled in the freezer. He took the bottle with a glass and walked past the cook toward the back door leading to the pool. He ignored her as she looked up from chopping ingredients for the salad, "Good evening, sir, welcome home."

***

It was five p.m. when Petronovich pulled into the parking lot in front of the Tverskaya Residence. The listening device he had planted had an effective range of three hundred yards and the ability to pick up both sides of the cell phone conversation that Natalia would have with her son in the next few minutes. Petronovich activated the recorder in preparation for the call.

Natalia sat on her sofa with her phone on the coffee table. She was reading the novel she had started the day before, which she was now more than halfway through. Reading was how she spent most of her day after breakfast at the condo restaurant and a trip to the local store for the night's dinner and essentials. She glanced at the time on her phone, it was nine past five. She picked it up and waited. At precisely ten past five, it buzzed.

"Sergey, how are you?" she asked.

"I'm fine, Mother, how was your week?"

Natalia began with a brief replay of the events that had occurred that week.

Naryshkin listened, fidgeting as the same story as last week, and the week before that, was told. He was about to end the call when Natalia said, "Oh, I almost forgot. A friend of yours was working in the building and stopped by my unit to check my heating and air."

Naryshkin felt the hairs on the back of his neck rise as he answered, "What was this person's name, Mother?"

"His name is Vladimir Petronovich. He was very nice. He asked me to tell you that he said hello when you called."

Naryshkin was silent for a good minute.

Finally, Natalia responded with, "Sergey, are you there?"

"Yes, I'm here. Petronovich is not a good man. Do not let him into your apartment again. If he should come to the door, call security, and have authorities remove him. Do you understand?"

"You're scaring me, Sergey. Do I need to worry?"

Naryshkin couldn't speak openly on the phone, given that it was most likely tapped. "No, Mother you don't need to worry, just do as I say. We're on the same page, right?"

"Yes. When will you call next?" Natalia asked, disturbed by her son's response.

"I'll be in touch before our regular call. Remember what I said. I'll call you soon."

"Be careful, Sergey. I love you," Natalia said.

Petronovich listened as the call was terminated. Naryshkin was obviously taken aback, which was the desired effect he had hoped to achieve. *Now he might come and check on his mom,* Petronovich thought as he turned off the recorder and drove out of the lot, back to the Hotel Ukraine.

With the small machine still recording, Volkov asked, "What is your cell number?"

Kozlov gave the number. "Now, what do we do?"

"Drive back to headquarters and drop me off. Once I've talked with my superiors, I'll be in touch."

Kozlov backed the vehicle and did a three-point turn, heading out of the forest. Twenty minutes later, they were in the lot. Volkov opened his door. Before leaving, he said, "Keep your phone near you. Do not talk to anyone about our conversation. If we suspect the SVR knows anything about us, you and your entire family will be eliminated. Do you understand what I've just said?"

"Yes," replied Kozlov as he nodded. "I understand. I'll wait for your call."

Hearing the affirmative answer, Volkov got out of the car and closed the door. As he watched Kozlov drive off, he pulled the slip of paper from his pocket and, sitting in his rental, dialed the number. The call was answered immediately: "How can I help you?"

"I'm assuming you know where Petronovich and McClintock are staying?" asked Volkov.

There was a slight hesitation. "Yes, the Hotel Ukraine."

"I'm changing hotels and moving over there. For now, this is between you and me. I need to speak with them personally before they are aware that I'm in town, understood?" Volkov asked knowing that he had some explaining to do regarding his death, or rather, life.

"Do you need help making the reservation?"

"No, I will take care of that. How did they register?"

"I reserved the rooms under my name, Vachovska. How they paid, I do not know."

"Probably a corporate credit card. Do you know their schedule?" Volkov asked.

Vachovska explained Petronovich's need to be at the Tverskaya Residence that afternoon, but nothing beyond that.

"I can't imagine he's going to be too late, it is, after all, Sunday."

Pleased with the answer, knowing he'd be able to meet Petronovich and McClintock this evening, he answered, "Very good. I'll contact them tonight. We'll be in touch."

Volkov had planned to leave Russia that afternoon after eliminating Kozlov. The change in plans required a call to Whittington. Petronovich and McClintock could help with the developing situation and Kozlov. He had his bag in the car and drove directly to the Hotel Ukraine.

***

Naryshkin stared at his phone, stunned by the call. He knew his options were limited. He couldn't go back to Moscow easily. If he did, he would need to drive the one thousand, six hundred and forty seven km or a little over one thousand miles. Flying was out of the question. The drive would take close to fifteen hours but could be done in one very long day. After some thought, maybe the best option was to get his mom out of Moscow, to Sochi. He filled the glass with vodka to the brim and proceeded to self-medicate using the alcohol.

By seven p.m. the caretakers called Naryshkin for dinner. Having not received a response, the couple went out to the pool. The bottle of Ciroc X was empty on its side by the lounge chair where Naryshkin was passed out cold. The husband was a burly man, about sixty years of age. He hefted the limp body over his shoulder while his wife scurried ahead, holding the back door open. They brought Naryshkin upstairs to his room where they simply laid him on the bed and covered him with a throw.

***

After self-parking his vehicle, Petronovich entered the hotel lobby and headed for the bank of elevators. There were several patrons at the front desk as Petronovich approached. He couldn't see the face, but one person, a male, had long blonde hair, reminding him of his friend, Vasily.

The man turned, ready to leave with his room key and paperwork when their eyes met.

Petronovich stopped in shock. He stood still briefly, then stepped forward and wrapped Volkov in a huge bearhug. Neither man said a word, but a single tear trickled down Petronovich's cheek. He finally cleared his throat, stood back with his hands on Volkov's shoulders and said, "You'd better have a good explanation for this."

"I will tell you everything. I thought you were already checked in?"

"I am. I was over at the Tverskaya Residence listening to a conversation between Naryshkin and his mother. I'll follow you to your room so you can drop your things off. Then we'll go to Jason's room, pick him up and head to the bar for a few drinks as we listen to the story you will tell."

Chapter 15

Jason had purposely left the door to his room ajar. Petronovich tapped and then stepped inside, followed by Volkov.

"Did she mention you on the call with her son?" Jason asked as he turned to the door, spotting Vasily and looking as though he'd seen a ghost.

Volkov stepped forward and gave him a brief hug. "Good to see you, Jason."

"What happened? You were supposed to have been killed?"

"He looked like it. There was so much blood and the tech confirmed it," Petronovich replied.

"I was wearing a medallion which deflected the round down and out my back without hitting any major organs, arteries, or bone. I was lucky. Whit wanted Naryshkin to believe I was killed, that's why he didn't say anything."

"So, what are you doing here?" Jason asked.

Petronovich jumped in. "That's what he's going to tell us in the bar. Let's go."

***

Naryshkin awoke, feeling as though someone had taken a hammer to his head. He stumbled out of bed, went into the bathroom, and took a long, hot shower, hoping that freshening up would help. To a certain extent, it did. But he knew what he needed most. He dressed in sweats and then headed for the liquor cabinet in the kitchen. After pouring freshly squeezed orange juice halfway into a tall glass, he topped the remaining half with vodka. After a couple of long sips, his headache began to subside.

He went into his study, closed the door, and sat at his desk. He began to turn red with rage as he thought of Petronovich talking to his mother in her home. What was more infuriating to Naryshkin was that his mother seemed to like him. Finally, he looked at his iPhone and dialed Kozlov's cell. It was ten a.m., he'd probably be in the office.

Kozlov answered his phone without looking at the number. "Hello?"

"Mikhail, we need to talk. Petronovich is in Moscow and he may have plans to kidnap my mother. I need your help."

Recognizing Naryshkin's voice, Kozlov answered, "I cannot be involved."

"I'm not asking you to get involved. I need you to go to my mother's apartment, right now. Pack a suitcase and take her to the airport. I've booked a flight for her on Pobeda Air to Sochi. You will forget you heard that city, correct?"

"Yes. What time does her flight leave?" asked Kozlov.

"Two p.m. You will have plenty of time. Tell Mom you are doing this for me and that I will meet her plane. Any questions?"

Kozlov had many, but none that he could ask Naryshkin directly without putting his life in jeopardy. He answered, "No. I'll do it."

***

The three men entered the dimly lit hotel bar.

"Glenfiddich?" asked the waiter, knowing Jason's preference.

"Please," Jason responded.

"And Grey Goose?" asked the waiter, looking at Petronovich and then Volkov. "What will you have, sir?"

Petronovich answered, "Grey Goose for both of us, please."

After the waiter, who happened to be the bartender too, was behind the bar, Petronovich said, "Okay, let's hear what happened and why you're here."

Volkov told the story of finding Naryshkin in his home. He then followed with his meeting with Whittington and the reason he was in Moscow.

"Did you confront Kozlov?" asked Petronovich.

"I did, and here's where it gets complicated," replied Volkov as he placed the small recording device in the middle of the table adjusting the volume so it was loud enough that only they could hear it. "Listen to this."

The three men listened to the conversation Volkov had had with Kozlov, including the name of the mole inside the CIA who had given up their contact information and home addresses.

"I need direction from Whittington as to how he wants us to play Kozlov. I simply couldn't eliminate him with so much information at stake, including other sleeper agents inside the agency."

"You did the right thing," said Petronovich as he sipped his drink. "Does he know where Naryshkin might be?"

"I didn't ask. He's waiting for my call and instructions as to how we want to proceed."

"It's nine a.m. in L.A. I suggest we finish this drink and then go back to the room and get Whit on the phone," Jason said as he looked at the other two.

"Agreed. Drink up, gentlemen," Petronovich replied.

212

Naryshkin had a second thought immediately after terminating the call to Kozlov. He dialed the office number once again, and Kozlov picked up with Naryshkin speaking, "One more thing. I've been thinking, we know Petronovich is in Moscow, but where are the McClintock brothers? Do we still have an asset inside the FBI?"

"Yes, several," answered Kozlov.

"Good. We must assume that the McClintocks are being protected by federal agents. The question is where? They certainly wouldn't be at their homes. Are our sources in positions high enough to uncover this information?" Naryshkin asked, waiting impatiently for the answer.

"I believe so. But, as I said before, I can't be part of your personal vendetta."

Naryshkin listened, then replied, "Kozlov, if you don't get this information for me, you will be living the rest of your days, however few there may be, looking behind your back, wondering when I will show up. And I will show up, I promise you that."

Kozlov listened, then replied in a measured tone, "I will make some calls and see if I can locate the McClintocks."

"Good! Make the calls and then get my mother to the airport. You made the right decision, Kozlov. I'll phone you tomorrow."

***

Petronovich and Volkov sat at the small table in Jason's room while Jason sat at the end of the bed. The phone was on speaker.

Whittington picked up after the first ring. "Is the task taken care of, Vasily?"

"That's the reason for my call. I want you to listen to a short recording. I have Vladi and Jason here as well."

"Let's hear it," replied Whittington as he listened without commenting. When the tape ended, Whit replied, "This does change things. Contact him and tell him we want the names of those that have been compromised in the agency as well as the FBI. In addition, pressure him on Naryshkin's location. We know from our sources that he's gone rogue and the SVR is looking for him. I doubt Kozlov will know anything, but it doesn't hurt to ask. After we get the names, we'll get him out. Any luck approaching Naryshkin's mother?"

Petronovich answered, relaying the conversation he had had with her and the subsequent call Naryshkin had with his mother.

"Naryshkin keeps his location and even his phone numbers from her. She believes he has an apartment near SVR headquarters."

"He probably did at one time," replied Whit. "Get me the information from Kozlov as soon as you can. We don't need any of our operations compromised more than they've already been. If that's all you have, I have a meeting here in five minutes."

The call ended with Petronovich looking at Volkov and saying, "You'd better contact Kozlov."

***

Mike Nielsen worked in a senior management position with the FBI at the headquarters in Washington D.C.

Kozlov sent an encrypted text message to Nielsen's cell, requesting the current location of Mike and Jason McClintock and their families. The note was short, marked 'Urgent' in the subject line. Once finished, Kozlov noted the time, thinking he would need to move quickly to get Mrs. Naryshkin packed and to the airport. The drive to her apartment would be only fifteen minutes, so he should have no timing issues, assuming Mrs. Naryshkin went along willingly.

The doorbell rang and Natalia shuffled to the door and then opened it after peering through the peephole. The man on the other side was wearing a suit.

She opened the door and then asked, "Can I help you?"

"Hello, Mrs. Naryshkin, my name is Mikhail Kozlov. I work with your son, Sergey. He has a plane ticket waiting for you at the airport. He asked me to assist you in packing and getting to the plane."

"I don't know. Sergey didn't mention this," replied Natalia. "Do you know where I am flying?"

"Sergey said he would meet you in Sochi. The plane leaves at two, so we must get ready," pressed Kozlov, hoping she wouldn't say no.

"I've never been to Sochi. It's supposed to be a nice resort city. Do you know why Sergey is there?" asked Natalia.

I'm pretty sure I do, he's in hiding,

"No, I do not," replied Kozlov. "Please, ma'am, you must start packing. You will not need the winter clothes you wear here. Pack so you will be comfortable in a mild climate. Do you need me to help?" Kozlov asked.

"No, Mr. Kozlov, I will be fine. I'll be with you in about an hour. I wish I'd have been given more of a notice," Natalia said as she shuffled down the hallway to her bedroom. "Make yourself comfortable. There's water in the fridge."

After ninety minutes, Natalia called for help with her luggage. Kozlov assisted with the luggage, and they were finally out the door.

After checking Natalia in at the Pobeda counter and having made certain she was cared for properly, Kozlov headed back to the office.

Kozlov was about to power down his computer when the text came through from Nielsen. The message was one line only. It read, 'McClintock address: safe house; 1212 Fiery Dawn, Vail AZ.' He wrote the address on his legal pad, threw it in his briefcase and left the office for the evening.

***

Volkov was in his room when he dialed the cell number Kozlov had given him. Sitting in his home office, Kozlov answered, "Hello?"

"This is Volkov. You have a deal. Once we have the names of the assets that have turned, we will get you out. We also need Naryshkin's location. Can you get that?"

Kozlov hesitated, then offered, "I do not have an exact location, but I can offer a general proximity."

"Where is that?" Volkov asked.

"Sochi, a resort city on the Black Sea."

"How is it that you have the city, but not the exact address?"

"I was only given the city," Kozlov explained.

"Given, by whom?" Volkov asked.

Kozlov decided that it was in his best interest to tell the truth, at least, most of it. "By Naryshkin. He flew his mother to Sochi this morning. I drove her to the airport." Kozlov failed to mention that Naryshkin had asked for the location of the safe house occupied by the McClintocks.

Volkov thought for a moment then followed with, "I will call you tomorrow. Have the names of the FBI agents and CIA

216

officers that are compromised."

Kozlov dropped the call and thought, *Tomorrow is going to be a busy day.*

***

Naryshkin was in the baggage claim area, waiting for his mother to be brought down in a wheelchair. She could walk but not great distances without assistance. The elevator doors slid open with Natalia emerging in a chair being pushed by a Pobeda airline employee. Her eyes lit up when she noticed Sergey.

"Sergey." She waved with a smile.

With her luggage in hand, Sergey walked over and gave his mother a kiss on the forehead.

"Hello, Mother, I'm glad you are here." To the attendant, Naryshkin said, "My car is outside, can you wheel her to the curb?"

The traffic was light as they drove away from the airport. The Black Sea was on the left and foothills, leading to mountains in the distance, were on the right. They drove in silence until it was broken with a question from Natalia.

"Sergey, why am I here?"

"For your protection, Mother. Petronovich is dangerous and since I can't be in Moscow, you can stay with me in Sochi."

"But isn't your work for the SVR at the headquarters?"

"I've been assigned to Sochi," answered Naryshkin, not adding anything more and wanting to put an end to the inquisition.

The silence returned.

***

Volkov knew it was important to get the names of the American assets who had turned. He also knew that Kozlov could not be allowed to live. He wouldn't tell Petronovich or McClintock, but after he received the list of names, Kozlov would have an 'accident.' He thought about that for a few more minutes and then went back to Jason's room.

Petronovich looked up. "Did you speak with him?"

Volkov relayed the conversation, concluding with the fact that Naryshkin was somewhere in the city of Sochi and his mother was with him.

Jason asked, "So, we have a city, but no address? That's like looking for a needle in a haystack. Sochi is not Moscow, but it is a large city."

"The only way we are going to get him is if he comes for us," said Petronovich. "I think we should get the names from Kozlov and get out."

"I'm all for that, but I'm having a difficult time bringing Kozlov with us to the U.S., knowing he was instrumental in Kamarov's death and almost mine."

"What do you propose?" Petronovich asked.

Volkov didn't hesitate. "Once he has the names, I will meet him and get the list. After that, the less you both know, the better."

Petronovich looked at Volkov, understood where he was coming from and simply nodded.

Jason said, "You have to do what you need to do."

"All right, now that this is done, why don't we go downstairs and get dinner?" suggested Volkov.

***

218

Naryshkin was in his office, about to phone Kozlov, when he heard his mother talking with the staff in the kitchen.

He shut the office door and dialed the cell. Kozlov answered and Naryshkin didn't hesitate. "Give me the address."

Kozlov read it back, then hung up, not wanting any further communication with Naryshkin.

Naryshkin looked at the phone and smiled at the brazen attitude that Kozlov displayed. *He certainly wouldn't act that way if he was sitting across from me,* thought Naryshkin.

Naryshkin rose from his desk and walked to the sidewall with the seascape painting. He pulled the painting back, revealing a wall safe. After spinning the dial to the appropriate numbers, he opened the safe and withdrew two new passports and credit cards, one in the name of Victor Heraskova. He then sat back down at the desk and pulled up the location of Vail, Arizona. He checked the map and noted it was a small town outside Tucson, in what looked to be the middle of nowhere.

After some thought, Naryshkin began to formulate a plan. He would retrace his entrance into Sochi using the same fishing boats he had used to get in. He knew where the vessel *Kalinovka* was berthed, and he knew both captains. He was certain that passage across the Black Sea to Trabzon, Turkey, would not be an issue. From there, he planned to fly to Mexico City and then on to Nogales, Mexico, a small town on the U.S.–Mexico border. Vail was only sixty miles from the Nogales. Once on the ground, he would purchase a car with cash and then drive sixty minutes to his destination. He planned to leave the day after tomorrow. This afternoon, he would make a trip to the marina and arrange passage to Trabzon with the captain of *Kalinovka*.

***

Volkov phoned Kozlov.

"Do you have the list?" Volkov asked after the cell was answered.

"Yes, it's not long, three names."

"Meet me in Bitsevski Park where we had our last conversation. One hour, don't be late," Volkov said evenly.

Kozlov hesitated, then replied, "Why not meet somewhere closer? I can even come to your hotel." The thought of being deep in the woods with Volkov was unnerving.

"Be at the park, one hour," Volkov responded and then terminated the call.

Kozlov shook his head as a bead of sweat began to trickle down his forehead. *At least I'll have a weapon,* he thought.

***

Naryshkin was waiting at the marina when the Kalinovka eased into the slip. After assuring the lines were secure, the captain cut the engines and stepped out of the wheelhouse. Standing next to the secured lines was Naryshkin. The captain noticed him and said, "It's Ivanov, correct?"

"Yes, good memory, captain," Naryshkin replied.

"Why are you here, Ivanov?"

"I need a ride back to Trabzon. I was hoping you could take me halfway like before and meet the other captain from Turkey for a ride the rest of the way. I would pay both of you ten percent more than I did the last trip."

The captain thought for a moment, then asked, "When do you want to go?"

"Day after tomorrow."

"I'll arrange it. Be here at forty forty-five, we leave at five a.m.," said the captain.

***

Volkov stood outside his car with the Udav in his windbreaker pocket, out of sight and easily accessible. He looked at his watch, Kozlov had five minutes.

Volkov listened and heard a car coming. He could see the dust in the distance before he saw Kozlov's vehicle. He came to a stop ten yards from Volkov and got out. He walked around the front of the car and toward Volkov with the slip of paper in his hand.

"Let's see the list," demanded Volkov with his left hand outstretched and his right in the jacket holding the gun which was directed toward Kozlov.

Kozlov handed the paper to Volkov and was about to say something when Volkov pulled the trigger. The hollow point hit the center chest and lifted Kozlov into the air, throwing him backwards to the dirt. He was dead before he hit the ground.

Volkov got in his car and drove slowly past the body, down the dirt road. Before leaving the park, he threw the Udav, wrapped in the windbreaker into some dense underbrush, where the jacket and gun would most likely never be found.

Volkov was on the highway when his phone vibrated.

Petronovich had sent a text: *Meet us in the bar.*

***

McClintock and Petronovich were at the same table in the back when Volkov walked in. He sat down, placing the slip of paper in the middle of the table. Petronovich picked it up and scanned the names. He didn't know any of the men.

"We'll have to call Whit with these names. It's four in the morning there, but this can't wait, we need to call him.

The waiter walked up and placed a Grey Goose in front of Volkov. "I'm assuming this is right?"

"Yes, thanks," Volkov replied, then looking at Petronovich and McClintock. "Kozlov won't be making the trip with us to the States."

Petronovich nodded without replying and Jason didn't respond.

Petronovich picked up his phone and dialed Whittington's cell phone. The phone rang several times and was then answered with, "Hello?"

"Whit, this is Petronovich. I'm sorry to be calling so early, but we felt that you should have the names of the compromised individuals we were given."

"Give me a second to get a pad of paper and pen." Everyone waited and then, Whit said, "Okay, is the list long?"

"No, three names."

"I'm ready, go," said Whit.

Vladi gave him the first two names and then followed with, "The last name is Mike Nielsen, that's it."

"Good job. I'll make some calls and have them arrested before sunrise. We will be interrogating them this morning to try to determine how much damage has been done. Tomorrow morning, your time, I'll have a plane at the FBO at Sheremetyevo International. I'll let you know when the jet is wheels up from D.C. so you'll have an ETA. Have Kozlov ready to go."

Volkov spoke up. "Kozlov won't be making the trip, he had an accident that was fatal."

222

There was a hesitation and silence at Whittington's end and then he responded with, "I'm not going to ask any more questions. But when you are working for me, going forward it's by the book and my rules, is that understood? I want an answer from each one of you, including you, McClintock, I assume you're on the call?"

Jason answered, "I am, and it is understood, sir."

"Petronovich?"

"Understood."

"Volkov, are we on the same page?" asked Whit.

"Yes, sir, understood."

"Good. I'll text as soon as I know your estimated departure time," said Whittington. "Have a good evening."

Chapter 16

Sergey and Natalia sat at the dining table, waiting for the chef to serve her specialty, which was borscht. Her beet soup was loaded with potatoes, cabbage, carrots, celery, and lamb. She placed a bowl on each placemat and then followed with a dollop of sour cream. After the chef had left the dining room, Sergey put his spoon down and said, "Mother, I have a business trip I must make. I will be leaving tomorrow."

Natalia looked up. "Where will you be going?"

"This is official business, I am not at liberty to say. I should be gone no longer than a week. You will be taken care of by the staff. Whatever you need, simply ask."

"This is so sudden. I wish I was at my home in Moscow. I don't know anyone here," Natalia explained. "With you gone, what will I do?"

"You will be fine, Mother. When I get back, I'll show you all there is to see in Sochi," Sergey replied.

Natalia didn't care if she saw the city of Sochi. She ignored the last statement. "When do you leave?"

"I have a car picking me up at four in the morning to take me to the airport," Sergey said, even though he would be taken to the marina.

Natalia picked at her food for the next few minutes without saying a word. Finally, she looked up and said, "Have a safe trip," then began in earnest to work on the tasty meal in front of her.

***

Whittington stood on the other side of the glass window and watched as the six sensors were attached to Nielsen. The room was sterile, with a small table and monitor for the examiner, and a chair, which Nielsen sat in, directly in front of the desk. The sensors monitored Nielsen's breathing rate, blood pressure, pulse, and perspiration. The questioner asked Nielsen three simple questions to establish a baseline; "What is your name?" "Where were you born?" "What is your wife's name?"

Nielsen answered calmly and evenly.

"Why are you doing this?" Nielsen asked.

The examiner responded, "Just answer the questions, don't ask. Have you had any communications in the past with foreign government officials?" The examiner watched the charts on the monitor in front of him.

Every sensor spiked as Nielsen replied, "No."

"Have you communicated in any fashion with the Russian government or someone you might assume represented the Russian government?"

Once again, the sensors spiked, only this time higher as Nielsen responded, "No."

The examiner glanced at the window, where he knew Whittington would be watching. He rose from the desk and walked toward the door.

"I'll be just a minute," he said to the subject.

Outside the door, Whittington asked, "Well?"

"He's definitely lying. I'll try one more time to elicit a truthful response."

"If that doesn't work, we'll do it the hard way," Whit responded.

Back in the room, the examiner stated, "The sensors are indicating that you are not telling the truth. We'll try one more time. If the machine doesn't come back with a positive response, we will use other methods to extract it. I think you know what that means."

"I've done nothing wrong."

"Have you passed any information to foreign government agents or representatives?"

Nielsen breathed in deeply, letting the breath out slowly as he tried to slow his heart rate and lower his blood pressure, "No."

The sensors spiked, but not as highly as they had with the previous question. The examiner watched the monitor and simply said, "Fail." He looked at the mirror and motioned for an agent to come in.

Nielsen was placed in handcuffs and walked out of the room to a cell down the hallway.

Whittington walked in. "Is the safe house ready?"

The agent that had conducted the polygraph looked up from the machine and replied, "We anticipated this result. The team is at the off-site location waiting for Nielsen."

***

Naryshkin was at the marina at four forty. Through the fog, he could see the *Kalinovka* lit up like a Christmas tree, with men on deck seen preparing the boat to get underway. With the cash in hand, he approached the vessel and asked loudly, "Permission to come aboard?"

The captain poked his head out of the wheelhouse. "Come aboard, Ivanov, we are ready to go."

Naryshkin stepped onto the deck and climbed the steps to

226

the wheelhouse, placing the cash on the table next to the captain.

"Make yourself comfortable, we're going to be several hours before we transfer you to the *Trabzon* vessel."

***

It was still early morning when the agents escorted Nielsen out a side door to a waiting black Suburban. Still handcuffed, they placed him in the backseat and drove away from the facility. The safe house was in the country about an hour from the city. They turned off the two-lane highway onto a dirt road. A small house sat on the hill, about a half mile from the exit. As the Suburban came to a stop in front of the home, two agents stepped out of the house and approached the vehicle. The driver of the Suburban asked, "Are you ready?"

"Bring him in. We will start when Whittington gets here, he should be here any time," replied the agent. As they approached the house, the rumble of a car coming up the hill could be heard. "That's him, we might as well get started."

"You can't do this! I've done nothing wrong," whined Nielsen.

The agents ignored him, forcing him forward. Inside the main room was a long table with straps for the head, legs and arms. The agents uncuffed Nielsen and moved him to the table, with Nielsen resisting in every way possible with each step. It took three agents to force him onto the table and strap him down.

Whittington watched from across the room. A towel was placed over Nielsen's face. The table was slightly elevated with the feet up higher than the head. A bucket sat underneath the table at the head's end to collect any water that would dribble down.

One of the agents had a gallon of water in hand, ready to

pour over the towel. Before doing so, a second agent asked Nielsen, "Did you give any confidential information to representatives of foreign governments?"

"No!"

The agent with the water jug began pouring.

Nielsen squirmed, trying to turn his head away from the pouring water. The straps securing his head prevented any movement. The pouring stopped and the towel was removed.

Nielsen was gasping for air.

The second agent asked once again, "Have you passed sensitive information to foreign governments?"

"No! Please stop this!"

They placed the towel over Nielsen's face once again and began pouring.

Nielsen struggled and flailed as much as he could against the straps. The pouring stopped and the towel was removed. Nielsen coughed, choked, and tried to breathe, finally whispering, "Okay, yes, I passed information."

"To whom?"

"The Russians."

"What information?"

"The home addresses for the McClintocks and Petronovich," Nielsen sputtered, still trying to breathe.

"Anything else?"

"The safehouse address where the family is located in Arizona."

The agent looked across the room at Whittington, who shook his head and turned away, not wanting to look at the traitor.

"Take him away."

***

228

McClintock, Petronovich and Volkov sat in the lounge of the FBO at Sheremetyevo International. A self-serve minibar was set along one wall, offering water, soft drinks, beer, and alcohol.

Each man had a drink as they sat in overstuffed chairs facing the tarmac. Whittington had texted the estimated arrival time prior to the Nielsen polygraph. If the plane was on time, it would be arriving in the next twenty minutes. They would be wheels up no more than thirty minutes after landing.

Petronovich was sipping his vodka when the cell vibrated. He looked at the phone.

"It's Whittington," he said to the others.

"Hello?"

Whit got right to the point. "We interrogated all three men. The last one, Nielsen, had to be waterboarded. He finally admitted to giving the Russians, by that I mean Naryshkin, each of your home addresses, which we know he already knew, but also, the address of the safe house."

"How long ago was this?" Petronovich asked.

"Two days."

"Then he could be in Arizona right now."

"Correct. We've alerted the team keeping watch over the family. They are packing and will be moved shortly."

"Where?" Petronovich asked.

"Prescott, about four hours north. We have a house there. I'm having the three of you flown into Tucson. The drive to Vail is about twenty-five minutes. If Naryshkin shows up at the house, he won't find the family. He'll have to deal with you three and a team of agents. If possible, I want you to take him alive."

Petronovich clicked off the cell. McClintock looked out the window as a Gulfstream G550 with an American flag on the tail

229

pulled to a stop not far from the FBO entrance to the flight line.

He commented, "I think this is our ride."

***

Naryshkin had a slight advantage in the travel west. His flight from Trabzon to Mexico City included a brief stop in Istanbul.

The first-class seat made the nineteen-hour flight bearable. Having the seat next to him vacant made the trip almost pleasant. The premium vodka proved to make the trip outstanding. He sipped his drink and thought about how he would abduct the McClintock family and use them as bait to lure in and kill Petronovich, Volkov and, of course, the McClintock brothers. Finally, the girlfriend, wife and children would die... collateral damage.

Going through customs in Mexico City proved to be uneventful. The Russian passport under the name Victor Heraskova was authentic and produced under the table by the same company the SVR contracted to make multiple passports for their agents. The job had been accepted after a large sum of money had been offered by Naryshkin. His connecting flight to Nogales was on time and, with any luck, he would be on the ground by eleven a.m. and crossing the U.S. border by eleven thirty. At that point, the driving time to Vail was only one hour.

***

It was late morning when the doorbell rang. The temperature outside was already ninety and the kids were getting their suits on for the pool. Mike looked through the peephole, and, recognizing one of the agents, opened the door.

230

"Mike, we have a situation. We're going to need to pack quickly and go," said the agent.

"What's the problem?"

"Our location has been compromised and we believe Naryshkin may be on his way here from Sochi."

"Can't you put an alert out with his picture and have him taken into custody once he tries to enter the country?" Mike asked.

"You know we will do that, but Naryshkin is smart enough to avoid the obvious routes in. The bottom line is we have to go. Get everyone packed. We leave in two hours."

"What's the destination?"

"We have a safe house in Prescott. That's where we are going."

"That's where you are taking my family. I'm staying here," Mike replied.

"My instructions are that everyone goes," the agent responded.

"I'm familiar with operations like this. Take my family to safety. I'm staying, end of discussion."

The agent shook his head. "Have the family ready to go in two hours." He turned and walked out the door to the home across the street. The FBI already had agents posted in front and back of the house.

Mike shut the door and found Julie helping Sam pick out the swimsuit to wear. "Julie, we need to talk, where's Brenda?"

Julie looked up. "She's outside by the pool, what's wrong?"

Mike explained what the agent had said, and the urgency of the situation. "You are going to be moved to a house in Prescott. We need to be packed and ready in the next two hours. You get Zach and Sam going and I'll tell Brenda. Then I'll help pack your things."

"I can do my own packing, you pack yourself," Julie responded.

"I'm staying, Jules. You, Brenda, and the kids are going."

"We won't go without you, Mike."

"I need to stay. If I can help put this thing to rest by killing Naryshkin, that's what I have to do. You will be safe in Prescott. I'll tell Brenda," Mike said and walked away.

***

Naryshkin was out of the airplane and walking down the short concourse to a line of cabs. He waited for the next available ride and drove the ten minutes to the port of entry at the U.S. border. He planned to walk across. The line of people waiting to enter was long, but Naryshkin slipped a young Mexican lady with two children, $20 to step in front of her in line. There were a few mumbles from the crowd behind him which eventually subsided as the line inched toward the door and the two customs and border inspection counters that were manned. The border agents were overwhelmed and worked as quickly as possible to pass people through. When it was Naryshkin's turn, he stepped up to the counter with his passport in hand. The agent had his hand held out ready to receive it. He glanced at Naryshkin, then the passport, and passed him through.

Once outside, Naryshkin noticed several dirt parking lots where Americans used to park and walk into Mexico. Many were there for dental care or prescription medication that was a fraction of the cost in the U.S. for the exact same drug or dental care. He noticed a young kid walking toward what was probably his old Toyota.

He approached the kid, "Is this your car?"

"Why?"

"I would like to purchase it from you," Naryshkin replied. "I will give you $10,000 US for the car. The true value is really only $1,500 if that."

"If I sold it, how would I get back to Tucson?" asked the kid.

"I'll throw in another $100 for the Uber ride. Deal?"

The kid thought for a moment, looked at his car, then back at Naryshkin. "Deal."

Naryshkin had already put the safe house address into his maps app on the iPhone. He would head north on I-19. The directions put him at the safe house at twelve thirty-five.

***

The flight from Moscow to Tucson was six thousand and ninety five miles. With a range of over seven thousand, seven hundred miles, the trip would be direct without a need to stop and refuel. The men slept most of the way. About two hours from their destination, the cabin steward walked through, offering lunch and cold drinks. Petronovich and McClintock declined, but Volkov took advantage of the BLT and Coke.

"Whit said he would have a car waiting at the FBO. If we are two hours out, we should be at the house about two," said Petronovich.

"We can get details of the neighborhood from the agent that picks us up," said Volkov, through bites of his sandwich. "It's supposed to be a gated community, so hopefully the options for ingress and egress are limited."

"It will be nice to have several agents with us to help monitor the cars entering the community. The house is supposed to sit on

233

a golf course fairway, so that could be an issue," replied McClintock.

"We will assess the situation when we get there," Petronovich commented.

***

Naryshkin waited near the entrance for a car that had a gate opener. When the old guy in the Cadillac reached for the visor, he knew he was going to open the gate, so he eased in behind the vehicle.

Once inside the gated community, the Cadillac took the second left.

Naryshkin drove on, the directions putting him a half mile away from the house. He followed the road to a point where it dog-legged to the left. At his immediate right was a street with homes ending in a cul-de-sac. He made the right turn, then parked back four houses, but with a view of the home he assumed was the safe house. A black SUV backed up to an open garage with people moving back and forth with suitcases, loading the vehicle.

They are moving. Why? thought Naryshkin.

***

Mike loaded the last suitcase in the vehicle.

"Julie, I'd like to talk to you and Brenda for a minute in the bedroom. Kids, get in the car," said Mike as Agents Silva and Moniot helped the two kids into the far back seat.

In the bedroom, Mike had a Benelli M4 short-barreled 12-guage shotgun and a Glock 17 9mm handgun. He picked the shotgun up and handed it to Julie, then gave the Glock to Brenda.

234

"I have a box of shells in the trunk for each weapon. I don't care what Silva or Moniot say, when you get to Prescott, load the weapons and keep them in a place that is easily accessible."

"They won't like us having them," Julie commented.

Brenda took the handgun, released the magazine, and then pulled the slide back to be sure a round wasn't chambered.

"I'm keeping this with me," she replied.

"Okay, let me carry the weapons out to the car. I'll talk to both agents," said Mike as the women handed him the guns. As they walked through the house, Mike continued, "You will be safe in Prescott. I'll be up to get you as soon as I can."

Brenda asked, "Have you heard from Jason or Vladi?"

"I haven't, but I would think they would be making their way back here, especially if the authorities believe Naryshkin may be coming back."

As Mike approached the Suburban, Agent Silva noticed what he was carrying.

"They won't be needing those, Mike."

"The weapons go, or the family stays here," Mike replied as he placed the guns in the back, ignoring Silva, who was staring at him.

Finally, Silva relented, "Get in the car ladies, it's time to go."

Brenda climbed in the back seat in front of the kids, while Julie gave Mike a kiss and hug and then followed. Once the back door closed, the big SUV eased forward onto the street and away from the house.

When the car was out of sight, Mike turned to the agents who had stayed.

"What's the plan?"

"The house will be watched twenty-four seven, front and back. We already have a team in place. Naryshkin can't get within

235

a half mile of this place without us knowing it."

"That's good, but I also don't want the security to be so tight that it scares him off," Mike commented.

"Our guys are good. They are not obvious," the agent said, nodding toward the community landscape maintenance team working in the common area a few doors down.

***

Naryshkin slid down in the seat as the black Suburban passed the cul-de-sac. He waited a minute and then followed the slow-moving vehicle at a distance. After three miles, keeping four to five cars between them, they entered I-10 West toward Phoenix.

Naryshkin was very good at his tradecraft, having learned from the best in the world with the KGB. He used the other vehicles, especially the many semis traveling west, as cover. With the distance and number of vehicles between him and the Suburban, he would be difficult to spot. The tricky part would be when they left the freeway. By necessity, he would then need to maintain an even greater distance between them.

Two hours into the drive, Naryshkin found himself in the middle of Phoenix traffic. After twenty minutes, they merged onto 17 N, toward Flagstaff and the mountains. It was still a freeway with plenty of traffic for cover.

After another long hour, the Suburban took the offramp for 69 N with a sign indicating the city of Prescott in the distance.

Naryshkin slowed significantly on Hwy 17 when he saw the Suburban signal right toward the exit. He allowed three cars to move in front of him, all taking the same exit. The two-lane highway was busy, which enabled Naryshkin to drop back further while keeping the black vehicle in sight.

Three miles south of Prescott, the Suburban turned left onto a dirt road. Naryshkin noted the mile marker and continued past, following the other cars into town.

The terrain was rolling hills with Ponderosa Pines. At an elevation of five thousand, three hundred feet, the temperature was significantly cooler than in the southern Arizona desert. Naryshkin needed fuel and food. After sunset, he would go back to where the Suburban turned and try to find their location.

***

The Gulfstream landed smoothly, then taxied the short distance to the FBO at the small Tucson airport.

McClintock looked out the window as they slowly pulled in toward the ground crewman with the orange batons, motioning the pilot forward, as a second crew person, a female, waited off to the side with chocks ready to be placed in front and back of the aircraft nose tire.

McClintock noticed the black SUV parked directly outside the chain-link fence and closed gate. Two men in suits exited the large vehicle when the G550 came to a complete stop.

"Well, that was one long trip," said Petronovich as he rose from the leather seat and stretched.

"I'm ready to see what the surroundings of the house look like and determine how difficult it will be to protect," Volkov responded.

Vladi replied, "The FBI at the house must have a handle on what we're up against."

"In either case, we'll be able to ask the two guys who are walking to the plane. They must be the drivers that Whit promised would meet us," said McClintock.

Volkov bent down and looked out the window. "No doubt, FBI."

The plane's captain opened the exterior door and the stairs folded down and out. "Welcome to Tucson, gentlemen. I hope your stay is safe and productive."

"Say a prayer, captain, thanks for the ride," said Petronovich as he inched by the pilot.

The two men waited at the bottom of the stairs as Petronovich ducked out of the doorway, followed by Volkov and McClintock.

At the bottom, the first suit stepped up.

"I'm Agent Ballard, Tony Ballard," he said, "and this is Agent Beckmann, Michael."

The men shook hands, introducing themselves.

Ballard said, "The car is right outside the gate, we better get going."

***

The Suburban moved at about twenty-five mph down the dirt road, past a sign that read, 'Dead End.' They veered left and then right, trying to avoid the potholes. After cresting a hill, the home could be seen at the top of another rise, though lower in elevation.

"This place certainly is remote," Julie stated.

"By necessity," Agent Moniot replied. "Sorry, no pool, kids," which elicited the expected moans as a response.

"That's okay, we'll keep busy, right, guys?" Brenda suggested, asking Zach and Sam.

"I guess," Sam said.

Zack asked, "When are we going home, Mom?"

Julie answered, "When Dad and these nice gentlemen say

238

it's time. It might only be a few more days," she added, hoping to give them something to hang on to.

Agent Silva, riding shotgun, added, "Your mom's right, it shouldn't be too long. We just need to be sure it's safe when you go home. We wouldn't want it any other way, right?"

"I guess," Zack replied.

Agent Moniot drove down a slight hill, and then climbed up the other side, toward the home and a paved driveway.

"The house is bigger than it looks. It has five bedrooms and three baths. One bedroom, at the front of the house, will be used by us. Each of you will have your own bedroom. The only house rule is that if you go outside, it's during daylight and you must stay near the house. That means no exploring. Also, and this is the most important rule, if we give you instructions to do something, you obey without question. Does everyone understand?"

"Agent Moniot, we're not all kids, we get it," replied Julie.

The vehicle stopped near the garage.

Silva jumped out, walked to the garage keypad and tapped in the code to open the garage door. The door slowly opened, exposing what looked to be a Jeep Grand Cherokee, 4x4, which took up most of the space.

Moniot met Julie and Brenda at the back of the vehicle. He knew what they wanted, and handed the weapons to them, along with the two boxes of shells.

"We'll bring in the luggage. Take the kids inside and get settled."

***

The black SUV with Petronovich, McClintock and Volkov drove

239

past the gate as it opened inward. Passing the community pool, the driver, Tony, pointed and commented, "We have an agent inside the pool fence behind the shrubs with a view of the gate. If he spots anything suspicious, he notifies us by radio. We also have agents positioned behind the house and across the street. There's no way Naryshkin is getting near you without us knowing."

Tony parked on the street in front of the house. "This is your place. We are right across the street. Michael can let you in."

As the men walked up the driveway toward the front of the house, the door opened.

Agent Beckmann was surprised. "Mike, you're supposed to be in Prescott."

"I've already had that discussion," said Mike as he moved past the agent to Jason, giving him a hug. "How have you guys been? Come inside."

Beckmann made sure the front door was locked before crossing the street to the other house.

Mike led the men into the house. Volkov went immediately to the sliding glass door leading to the backyard and pool. He stepped out and walked the perimeter. The fence was four feet high, made of decorative steel with a wire mesh backing painted to match the house. He thought, *This is no protection at all. There's no barrier between the house and golf course two hundred yards away.*

He saw Petronovich come out of the house followed by Jason and Mike. "This place is going to be difficult to protect from an intruder."

"Ballard said they had a man in the back. He must be out there somewhere," Petronovich replied.

"I say we put two men on the roof, front and back and two inside, also front of the house and back. We can rotate every two hours, that way nobody becomes complacent and the view changes," said Volkov.

Mike added, "That sounds good to me. I have one AR-15 and a short barrel shotgun. We need two rifles on the roof. The shotgun stays inside. I'll talk to Ballard and see if we can get another AR with ammo."

"Mike, why don't you call Tony, while we check the house out? You might also request night vision goggles. With any luck they will have an extra set," Jason suggested.

Petronovich said, "We have a few hours before it gets dark. Is there any beer in the fridge?"

"I have a six-pack of Dragoon IPA, brewed about forty-five miles east of here. After you have had a look around, help yourself."

***

Silva carried the first load of bags inside, dropping them inside the door. He then went to an alarm pad next to the door and activated the external Infrared Perimeter System.

After the last of the bags were inside, Silva suggested, "Why don't you watch the panel. I'll start at section one, about a quarter mile away and move around the home, breaching each section. The pad shows each of the twenty sections. The blue light means no breach. A blinking red light, with a corresponding chirp, indicates a breach and needs to be acknowledged and then reset to start. You know the drill. Use your radio and let me know when a breach is indicated, and I'll confirm. Then you can reset the section."

"Okay, let's get this done," said Moniot.

Silva walked down the driveway and noticed the first sensor, about four and a half feet up a pine tree, facing the dirt road. It was positioned high enough to avoid most animals, but low enough to sense a car or individual walking. Silva stepped in front of the sensor. His radio immediately crackled: "Section one breached."

"Correct. Reset and wait for section two."

This went on for the next forty-five minutes. After the last section was tested and reset, Silva radioed, "Test complete. Keep the system activated, I'm coming in."

"Roger that."

Julie was standing behind Agent Moniot, watching the progressions and testing of the system. "It looks like we're pretty secure here."

Moniot looked back at Julie. "We are. In fact, if we don't respond to the system in ten minutes, an alert is sent to our office in Phoenix and the closest available assets, or agents, are diverted to this location. You guys are safe here."

"Good to know," she said and then went back to her room.

The shotgun was in the closet. She was about to retrieve it when there was a tap at the door.

"Come in."

Brenda poked her head in. "Okay if I come in?"

"Sure. I was about to load the shotgun. What are the kids doing?"

"Sam is playing with her dolls on the bedroom floor and Zach, I think, is playing a game on his pad."

"Then it's a good time to get this done. Did you load the Glock?"

" Fifteen in the magazine and one in the chamber, I'm good to go. I sure hope we don't have to use the weapons."

"Better safe than sorry," said Julie as she chambered five shells. "The security system here looks to be pretty good. I watched Agent Moniot as they checked the perimeter motion sensors. Now that the guns are ready, why don't we check the kitchen and see what we can come up with for dinner?"

"Good idea. I don't think the FBI Academy has a course in culinary skills," quipped Brenda with a smile.

***

The sun was about half an hour from setting. After filling the car and getting a bite to eat, Naryshkin had found a park which was somewhat secluded. He sat back in the seat and took a thirty-minute power nap. Feeling rested, he started the car and headed back toward 69 S. When he reached the mile marker where the SUV had turned, he slowed and moved onto the dirt road. He passed the 'Dead End' sign and eased forward, careful not to kick up dust.

After a quarter of a mile, he pulled the car to the side and decided to walk. He checked his handgun, making sure he had a full magazine, then attached a suppressor and chambered a round. Satisfied, he put on a black windbreaker and moved toward the tree line along the road.

After moving out of a gulley to the top of a rise, he could see a home on a hill with the interior lights on. He knew there would be perimeter security, most likely laser or infrared sensors.

After each step that he took, he would stop and scan the trees for sensors with a pen light. With none located, he would take another step. It took almost an hour, at this pace, until he spotted a small box attached to a pine tree, facing the road.

Naryshkin slowly moved down to the ground and belly-crawled under the sensor about ten yards past, before rising slowly to his feet. He moved deeper into the tree line for better cover as he approached the home. He stopped about three hundred feet away from the house with a clear view of the living and kitchen area. He was surprised at the lapse in judgement, that the FBI hadn't secured all window coverings, or maybe it was simply arrogance. Either way, he could make out two women in the kitchen. What he couldn't see, which was his main concern, were the agents responsible for protecting the family.

***

Brenda looked through the fridge. "There's plenty of fresh hamburger, with frozen steaks in the freezer."

The pantry door was open, with Julie inside, browsing, "I have a couple of packs of meatloaf mix with a sack of russet potatoes. I guess our choice is hamburgers on the grill or meatloaf."

"Knowing Silva and Moniot, they'll want to be indoors. Don't even ask. Let's get to work."

Before leaving the pantry, Julie noticed the key hook on the wall next to the door. "Just so you know, the keys to the Jeep in the garage are here on the wall."

***

There were no streetlights in the gated community, only porch and garage lights, up and down the street. Petronovich had night vision binoculars which he used to scan the street from the roof. He then moved toward the back of the house to take in the golf course and community common grounds beyond the home's fence.

"Nothing so far," commented Petronovich to Jason who was kneeling, resting the AR-15 with night scope that Mike had secured from Agent Ballard, on the short wall of the flat roof.

Jason continued to scan. "I'm glad it's not winter. They can get snow here."

Petronovich used a portable radio and transmitted, "In fifteen, let's rotate. Jason goes inside and Vasily comes up with me. We will change every two hours."

244

***

Naryshkin came out of the woods, behind the SUV. Crouching low, he quickly moved to the side of the vehicle. He took a switchblade from his pocket, pressed the button exposing the blade and proceeded to slash the front and rear tires on his side of the car.

There's no way they are driving this away from the property, he thought. He lifted his head slightly to get a view of the house. There were still no agents in sight.

Just as he was about to move, the back door opened and a man with a rifle stepped out. He walked down the driveway and then crossed the front lawn and began to circle the house.

Naryshkin went the opposite way, keeping his handgun holstered, but opening the switchblade. He was at the back corner, bending low, ready to spring.

As Agent Moniot turned the corner, Naryshkin jumped, leading with the knife in his right hand, severing Moniot's carotid artery, and, with his left hand, he ripped the rifle away before it could be discharged. He pulled the knife out of Moniot's neck and then slashed his throat. Moniot gurgled, sucking blood into his lungs, with eyes wide open in surprise and disbelief.

Naryshkin whispered, "Relax, don't fight it. This will all be over soon."

Naryshkin watched as a single tear rolled down Moniot's cheek. His body went limp as he died.

The assassin dragged the body to the trees just beyond the grass, being careful not to stand upright and trigger the alarm which he knew was about four feet high. He placed the body on the other side of a pine, positioned so that it could not be seen from the house. He then waited.

Inside, Silva looked at his watch. Thinking Moniot should

have been back by now, he used the radio and called, "Moniot, come in." He waited, with no answer. Then again, "Moniot, come in." Still no answer.

He phoned the Phoenix FBI field office and explained the situation. Then, he moved quickly down the hall to Julie's bedroom, tapped on the door and opened it.

Julie was lying in bed with a night light on, reading a book. She had the shotgun on the ground by her side.

Silva stepped in. "Moniot's not answering the radio outside. I'm going to check on him. If I'm not back in half an hour, get the kids and get out. Keys to the SUV are on the counter. I've already called Phoenix to let them know we may have an issue. If they don't hear back from me in thirty minutes, a team will be flown in by helicopter. They will be here within the hour. Wake Brenda and get the kids dressed, just in case. Leave everything if you need to go. I see you have your shotgun. Follow me with the weapon and lock the door behind me."

Silva turned and went down the hall through the family room and kitchen to the back door, picking up the Browning handheld spotlight from the table next to it. He had his Glock 17 out and ready. With the light switched on, he exited the door and quietly closed it tight, listening as Julie snapped the deadbolt into place.

Chapter 17

Julie looked at her iPhone, she had twenty-five minutes to wait before she left quickly with the kids or went back to bed to read. She hoped it was the latter. To be safe, she tapped on Brenda's door opened and told her what Silva had just said.

Brenda jumped out of bed and dressed quickly, saying, "I'll be right there to help get the kids ready."

Julie went into each of the kid's rooms, switched on the light and whispered, "Zach, honey, get up, we may need to leave soon." Hearing that, Zack hopped out of bed, dressed quickly and then sat on the floor as he laced up his shoes.

Sam reacted a little more slowly, still yawning as she dressed. "Where are we going, Mom?"

"I don't know, Sammy, but we need to be quick."

Just then, they heard two loud cracks. It was the distinct sound of a weapon being discharged.

"Oh, crap," Julie exclaimed as she jumped at the noise.

Brenda ran into the room. "That sounded like it came from the front. We can't get to the SUV."

"What about taking the Jeep in the garage? It's off to the side."

"I think that's the plan. Let's get to the Jeep. If Silva isn't back in three minutes, we leave," responded Julie. They each grabbed a child's hand and rushed them through the house.

Julie had the shotgun and Brenda had the Glock.

Brenda stopped by the pantry and took the car keys off the

ring.

***

Silva stepped outside and moved cautiously around the house and toward the front. He scanned the tree line beyond the property and could see nothing.

Naryshkin watched the beam of light and stepped behind a tree as it approached. With the advantage of surprise gone, he had the handgun with suppressor out and ready. As the beam passed his position, Naryshkin stepped out and squeezed off two quick rounds with a *pfft, pfft*.

The first round hit Silva's arm, holding the light, which sent it flying. The second round hit Silva center mass, throwing him backwards. His hand muscles tightened around the trigger, sending two rounds skyward as he landed on his back with eyes staring at the clear night stars.

Silva twitched once and then exhaled his last breath.

Naryshkin approached the body carefully, kicking the handgun away from the FBI agent. As he did so, he heard a low, soft rumble and watched as a dark-colored jeep sped out of the garage with tires squealing on the pavement, then rocks and dirt flying as the vehicle sped down the dirt road.

Naryshkin fired three quick rounds with two hits in the rear and one miss. The bullets didn't slow the car, in fact, it sped up.

Naryshkin knew that there were only two agents and that nobody would be in the house. He holstered his weapon and sprinted to his car, probably half a mile away. He was certain that additional FBI assets were on the way, and he needed to be gone.

***

As the sun began to rise, Mike and Volkov were on the roof, alert, scanning the neighborhood, looking for any signs of unusual activity. At this time of night, or early morning, nothing was happening.

Mike got on the radio. "Tony, come in?"

Agent Ballard answered, "Tony."

"It's pretty quiet. I don't think Naryshkin is coming here."

Ballard responded hesitantly, "Mike, I just got off the phone with the Phoenix field office." Tony hesitated.

"What did they say?"

"The safe house was hit. We have two agents dead. Your family was not on the premises." As Tony was speaking, Mike's iPhone rang.

"Tony, Julie is on the line, I'll call you right back."

"No, wait, Mike! Answer the call and then bring me on as well," said Tony.

"Give me a second to figure this out." Mike answered Julie. "I just heard. Are you guys okay?"

"I'm too old for this shit, Mike. I've put Vail in the maps app. and it says we are three hours away."

"Julie, I have Agent Ballard on the line, I'm going to bring him into this conversation. When we are finished, we'll talk on our own." Mike pressed the button to allow a second line in. "Tony are you there? I have Julie on the line."

"Julie, is everyone okay?"

"Yes, just upset."

"Tell me what happened, please. I'm recording this."

Julie recapped what had happened and what Agent Silva had told her to do. "I couldn't take the SUV as he suggested, it was in front of where the gunfire was coming from."

"You did the right thing. Did you see Naryshkin?" asked Tony.

"No, it was dark, and we were getting the kids into the car. When we knew Agent Silva wasn't coming, we made a break for it."

"Where are you now?" asked Tony.

"We're an hour outside Phoenix, three hours from Vail."

"You're not going to Vail. Did Naryshkin see you leave?"

"Yes, he shot at us and hit the car twice. Thank God, nobody was hurt."

"Good. Open your maps app and input the address I give you. Let me know when you're ready."

"Okay, go."

"21711 N. Seventh Street, Phoenix. That's our office in Phoenix. Head there. Since Naryshkin saw the car, he'll think you'll go back to Mike in Vail. Once you're here, we'll have a detail bring the car to the safe house in Vail. By the way, did you happen to see what Naryshkin was driving?"

"There was a car parked by the side of the road leading to the house. It was dark, Brenda was driving, probably doing seventy. It was a beater, maybe an old Toyota; dark-colored. I couldn't tell if it was blue or black. I just thought it was odd seeing the car sitting on a dead-end road. I didn't put two and two together until now."

"Okay, that helps. I'll let the Phoenix office know that you are coming in. In the meantime, you and Mike catch up. I'm glad you're safe."

***

Naryshkin didn't realize it, but he was only ten miles behind Julie and the kids heading toward Phoenix. He thought the women would most likely go back to Vail. He had no intention of following. The FBI would have surmised that he was in the vicinity of the Vail safe house two days before. The only way Naryshkin could have known about the Prescott home was if he'd followed Silva, Moniot and the family to the property from Vail.

He'd decided that he'd pressed his luck and it was time to regroup. The trip to Southern California from his current location would take about seven hours. That was where he was headed.

First, he needed to make a brief stop in the outskirts of Vail, which was two hours away.

**

Julie, Brenda, and the kids arrived at the Phoenix headquarters. When they entered the lobby, they were recognized immediately and whisked down the hall into a conference room toward the back of the building.

"Have a seat, someone will be in to see you shortly," said the tall, blonde, female agent. "Can I get you something to drink?"

"Coffee, if it's not too much of a problem and water for the kids?" Julie answered.

"Coming right up," smiled the agent as she closed the door.

"Mom, what's going on?" Zach asked. "I want to go home."

"Me too," Sam followed.

"Take a deep breath and let's just wait and see what these nice people have to say," Julie assured them, but not really convincing herself, or Brenda, for that matter, who listened, nodded, and smiled.

Brenda added, "This is almost over. The agents are looking out for our safety. We will listen to what they have to say.

251

Remember, your dad worked for the FBI in Chicago. He'd want us to follow instructions, right?"

"I guess," said Zach and Sam at the same time.

The conference room door opened with two agents each carrying a tray. One had doughnuts, milk, and water, while the other had a pot of coffee with two cups of creamer and sugar.

The blonde agent said, "I thought this would be a little more appropriate," as she placed the sweets in front of the kids.

Sam looked at Julie before reaching. "Mom, can we have one?"

Julie smiled. "Sure, but drink the milk too."

As the two agents opened the door to leave, a third, older gentleman in his sixties entered. He smiled, looking at the kids and Julie.

"You must be Mike McClintock's family. I'm Agent Ed Pena. The Phoenix office is my responsibility."

Julie smiled. "I'm Julie, this is Zach and Sam, our children, and Brenda, Jason McClintock's better half from Montana."

Pena shook each of the family member's hands, including the kids. He sat with them and reviewed what he knew about the incident in Prescott, mindful that the kids were present. He then followed that with, "We believe Naryshkin will follow you to Vail, thinking you will want to be with Mike and Jason. The few belongings you took from Prescott have already been removed from the vehicle and two of our female agents are driving, as we speak, to Vail. The car will remain in plain sight in front of the house, hoping to entice the subject to attack."

Julie listened, then spoke. "He's not that stupid, Agent Pena. I think you had your chance to get him when he followed us from Vail to Prescott."

"You may be right, but we have to take the chance that he'll

252

bite. If he doesn't, we will have another discussion. It might take a couple of days. So, we have you booked at the Mountain Shadows Resort in Paradise Valley. We have you in a Cabana room next to the pool. You and the kids will love it. You will be registered under an alias, and it goes without saying that you will be provided twenty-four-hour protection. After you're finished with the coffee and sweets, we'll get you out of here."

***

Whittington sat at his desk, reviewing the steps they had taken to apprehend Naryshkin and where they had failed to keep the safe house in Prescott off the grid and known to only a handful of people. His intercom buzzed, with his secretary at the other end.

"Yes, Nancy?"

"Sir, there is a call from the State Department, a Mr. Jackson is on the line."

"Send him through."

The phone buzzed. "This is Whittington."

Jackson identified himself. "The reason for my call is simple. Two weeks ago, we had a fishing boat captain from Trabzon, that's in Turkey, come to our embassy in Ankara. The reason this caught our attention is that Ankara is an eight-hour drive from Trabzon and this captain must have thought the information he had for us was important."

"What does this have to do with my office, Jackson?" Whit asked.

"We know that you have had people in Russia, looking for a Russian national by the name of Naryshkin. After speaking with the captain, he mentioned that he was initially approached to ferry an individual from Trabzon to Sochi, Russia. This captain assisted the man in avoiding Russian Port Authorities by transferring him to a Russian fishing trawler in international waters. They took him into Russia, thereby avoiding the authorities."

"Did he provide a picture of his passenger?" Whit asked.

"As a matter of fact, he did. We identified him as Naryshkin. When we get off, I'll email you the photo. It was taken by one of the crew. Naryshkin wasn't aware the pic was taken."

"When did this occur?"

"The captain transported him once from Trabzon to Sochi, a month or so ago, and then a second time, he met the Russian fishing trawler and brought him into Trabzon. This last trip occurred two weeks ago. The captain said he expected to transport Naryshkin back to Sochi in the next few days."

"Why is this guy so invested in this Russian?"

"I asked the question. The captain says he's a NATO patriot. He believes his Russian passenger is up to something not good, his words. Now that we know the guy is Naryshkin, the captain's intuition was spot on."

"Why wasn't this brought to my attention right away?" asked Whittington, not pretending to hide his frustration.

"The State Department is a large, bureaucratic organization. The report arrived on my desk this morning and we're talking. Get off my back, Whittington."

Whit took a deep breath. "We know Naryshkin is in the U.S. If we don't nail him in the next day or two, he probably will head back to Russia. You said this captain works out of the marina in Trabzon?"

"Yes. The name of his boat is *Sansli*. If I get any additional information, I'll contact you. Good luck, Whittington. This guy needs to be apprehended. You didn't mention what happened in

254

Prescott last night, but we are aware of the hit. I'm sorry for the loss of American lives," said Jackson as he ended the call.

Whittington stared at the phone. This was the link he needed to take Naryshkin down. He knew he should have assets in Trabzon, but he needed to see what the FBI had in mind right now before he committed any manpower. His hope was that Schumacher could apprehend Naryshkin on U.S. soil. Whit knew that Schumacher must be in turmoil after what happened in Prescott. They needed to talk. Whit picked up the phone and dialed Jack Schumacher.

Chapter 18

Vail, Arizona, is a bedroom community about twenty miles east of Tucson, which is a college town, home to the University of Arizona. Vail has a small strip mall with a Safeway, along with two pizza joints and a couple of fast-food Mexican outlets. One of the Mexican drive-throughs is family-owned and offers traditional Mexican fare at reasonable prices. It is also a hole-in-the-wall type of place.

As Naryshkin turned off the freeway and drove toward Vail, he noticed this business. It was busy, given the noon hour approaching. It appeared that many of the clientele were Hispanic and worked in either the trades or landscape maintenance. One guy stood out from the rest. He sat alone on the front fender of a chevy truck which must have been from the early sixties, eating what looked like a burrito. The truck was rusted and had more body damage than any vehicle Naryshkin had seen in a long time. Then he noticed the plates. The truck was registered in Sonora, Mexico. *This guy must cross the border every day for work,* thought Naryshkin.

He pulled into the lot next to the young kid.

The kid looked up. "Hola."

Naryshkin ignored the greeting and asked in English, "Do you have a minute to talk?"

"Si senor," replied the kid as he put down his lunch.

"There is a house about two miles from here. I'd like you to deliver a note using my car. If you do this, I will give you $1,000

U.S. and you can keep the car. I will take your truck. Do we have a deal?" Naryshkin asked, not having to wait for a reply.

In English, the young guy said, "Sure. What is the address?"

Naryshkin smiled and pulled a sealed envelope out of his pocket. "The address is on the envelope. Hand it to the owner of the house and drive away. It should take you no more than ten minutes."

The kid took the envelope, reached into his pant pocket and handed Naryshkin the truck keys. Naryshkin, in turn, handed the kid the keys to his car along with ten Franklins.

"If you should want this piece of shit back," (referring to the truck) "it will be in the long-term parking lot at the Nogales airport."

The kid nodded. "I will do this right now, senor," he said as he jammed the last of the burrito into his mouth and walked toward Naryshkin's car.

Naryshkin watched as the vehicle eased out of the lot onto the empty street. He climbed into the beat-up truck's cab and tried to turn over the engine. After three tries, the engine caught, burped out black smoke from the exhaust and began to idle roughly. Naryshkin turned onto the road heading out of Vail, south toward Nogales, Mexico, which was about sixty miles away.

***

Schumacher's cell buzzed. He looked at the phone and recognized the number. "Schumacher."

"Jack, I'm sorry about the Prescott situation. Have you found the family?" asked Whit.

Schumacher filled Whittington in and then asked, "Do you

have anything on Naryshkin?"

Whit brought Schumacher up to speed on his recent call from the State Department, then followed that with, "Jack, if you can't get Naryshkin today, I'm certain he'll head back to Sochi. I need to be ahead of this and have men in Trabzon before he arrives. If he's even a half day ahead, he could give us the slip once again."

"I agree, Whit. If Naryshkin doesn't show in Vail by this evening, he's most likely not coming. It's one p.m. Let's give him until midnight. If nothing happens, it's your show. I'll keep you posted."

"Okay, good luck, Jack," Whit replied as he cut the call.

Schumacher dialed Tony Ballard to get an update.

***

Agent Ballard walked across the street to see how the McClintocks and the Russians were doing. He knew Petronovich by reputation but that still didn't put him at ease when he was near the tall, stoic individual. He was Russian KGB, and, as rumors have it, was very good at what he did. Tony tapped the door and then tried the handle. It was locked. *Good,* he thought as he heard the deadbolt swing and the door open.

Petronovich stood in front of Tony.

"Can I come in?" asked Ballard.

Petronovich stepped aside and motioned him forward.

The McClintock brothers in the kitchen making sandwiches and Volkov was sitting on the sofa, drinking a soda.

"I wanted to see if you guys needed anything. One of the other agents is heading to the store," asked Ballard.

As Jason was about to respond, Tony's cell vibrated. He

answered, "Ballard."

"Ballard, this is Schumacher. We believe Naryshkin will try to hit the Russians and McClintocks today. Do you have all avenues of ingress covered?"

"Yes, sir. There is no way he can get into the community without being spotted."

"I believed that once, Ballard, and now we have two dead agents in Prescott. I don't care what the cost is, I'm doubling the boots on the ground. They'll be arriving in two hours. Review your current watch positions and see where the extra resources will be most effective. I'm counting on you to get this done, Tony," said Schumacher. "Any questions?"

"No, sir. We'll be prepared to accept the extra help," responded Ballard as he terminated the call and looked across the room at the men who were listening. "Command believes that Naryshkin will strike today. I've got to check our perimeter watch sites. You men maintain your position here. Your rotation last night seemed to work well," said Tony as he turned to leave.

***

The drive from the Phoenix FBI office to Mountain Shadows Resort should have taken thirty minutes. Three large, black Suburbans left the FBI complex with one car leading, followed by the McClintock family in the middle vehicle and a third SUV bringing up the rear. The trip took twenty minutes at speeds in excess of the posted limits, with all lights flashing. When they pulled in front of the two large doors leading to the hotel registration area, two agents came out of the building, motioning the bellhops away and opening the passenger doors for the McClintocks.

They stood next to the front entrance and took in the view of Camelback Mountain as it rose above the posh complex.

Julie commented, "This must cost a pretty penny."

"SAC, or Special Agent in Charge, Pena, thought this would be a well-deserved break for you given all that you've gone through. We have you located in two Cabana rooms with the pool right outside the rooms. Agents will occupy the rooms next to yours, as well as two across the complex on the other side of the pool. When you are not at the pool, you must be in your room, or, with advance notice to us, going to the dining room. We want your stay to be as pleasant as can be, given the circumstances. Hopefully, you won't be here more than a day or two. Any questions?" asked the agent.

Sam raised her hand tentatively.

"Yes, honey?" responded the agent.

"Can we go to the pool now?"

The blonde agent smiled. "You bet, let's get your things. "

***

The FBI agent positioned on a rooftop among the first row of homes nearest the community gate entrance, picked up his radio and called, "There is an older, dark blue Toyota that just turned into the complex. He's following a car that just put in the gate code now."

Ballard responded, "I don't want that older vehicle near the safe house. After he's a block in, I want one vehicle in place to block his approach and a second in the rear to prevent him from leaving. You know the drill, understood?"

"Understood," responded one driver.

"Roger," came from the second.

The kid waited for the gate to swing open.

He eased the car toward the entrance and moved slowly across the threshold as the gate widened. He began to accelerate as he passed the gate, listening to the directions being given by the maps app on his iPhone.

He passed the first side street in the complex on his left, a half block from the gate. As he rounded a curve, a black SUV darted from the street on his right and came to a complete stop.

The kid slammed on his brakes, fishtailing slightly as he stopped. In the rear-view mirror, he noticed a second black SUV hemming him in. He wanted to move the car, but he couldn't.

The kid began to shake as he watched two men in suits, with guns raised, pointed directly at him, hollering, "Put your hands on the wheel where we can see them! Don't move!"

The kid glanced in the rear-view mirror and saw two suits, also with guns raised, off to the far left and right of his car, in position to fire at an angle if necessary. The first agent, the one in front, approached the passenger side. The window was down.

He looked inside. The driver was not Naryshkin.

"Do you live in this complex?"

"No, sir."

"What are you doing here?"

"I was asked to deliver a letter?"

"To whom?" asked the agent.

"I don't know, sir. The man said to give it to the homeowner. The address is on the envelope," said the kid, shaking. "The letter is on the passenger seat in front of you."

"Don't move," said the agent as he opened the passenger door and picked up the envelope.

Only three minutes had passed since stopping the car.

Ballard's car came to an abrupt stop in front of the first SUV.

261

He noticed that the situation was contained with the Toyota driver shivering in obvious fear.

Tony walked up to the agent that had the envelope. "I'll take that."

The agent, keeping his eyes on the kid, handed Ballard the envelope.

Tony responded with, "Check the driver for any priors. Cuff him and transport him to Phoenix. Call a tow. I want this car in Phoenix asap where we'll go over it with a fine-tooth comb."

Tony got back in his car and headed for the safe house. He knocked on the door and Petronovich answered once again.

Tony didn't wait, he pushed past Petronovich and walked into the kitchen where Jason and Mike were sitting at the counter eating.

"We just stopped what we believe was Naryshkin's car heading here. The driver was a Mexican kid, not Naryshkin. He was told to deliver this letter to the house."

Tony had a pair of disposable safety gloves on as he opened the envelope. He unfolded the letter and read out loud, "I have exhausted my allotted time for now. But be assured, I will return at a time and place of my choosing. In my mind, all of you, Petronovich, Volkov and the McClintocks, are dead. I want you to remember Kolkov. He died when he least expected it. And so, it shall be with the four of you. The time will come, whether it be months or years from this day, rest assured, you will each see me again. It's initialed SN, Sergey Naryshkin."

"That confirms it, he's gone," whispered Petronovich under his breath.

"I need to call Pena. Stay put for now until we decide what to do. This may be a ploy to get us to let our guard down," Tony responded as he walked toward the door, dialing the SAC in

262

Phoenix, who, in turn, would phone Schumacher.

***

The Mexican kid sat handcuffed in a sterile room with an obvious one-way mirror, at a long table with six chairs. The door swung open, and two agents approached. One tossed a file on the table, taking a seat opposite the kid.

"You have no priors, so your visit with us will be brief," said the agent as he opened the file, withdrawing a picture of Naryshkin and holding it so it faced the prisoner. "Is this the man that gave you the letter to deliver?"

"Si, senor."

"Did he say anything else other than give you delivery instructions?"

"He only added that I could pick up my truck in the long-term parking lot at the Nogales airport."

The agent conducting the interview looked immediately at the second agent, who was already rising from his chair and heading to the door.

***

Naryshkin knew the window to get out of Mexico was short.

Flights out of Mexico City had destinations worldwide and there were many Russians conducting business in Mexico. With his undercover credentials, he would be hard to find. If he could get out of Mexico City unnoticed, he was confident he could get to Turkey, then home to Sochi. His flight landed in Mexico City on schedule, giving him time to transfer to the International Terminal and the gate for the late afternoon flight to Istanbul.

Naryshkin had seventy minutes before boarding. He smiled as he walked into the lounge, sat at the bar, and ordered a Ciroc X vodka.

***

Whittington was in front of his computer, responding to an email when the ping of an incoming email occurred and briefly showed the message coming in from Schumacher. He immediately exited what he was doing and accessed Schumacher's note. The subject line read, 'This just came in.'

Schumacher had scanned Naryshkin's letter and emailed it to Whittington. Just as Whit finished reading the short note, his phone buzzed.

He picked up and said, "Jack, I just read the note. I'll have my guys in the air to Trabzon within the hour."

"You better, Whit. We know that Naryshkin is in Mexico but heading out of the country soon. We confirmed a Russian under a different name flying out of Nogales to Mexico City."

"That's my concern. I'm certain he will have a couple of passports under various identities he will use, which will make it that much harder for us to follow, especially since there are so many Russian Nationals flying in and out of Mexico City every day. Our best bet is to get my team to the Trabzon marina before he arrives. He's flying public, but we fly private, so it should not be a problem. Can you get one of your guys to take Petronovich and Volkov to the Tucson FBO?"

"You bet. I'll call right now. Let me know if I can do anything else. Good hunting, Whit," Schumacher replied.

"Thanks, Jack. I'll have Petronovich and Volkov ready to go in the next thirty minutes," Whit replied as he dialed Petronovich

264

and explained the urgent situation.

***

The four men stood in the kitchen. No one spoke. The hum of a cell phone broke the silence with each looking at his phone.

Petronovich looked up. "It's Whittington." He answered and listened to Whit, then responded with, "Understood, we'll be ready. Get me the email with the details of the Trabzon marina and the boat we need to intercept as soon as you can."

Vladi looked up, then over at Volkov and said, "Get your gear together we leave in about twenty."

"Where's Trabzon?"

"Turkey. It's a city on the Black Sea. Directly across the water, about one hundred and eighty miles, is Sochi, Russia," Petronovich explained. "Naryshkin has been using fishing trawlers, Turkish and Russian, based in both cities, to get into and out of Russia, avoiding the authorities in both countries. Naryshkin would transfer from one boat to the other in international waters."

"They must have firm evidence that Naryshkin is headed that way," said Jason as he looked at Mike. "I'm going across the street to speak with Tony. We're out of here, one way or the other." Just as he finished the sentence, there was a tap at the door, which wasn't locked.

Tony walked in.

"We will have two SUVs ready shortly. One will take Petronovich and Volkov to the FBO in Tucson and the other to your families in Phoenix."

"I'd like transportation to Santa Barbara this afternoon or evening," Mike said, anxious to see his family.

"We anticipated that. Private air is not available. There is a two thirty flight out of PHX this afternoon which you would miss. The next available is the eight fifty tonight. It has a long layover in L.A. but lands in Santa Barbara at twelve thirty in the morning. You'd need to rent a car and then drive an hour home. I think the best option, which we already reserved, is the first flight tomorrow. It leaves Phoenix at eight fifty and arrives SBA at twenty-two past ten a.m. We have you and your families at a luxury resort. You could enjoy some pool time with drinks this afternoon and a nice dinner on the government for all you've done."

Mike responded with, "You're probably right, Tony. We could use a few hours to decompress. It wouldn't be fair to the kids. I'll get my things and be ready when you are."

Jason looked at Petronovich and Volkov. "Get that son-of-a-bitch, Vladi. No-holds-barred. After what he's done, mercy is not an option."

"He will rot in hell, and not quickly enough," replied Volkov, thinking about how close he came to being assassinated by Naryshkin.

Mike simply said, "Be safe," then gave each a handshake and hug, before turning and walking down the hall, toward the bedroom.

***

The uniformed lady at the gate picked up the mic and announced, "We are now ready to board our first-class passengers on KLM's flight 1212 to Istanbul. Welcome aboard."

Naryshkin heard the announcement from the lounge. He had a quarter of a glass of Ciroc X left and was not about to leave it

266

behind.

He slugged back the remaining clear liquid, then placed a $100 bill next to the empty glass. Glancing at his watch, he confirmed that the flight to Istanbul would be on time. Assuming his connection to Trabzon was on schedule, he would be sitting next to the pool at his home in Sochi the day after tomorrow. He walked to the counter and handed his ticket to the KLM employee, who scanned it in the system. After the slight *ping* sounded, she looked at the ticket and said, "Welcome aboard, Mr. Gorsky."

***

The G550 stood in front of the FBO office with the engines at ground, idle. The same crew who had flown Petronovich and Volkov into the States the other day were at the base of the stairs to the aircraft, waiting for their passengers. The black SUV drove through the gates, which were normally padlocked, directly onto the tarmac and the jet. Petronovich and Volkov both jumped out of the vehicle and strode briskly toward the plane.

The captain gave a brief salute. "Good afternoon, gentlemen, welcome aboard. Stow your gear in the back compartment and take a seat. After a short taxi, we'll be wheels up; about ten minutes."

The Gulfstream could carry eighteen passengers with a range of seven thousand, seven hundred and sixty-seven miles at an average speed of five hundred and eight-five mph. With such a light load today, the range would be extended and, given the distance from Tucson to Trabzon, Turkey being seven thousand and thirty-nine miles, this would be a nonstop flight.

The flight time would be twelve hours, with an arrival time

in Turkey of twelve p.m. Trabzon was exactly twelve hours ahead of Tucson. Petronovich sat back in his leather seat and thought, *This is going to be a long flight.*

***

Jason and Mike were shown to their respective Cabana hotel rooms. Before going into his room, he looked at Mike, who was about to enter the room next door, and said, "I'll see you on the patio as soon as I change into my swim trunks."

Jason stepped through the door to his room. The rooms offered what might be called industrial chic décor. The walls were cement with large stainless-steel ducting along the ceiling, pictures of desert landscape on the walls, a bar with drinks cart, and a refrigerator stocked with water, sodas and beer.

The bathroom was large, which included a shower with three sides which were clear glass, including a bench inside the shower, and an assortment of soaps and lotions which probably couldn't be found in resorts less than five star.

He threw his bag on the bed and looked out onto the patio through the sliding glass doors. Across the way, he could see Mike's kids splashing in one of the two seventy-foot pools which were adjacent to each other, with one being ten feet higher than the other. They were separated by a walkway and waterfall, with water flowing from the top pool to the lower pool, in constant circulation.

The kids were in the higher of the two pools. Julie and Brenda were inside a Cabana with the fan slowly rotating, sipping what looked like champagne. He could see a tray of appetizers on the coffee table in front of them.

Tony was right when he said this was a luxury resort, thought

268

Jason as he turned back to the bed and his bag.

Mike tapped on the sliding door. Trying the lock, he slid the door open, which pancaked wider for the outdoor living experience.

"That's cool," he said as he stepped in. "You about ready?"

"Let's go," Jason replied as they walked back outside. "I'm closing this sliding door back up. This is Arizona, for God's sake. Rattlesnakes, scorpions, tarantulas, you know, all the critters Brenda and Julie like."

"Not to mention you and me! I hate snakes."

Mike led the way as they took three steps down from Jason's patio, walking past a cigar-smoking area to which Jason noted, "We're going to need to light up a Padron tonight."

They then crossed the walkway to the gate for access to the pool area. As they walked through the gate, Zach saw the men and screamed, "Dad!"

Julie and Brenda looked up from the Cabana, with Julie jumping up, taking the ten steps down to the walkway two at a time, meeting Mike halfway across the walking bridge and into his arms as the waterfall streamed down to the side.

Brenda followed Julie, walking with a huge smile on her face.

Jason stepped past Mike and Julie and took Brenda into his arms.

She smiled, "Hello, handsome" and they kissed.

Zach and Sam were above them, looking down from the pool waterfall wall. They could stand on their toes in the three feet of water.

Sam smiled and said, "This is getting gross. Come into the pool, Dad! Let's play Marco Polo!"

"I'll be right there, cutie, give me a minute," replied Mike as

269

they followed Jason and Brenda to the Cabana. Just as they sat down, the Cabana girl arrived with extra towels, a fresh pitcher of water and plastic glasses. She then asked the question Mike and Jason had been waiting for, "Can I get you a drink?"

Both Jason and Mike smiled and ordered.

***

The flight from Tucson went quickly with Petronovich and Volkov sleeping on two sofas, opposite each other in the rear of the plane. When they woke, it was ten p.m. in Tucson, but ten a.m., bright and sunny, as they flew east over the Black Sea.

The co-pilot walked to the back of the cabin where both men had moved from the sofas to the large recliners, each with a window. He stopped in the aisle so he could see both passengers, one on each side.

"We're about two hours away. In case you didn't notice, there are cold cuts in the fridge with everything to make a pretty good sandwich. If you're at all hungry, you might want to take advantage of that. I'll let you know when we are twenty minutes out."

"Thanks," said Petronovich. "I'm good."

Volkov was up and out of his seat. "I'm going to make myself lunch."

"Grab me a water, Vasily."

With his sandwich in hand, Volkov handed Petronovich a water, put his tray table down and sat. He looked over at Vladi.

"What's the plan once we hit Trabzon?"

"I was thinking about that. Most fishing vessels leave the marina long before sunrise to get to their favorite fishing grounds, ready to fish, as the sun comes up. They also need to

270

off-load their catch in the afternoon and prepare for the next day. I would think the vessel would return sometime between three and four p.m. We will go directly to the marina and wait for the Sansli to return. There is no way that Naryshkin can reach the boat before us," explained Petronovich. "After we have a talk with the captain, we'll find a place to stay for the night, close to the marina. With luck, tomorrow will be a busy day."

"Sounds good. I can't wait to make it Naryshkin's last," replied Volkov as he took the last bite of his sandwich and rose from the chair, taking his plate to the galley.

Both men noticed the engines slowing down and the slight drop in elevation as they began their decent into Trabzon.

***

The Mountain Shadows Resort was located north of Scottsdale in Paradise Valley. Paradise Valley became a city in 1961. In homage to Paradise Valley residents, Mountain Shadows named their widely acclaimed dining room, Hearth '61 because of the year.

After an afternoon of sun and drinks, not to mention a well-deserved nap and shower, the McClintocks were ready for dinner.

The dining room had soft, elegant lighting with the vibe to match the classical piano playing softly in the background.

The round table with white linens was set for six. Zach and Sam sat between Mike and Julie with Jason sitting next to Mike and Brenda next to Julie. They promised to make this an event, not simply a dinner.

After drinks and an appetizer of charred octopus were served, they viewed the menu. A Caesar salad was ordered all around. The ladies ordered Hawaiian Swordfish with roasted sunchoke and Arizona citrus in a poblano cream sauce. Mike had braised short ribs and it was tenderloin of beef in a red wine demi-glace for Jason. Zach ordered a cheeseburger with fries and Sam had fries with her chicken nuggets, in that order of preference.

As promised, the dinner was relaxed and unrushed, completed with eggnog crème brulee and peppermint mocha cheesecake for the adults and a scoop of vanilla ice cream for the kids.

As the kids finished their ice cream, their eyes started to droop, and the yawns began. Mike noticed and said, "Let's get these kiddos to bed. With an eight fifty flight, we'll be up by six, no later."

"You guys take off, Brenda and I will follow. We'll see you outside in the morning," said Jason as he looked for the Hearth '61 manager. Since the tab was covered by the government, he wanted to make sure the staff was properly tipped.

He noticed the gentleman off to the side, viewing the dining room and walked to him.

"I want to thank you and your staff for a wonderful evening. Please share this with everyone who assisted us tonight," whispered Jason as he slipped the manager several one-hundred-dollar bills.

***

It was four p.m. when the KLM flight from Mexico City touched down in Istanbul.

Naryshkin looked at his watch. He had one hour to get to the gate for the flight to Trabzon. Given that he was among the first passengers off the aircraft, that shouldn't be a problem.

After exiting the plane, he checked the departures sign and

272

noted the gate number for Trabzon and, more importantly, that the flight was on time. As he walked down the concourse, he thought, *The flight is about an hour and a half. That would put me into Trabzon at six thirty. The captain of the Sansli may still be on board the boat if I get there at seven.* Naryshkin stepped up his pace, anxious to get home.

Petronovich got out of his seat and, without a word to Volkov, strode toward the front of the aircraft and tapped on the cockpit door.

The co-pilot opened it. "How can I help you, sir?"

"How far out are we?" asked Petronovich.

"About twenty minutes."

"Can you contact the FBO at Trabzon and have a car waiting to take us to the marina?"

"I can do that. It shouldn't be a problem," replied the co-pilot. "If not, there will be taxis available in the immediate area to take you wherever you need to go."

"It's a matter of time. I don't want to miss our contact."

"I understand, sir, let me see what I can do."

"That's all I can ask," said Petronovich as he closed the door and turned back to his seat, noticing the Back Sea giving way to land outside the cabin windows.

"What's up?" asked Volkov.

"Just trying to line up a ride to the marina once we land."

***

The black Suburban dropped the McClintocks off in front of the American Airline terminal. Two agents walked up to the SUV, one opened the side door to let the passengers out while the other, with the help of the driver, pulled the luggage from the rear.

An American Airline employee checked the bags at the curb and handed the receipt to Mike.

One of the agents spoke to the group. "Follow me. I'm taking you past security, directly to the gate." The agent held up his FBI credentials as he opened the gate, allowing the McClintocks to pass.

The DHS employee was about to say something but after receiving the glare from the FBI agent, he thought better of it. He escorted the family to the gate where they waited to board.

The agent sat next to Jason and Mike, saying, "A team from the Santa Barbara office will meet you and drive you to your home. We've arranged twenty-four-hour surveillance with the Santa Barbara County Sheriff's office."

Mike replied, "I don't think that's necessary."

"Out of an abundance of caution, they are going to remain on the premises for at least forty-eight hours or until we've heard from CIA that Naryshkin has been neutralized."

"We appreciate all you've done," said Jason.

"One more thing. Until the protection umbrella is lifted, you are not to leave the property. I understand you own a vineyard," said the agent, looking at Mike. "There must be plenty of work to do to keep you both busy for two to three days."

"That's an understatement," Mike said as the jet that would fly them to Santa Barbara was guided slowly up to the jetway position by the ground crew with orange batons.

The McClintocks incredible journey was almost over, they hoped.

***

Petronovich and Volkov sat in their thick, padded leather chairs and watched out the windows.

About five miles from the airport, the captain dropped the landing gear. They could see the flaps roll down, giving the aircraft extra lift as the plane slowed significantly. The glide path was at about three degrees, dropping five hundred feet per minute. *Not long now,* thought Volkov as he tensed a little, uncomfortable not being in control of his environment.

As the plane crossed the runway threshold, the captain allowed gravity to assist the landing as he gave the plane a little push forward with gas for the landing flare. The tires met the concrete with what might be called a slight kiss, nothing hard about it. The roll-out was short with such a light load and the G550 was parked in front of the Trabzon FBO office five minutes after touchdown.

The captain lowered the steps with Petronovich, followed by Volkov and the pilots walking down into the FBO office to clear customs.

The Turkish government was aware of the aircraft and its occupants, so once the passports were presented, they were stamped and allowed to proceed. One of the authorities spoke to Petronovich, assuming he was in charge, which was the correct assumption: "I have a taxi out front waiting for you."

"Thank you," replied Petronovich. Vladi looked past Volkov to the pilots. "Thanks for a nice ride, guys. We should be ready to return within forty-eight hours. Enjoy Trabzon."

Volkov retrieved his passport and the two walked out the front door to the taxi. Before they reached the vehicle, a young man in a suit called out, "Mr. Petronovich?"

Vladi turned. "You must be from the U.S. Embassy in Istanbul." Petronovich knew the kid was part of the CIA team located there. "What do you have for me?" Petronovich was referring to the briefcase that the man held.

"I believe you're going to need the items inside," said the thirty-something kid as he handed the case to Petronovich.

Looking at Volkov, who already knew what was inside, he said, "Whit said someone would meet us."

Petronovich took the case. "Have a safe trip back to Istanbul."

"I hope you are both successful in your efforts here in Trabzon," replied the suit.

Petronovich stepped toward the taxi, opened the front passenger door, and got in. Volkov sat in the rear. "Where to?" asked the driver in respectable English.

"The marina, please."

"Yes, sir, a six minute drive, no more."

Petronovich looked over at the cabbie. He appeared to be in his late forties, groomed well, hiding a rough exterior, evidence of a tough life. "Do you know a clean place to stay next to the marina?"

"Yes, sir. The Alesha Suite is nice hotel, overlooking marina. You can walk there, only a couple hundred feet."

"Sounds perfect," said Petronovich as the cab pulled in front of the gate leading to the marina office. He handed the driver the fare which was two dollars but added ten as a tip.

The driver was surprised, took the money, shook Petronovich's hand and said, "Thank you so much. May Allah bless you on your travels."

***

Naryshkin made the connection and was wheels up on time. He opened his phone and sent a text message to his mother in Sochi:

On my way home. Will see you tomorrow for dinner. Make one of your special plates. See you soon. SN.

Now Naryshkin could only hope that the captain of the Sansli would be on board the vessel when he arrived. *I'm going to be cutting it,* he thought.

***

To say the marina had an office was an overstatement. The small building was a shack.

Petronovich tapped on the door and walked in. A gruff-looking man in his late seventies, early eighties (but probably, mid-fifties) sat behind a desk. In Turkish, he asked, "How can I help you?"

Petronovich replied in Russian. "I don't speak Turkish. English or Russian?"

"English," replied the manager.

"Can you tell me if the vessel named *Sansli* is in port?"

The old man stood from his desk and looked out the window, then at his watch, "He's not back yet. Maybe one more hour."

"You can see the slip. Which one is it?" Petronovich asked.

"The *Sansli* slip is third from the end. You can clearly see it is empty. If you have business, come back in one hour." With that, the old man sat back down and opened an old newspaper, signifying the meeting was over.

Volkov held the door open for Petronovich as the two walked out. "Crotchety old guy," said Volkov.

"Look at his life. Wouldn't you be? Let's walk over to the Alesha and check in. It must be that tall building right across the street. If it is, it'll be perfect if we can get a view of the marina from the room."

277

***

As promised, agents from the Santa Barbara FBI office were waiting at the gate for the passengers to come off.

The McClintocks were seated in first class, so they were among the first passengers out. An agent stepped forward and asked, "Mike McClintock?" though he didn't have to ask. They had pictures of every member of the family.

"Yes," answered Mike.

"Please follow me," said the agent as a second agent in the distance held the elevator for everyone to enter. "The car is right outside. We'll get your luggage, then drive you to Santa Ynez."

"I can't wait to go home," said Sam.

Zach followed that with, "Me too."

***

Petronovich and Volkov walked into the lobby of the Alesha hotel. The space was airy with no less than eighteen-foot ceilings. The front desk was ornate with gold trim everywhere. There was a woman and a man attending.

Volkov walked up to the woman, speaking in English. "Hello, we'd like two rooms for tonight, and possibly tomorrow."

She responded in kind, "We have mountain view, which is $25 U.S. or marina view, which is $34. Which do you prefer?"

"Marina view would be perfect, thank you," replied Volkov as he placed the credit card on the counter with his passport.

Petronovich set his passport on the counter as well.

"You can put both rooms on my card, the company will cover both rooms," said Volkov as he looked at Petronovich and

278

smiled, knowing the lady was thinking that would be a corporate account, not CIA.

The registration clerk picked up the passports. "I'll be right back after I photocopy the passports." She came back, handed the documents back and proceeded to tap the keys on the computer in front of her. After a moment, the printer began to roll out the registration document. She placed an 'x' near the spots Volkov needed to initial and sign, then slid the paper over to him with a pen.

While he was signing, she handed one key to Petronovich and the other to Volkov. "Your rooms are on the seventh floor with views of the marina. The lounge opens at four and the dining room at five p.m. If you should need anything, do not hesitate to call. Once again, welcome to Alesha."

Petronovich opened the door to his room and Volkov followed, walking immediately to the window.

"The view is perfect. We have an unobstructed view of the slip that the *Sansli* will be using." Volkov yawned and turned toward the door. "It's three. I'm going to get about an hour of shuteye. Wake me if the *Sansli* comes into port." Volkov shut Petronovich's door and let himself into his room.

***

The black SUV entered the 101-freeway, easing over to the number one lane. The vehicle's lights were flashing as they reached the cruising speed of eighty-five mph. Cars in front cleared to the right with the Suburban passing unimpeded. The trip, which would normally take an hour, had the McClintocks turning into their long driveway twenty minutes early.

A Santa Barbara Sheriff's vehicle was already positioned

279

next to the house in plain view from Refugio, the road that ran in front of the vineyard.

"Welcome home," said the agent as the vehicle kicked up dust on the long dirt driveway.

"Thanks, it's good to be home. I don't think we'll need a vacation for quite a while," Mike replied.

"I hear you, sir. You folks have been placed through the wringer over the last few days."

"Try weeks," said Jason.

"Right," the agent followed as he pulled up next to the garage.

After the luggage had been brought inside and the FBI agents had departed, Mike looked at Jason. "Let's take a walk and see how the grapes are doing."

"Sure," said Jason as he followed Mike out the kitchen door.

***

It was four fifteen when Volkov woke with a start. He thought he was dreaming when he heard the knock at the door, then he remembered where he was and jumped up.

Petronovich was about to knock again when Volkov opened.

Vladi simply said, "Sansli is in the slip. Let's go down and talk with the captain."

The two men walked across the street, through the gate to the marina and then down to the slip where *Sansli* was tied off.

Two deck hands were visible, with one hosing down the deck and the other stowing gear that had been used during the day's fishing trip.

Petronovich called over to the men, "Is the captain on board?"

A young guy poked his head out of the wheelhouse window after hearing English being spoken. His men had no idea what Petronovich had asked.

He replied to Petronovich in broken English, "What you want with me?"

"Can we come aboard and talk?"

"Sure, be careful not to fall," replied the captain as he stood at the door, motioning them to the bench behind the captain's chair.

Petronovich and Volkov took a seat while the captain lifted himself onto his chair at the helm.

"What do you need?" asked the captain.

"We flew into Trabzon from the U.S. today, because of the information you had given to our people at the embassy in Istanbul. Have you heard from the man that you transported a week or so ago?"

"No. He not come yet."

"We believe that he will be contacting you either today or tomorrow. If he does, we will want to be on your boat, hidden, until we are in international waters. Do you understand, captain?" Petronovich asked.

"Yes, I know."

"How can you let us know if he will be on board in the morning?" Volkov asked, interjecting himself into the conversation.

The captain stood. "I have idea."

He walked over to a closet, pulled out a box, and rummaged through what looked like many different flags used on boats. He pulled out two flags and laid them on the table in front of the bench where Petronovich and Volkov were seated.

The first one was entirely red with what looked like a notch cut out of the right side.

"This flag called Bravo, means dangerous cargo on board. If I fly this late night, early morning, means man will be coming in morning."

"Snap a picture of this and take notes, Vasily," Petronovich commanded.

The captain moved to the second flag which had three horizontal stripes. The top one was yellow followed by a blue center stripe and below it, once again, a horizontal yellow stripe.

"This is the Delta flag. Meaning is, keep clear. I fly this flag and man not here."

Volkov snapped a picture and wrote what the captain had said.

"That seems clear enough, captain. We have rooms at the Alesha and can see your trawler from there. We will be watching for your signal. Assuming he will be on the boat tomorrow, what time should we be here?" Petronovich asked.

"Man come early. You be aboard by three-thirty in morning."

Petronovich and Volkov both stood.

Petronovich offered his hand. "You will be well compensated for the help you have given the United States Government. Thank you."

"I not do this for money, my friend."

Volkov replied, "We know that, and appreciate what you are doing all the more."

Petronovich patted the young captain on the shoulder and ducked through the door out of the wheelhouse onto the dock.

"We will be in touch, captain."

***

It was seven fifteen, with the captain about to lock the wheelhouse door and go home for the short night. The boats in the marina were illuminated by marina spotlights and a low fog was beginning to roll in. The captain had the key in the lock and had been securing it when he sensed someone on the dock next to the boat.

He glanced over and looked at Naryshkin standing on the dock. "Ivanov, you need ride tomorrow to Sochi, yes?"

"That's right, captain. For the ride you will be compensated the same," Naryshkin replied.

"Not this time, Ivanov. The captain of the *Kalinovka* and I have had a discussion. This doesn't feel right. The fee for both of us is double, 60,000 Turkish lira. No discussion. As they say in America, take it or leave it."

Naryshkin was annoyed and taken aback. He looked at the captain. "I will pay the fee this one time. Then I might find an alternate route."

"Your choice, Ivanov. In fact, I'd like that," replied the captain. "Be here at four forty-five, no later. We leave at the usual time." The captain turned to make sure the door to the wheelhouse was locked. When he turned back, Naryshkin was gone.

The captain opened the wheelhouse door, went inside to the table and picked up the red flag. Once again, outside the wheelhouse, he locked the door, stepped down onto the deck and fastened the red flag to the aft outrigger halyard, hoisting it to the top where it fluttered in the light breeze.

***

Petronovich and Volkov had a small table in the dimly lit lounge area toward the back. Volkov had finished his Grey Goose while Petronovich was still nursing his. Both men were in deep thought.

Petronovich looked over at Volkov. "Vasily, go up to your room and check for the flag on the *Sansli*. I'll order another round.

Volkov rose from the table without saying a word and headed out of the bar. It was dark outside, but ambient light entered the bedroom from the window when Volkov opened the door. He walked to the window and looked down towards the marina. The *Sansli* was dark, but he noticed the flutter of the flag aft. Looking closely, he recognized the red flag and smiled., *Dangerous cargo,* he thought. *Only it's not Naryshkin that is dangerous, it is us.*

Volkov took the elevator down and walked into the bar. A Grey Goose waited for him. He sat, took a sip and then, without looking up, said, "Naryshkin will be onboard tomorrow. A red flag is flying."

Petronovich smiled, raised his glass and said, "Here's to Naryshkin's last day."

"Na Zdorovie," replied Volkov, smiling widely.

"We'd better make this the last round. We've got to be on our A-game tomorrow," said Petronovich.

"Yes, sir," said Volkov with a grin.

***

Jason followed Mike to the tasting room where grapes were being fermented and were about two weeks from bottling. Mike took two glasses off the shelf and walked over to one of the oak barrels which would soon be bottled.

Using a long stem 'cheater,' he withdrew a half glass of wine and dropped it into one of the glasses. After handing the glass to

Jason, he repeated the process for himself.

"Let's walk outside and check the vineyard," suggested Mike as they headed for the tasting room door.

They walked for a quarter mile when Jason finally said, "What's on your mind?"

"You know, Jason, I think back on the last couple of years, and they sure have been interesting. It's all since Vladi, and now Vasily, have come into our lives. Those two are family and I wouldn't have it any other way. Do you know what I mean?"

"I do. And I know you're worried about them. You need to remind yourself that they are professionals. They'll be fine."

"You're right. I'm thankful that our families are safe. But, in the last three years, there have been many close calls. When I was with the FBI, I was okay with it, but not for my family."

Jason didn't hesitate. "Agreed."

"What do you say we get the oak pit going and the tri-tip seasoned?" suggested Mike, "Then open a bottle of the 2013 Syrah."

"I'm in."

***

It was dark when Petronovich walked next door to Volkov's room. He had the case that had been given to him by the guy from the embassy in Istanbul in his hand. He tapped lightly on the door, which swung open immediately.

Volkov motioned him in. "I was about to come over."

Petronovich walked past Volkov and set the case on the table in the corner. He opened it, revealing two Glock 17's and four magazines. He picked one gun up, handed it butt first to Volkov, and then placed two magazines for him on the table.

Volkov slid one of the magazines into the Glock and chambered a nine mm round. Petronovich did the same.

"Are you ready?" asked Vladi.

"Yes, let's do it."

The two men crossed the street. They were at the gate to the marina within ten minutes. They could see lights on inside the wheelhouse of the *Sansli*. They approached the vessel and Petronovich almost whispered, because of the echo in the fog, "Captain."

The captain came out of the wheelhouse and stepped onto the deck. "Come aboard." He walked over to the open hatch near the stern hold. Pointing down into the hole, he said, "I place two chairs, lantern and thermos of coffee down there. You go now. Climb ladder down. When we are out of territorial water, one of my men will open hold and let you out."

Volkov looked at Petronovich. "Sounds good to me," he said and was the first inside. Petronovich followed.

***

When Naryshkin arrived at four thirty, the deck crew was busy preparing the fishing gear. The captain was inside the wheelhouse when he heard, "Permission to come aboard?"

"Granted, Ivanov. Come up to the wheelhouse. Let me see your cash," replied the captain.

Naryshkin stepped onto the deck, climbed the four stairs into the wheelhouse and placed the wad of cash on the table.

The captain picked it up, once again without counting it, and placed it in a drawer near the helm.

"Have a seat, Ivanov, we will be leaving ahead of schedule."

***

It was cold and damp in the hold, with an overwhelming stench of fish. Both men had their jackets zipped and hoisted up high to cover their noses. The vibration of the engines began with quite a bit of movement on the deck above. They could hear the captain issuing commands as the engine vibration increased, and the low rumble of power echoed through the hold.

"We're underway," said Petronovich as he sipped a cup of the strong, hot coffee.

***

The *Sansli* eased out of Trabzon's small harbor. After clearing the no wake zone, the captain increased power and maintained a steady eight knots. The exterior lights illuminated the way out to sea as the fog began to lift.

Naryshkin sat in the corner on the bench, bundled in his jacket, head against the wall, dozing. Every few minutes, he would shake awake, get his bearings and then fall back to sleep. The interior of the wheelhouse was dark and quiet except for the periodic snore from the corner of the booth.

After two hours, the *Sansli* was fifteen nautical miles offshore, outside Turkish territorial waters. The captain stood, walked to the wheelhouse door, and motioned to one of the deck hands to open the hatch to the stern hold.

Petronovich and Volkov looked up as the hatch opened and the bright *Sansli* deck lighting poured inside.

The deckhand motioned for Petronovich and Volkov to come up. Both men stood, withdrew their weapons, and climbed the ladder up to the deck.

The captain glanced down and saw Volkov coming out of the hold with Petronovich following. Both men crouched and stepped quickly next to the stairs leading to the wheelhouse. The captain put the *Sansli* in neutral and stepped toward the door.

"Where are you going, captain?" asked Naryshkin.

"It's time to prepare the nets for fishing. The sun is about to rise."

The captain closed the door behind him and stepped down onto the deck. He whispered to Petronovich, who was standing next to the stairs, "He is all yours."

Petronovich nodded, climbed the stairs, and opened the door. Naryshkin was in the corner and appeared to be sleeping.

Volkov followed and quietly shut the door. Naryshkin sensed the abnormal sound of two people moving about in the wheelhouse. He opened his eyes to see Petronovich at one side of the bench and Volkov at the other, both with guns pointed at his head.

"Place your hands on the table where we can see them, Sergey," said Petronovich.

"If you hurt me, you'll cause an international incident Petronovich."

"You are an embarrassment to the Russian Federation, Naryshkin. We've been in communication with your country once we knew where to find you. They have given us the authority to permanently silence you. You've created a rogue insurrection, believing what you were doing to be in the best interest of Russia," said Petronovich.

"Everything I've done was for Russia. It is the two of you who are the embarrassment to the Motherland."

Petronovich looked over at Volkov and said, "Lay the options on the table, Vasily."

Volkov removed a plastic wrap from his coat pocket, carefully placing the contents on the table in front of Naryshkin. In front of him were a single nine mm cartridge and a small white capsule.

"These are your choices, Naryshkin," said Volkov. "Pick one."

Naryshkin began to perspire and whispered, "You can't do this. What is the pill?"

Petronovich replied, "You know what it is."

"Cyanide."

"That's right," said Volkov. "Choose."

Naryshkin's shoulders drooped in resignation. "Please hand me a piece of paper and pencil," Naryshkin asked, pointing to the desk next to the helm seat.

Volkov stepped over to the desk, tore a piece of paper from the pad and placed it, along with a pencil in front of Naryshkin.

Naryshkin quickly wrote down an address and pushed the paper toward Petronovich.

"What is this?" he asked.

"That is my home address in Sochi. My mother is staying there. Will you let her know that I died doing what I thought was right for my country?"

"No guarantees," said Petronovich. "Make your decision."

Naryshkin picked up the cyanide capsule, put it in his mouth and swallowed.

Petronovich and Volkov watched as Naryshkin's breathing became noticeably labored. He slumped to the side of the bench and began to convulse. This lasted no more than a minute when Naryshkin's eyes widened, and he took his last breath.

Petronovich checked the carotid for a pulse, then looked at Volkov. "He's dead. Get the captain up here with a tarp."

Petronovich used his camera to take a picture of the body and then pulled a piece of hair from Naryshkin's head for the DNA to confirm the identity.

He placed the hair in an envelope found on the desk and waited for the captain.

***

The captain's deck hands placed two heavyweights (normally used to drop the large fishing nets to the ocean floor) into the tarp with the body. They cinched the tarp closed with several ropes, top to bottom.

The captain looked at Petronovich "Good enough?"

"Yes, send the body overboard," replied Petronovich.

The deckhands, with the captain and Volkov's help, hefted the body to the rail and let it roll over into the Black Sea.

Petronovich watched as the body hit the water with a splash and sank quickly from view.

"Please take us back to the marina, captain," said Petronovich.

***

About a mile from the Trabzon marina, Petronovich was on deck and noticed his cell phone had two bars and access to a tower.

He dialed Whittington and gave an update as to what had happened. After he finished the briefing, Petronovich added, "Have the plane fueled and the crew ready to leave Trabzon in about two hours. One more thing, Whit. Get us clearance from the Russian government to fly into Sochi. I need to make a quick stop."

"What's in Sochi, Petronovich?"

"Natalia Naryshkin. After I meet with her, which won't take long, we will fly to Santa Barbara."

"You got it. Let me know when you leave Sochi," said Whittington as he terminated the call.

The captain was in the wheelhouse, lining up the trawler to enter the small harbor in Trabzon. Petronovich took the stairs two at a time, up to the wheelhouse.

Standing next to the captain, looking over the bow, Petronovich said, "I have something for you." He reached for his wallet and withdrew a U.S. Treasury check in the amount of $100,000, placing it face up for the captain to see.

"This, for me?" the captain asked, looking at the check and then Petronovich.

"Yes, for you. You were most helpful in apprehending a man who had caused more death than you know. The U.S. Government wants to thank you," replied Petronovich.

The captain smiled, took the check and placed it in the drawer, next to the cash Naryshkin had given him earlier that morning.

"Thank you," he replied.

***

The pilot was in the cockpit doing paperwork while the co-pilot was doing a pre-flight walk-around when the Uber pulled up at the FBO. Petronovich and Volkov walked through the small office out to the plane with their overnight bags in hand. The co-pilot looked up.

"We're set to go. I understand we have a stop in Sochi."

"Yes, it will be brief. In fact, Vasily will stay with you and

291

the plane, while I conduct my business. It shouldn't take more than a couple of hours," said Petronovich.

"Sounds good. The aircraft is in good shape. We're fueled and ready to get underway once you get situated," responded the co-pilot.

Volkov was already on board, followed by Petronovich and the co-pilot.

The flight time to Sochi was a quick forty minutes. The G550 had reached a cruising altitude of ten thousand feet when it began the decent.

"That was quick," said Volkov as he looked over at Petronovich. He was doing something with his phone.

"I just checked maps. It looks like the drive time from the airport to Naryshkin's home is about twenty minutes. I'll order an Uber once we land."

***

The Uber dropped Petronovich off in front of Naryshkin's house.

Vladi got out and looked at the large home, then across the road at the Black Sea. *This place is amazing,* he thought.

"Stay here, I won't be long," said Petronovich to the driver.

He walked up the steps to the large double doors and rang the bell. A lady in her mid-fifties answered, speaking Russian. "Yes?"

"Is Mrs. Naryshkin available?" asked Petronovich with a Russian accent that would place him near Moscow.

"May I tell Mrs. Naryshkin who is calling?"

"Yes, I am a friend, my name is Vladimir Petronovich."

"Oh, please come inside Mr. Petronovich. I will tell Mrs. Naryshkin you are here," said the lady who was obviously help.

Petronovich waited in the foyer, taking in the ornate furniture and pictures.

The lady returned and asked, "Mr. Petronovich, will you follow me to the pool patio? Mrs. Naryshkin is delighted you dropped by."

Vladi followed through the living room, past the dining room and through a back door next to a dining nook. "Mrs. Naryshkin is seated under the umbrella. Can I get you anything to drink?"

"No, thank you. I won't be long," Petronovich replied.

As he walked toward the table, Natalia stood, smiled, and offered her hand.

"Vladimir, you are a long way from home. Why the visit? Though I am happy to see you. Please sit," she said as she motioned to a chair.

Petronovich took and seat and said, "Mrs. Naryshkin, I'm sorry to say, I have bad news."

"It's Sergey?"

"Yes, ma'am. He was killed doing something very dangerous; something he thought was for the good of Russia. He won't be coming home."

"Where did this happen, Valdimir? What about the body?"

"That is classified. The body was not found. I didn't want you to get the news from anyone else. I have a plane and can fly you back to Moscow if you choose."

"So, you still work for the SVR, Vladimir, I knew it."

Petronovich smiled, letting her think what she wanted.

"But, no I have a nice couple that cares for me here, and I must say, that in the short time I've been in Sochi, I've come to like the mild weather. Would you like something to drink?" asked Natalie, trying her best to be strong after hearing the news.

293

"No, thank you. My plane is waiting, I must go," said Petronovich as he watched a tear roll down Natalia's cheek. He rose, took a business card from his pocket, with his name and contact information and placed it on the table. "If you need anything, call me."

Natalia remained seated but picked up the card. "This card says Long Beach. Is that U.S.?"

"Yes, I work around the world. Sometimes I get back to Russia. When I do, I will give you a call."

"That would be nice, Vladimir. You must go now and catch your plane."

Petronovich turned and walked back through the house to the car. "To the airport, please."

***

The G550 reached a cruising altitude of forty-five thousand feet. Petronovich rose from his chair and went to the galley. He came back into the cabin with two glasses and a bottle of Grey Goose which he set on a fixed table positioned between two plush leather chairs. Looking up toward Volkov, who was facing forward, about mid-cabin, he said, "Vasily, come back here and sit."

Volkov turned, looked back, and smiled. Without saying a word, Petronovich poured as Vasily sat in the opposite chair. No words could describe what they and the McClintocks had gone through in the last few weeks.

Finally, Volkov raised his glass. "Here's to life returning to some sense of normalcy."

Petronovich raised his glass and said, "To normalcy." Then, looking at Vasily, he added, "I've been thinking."

"That's never a good start."

"Hear me out. Because of me, Jason, Mike, and their families were put in grave danger. And you almost lost your life. It's not much but, would you consider going on a cruise with me and the McClintocks?" asked Petronovich.

"I've never been on a cruise ship. Where?"

"I don't know. We have a long flight. If you're in, I'll play with the idea."

"Count me in, Vladi."

After twelve hours in the air, the co-pilot came back into the cabin. Petronovich and Volkov had slept some, but not much, anxious to get home.

The co-pilot said, "We're about an hour outside of Santa Barbara. We will be touching down at about three thirty this morning. Mr. Whittington has been following our progress and said he would have a car waiting to take you to your homes in southern California, or up to the McClintock vineyard in Santa Ynez."

"I requested landing at SBA, so we could go to the vineyard," Petronovich replied.

"Mr. Whittington thought that would be the case. He asked me to tell you to take a couple of days off. The debriefing will take place in his office next Monday, ten a.m. In any case, you should be at the vineyard before sunrise," said the co-pilot as he returned back to the cockpit. Before closing the cockpit door, he turned and said, "Welcome home, gentlemen."

***

The Suburban turned off Refugio Road onto the dirt driveway.

"Kill the lights and drive slow, I don't want to wake the

295

family," said Petronovich to the driver.

In the distance, they could see a Santa Barbara County Sheriff's car. The deputy saw the vehicle turn in. He opened the door, extinguished the interior light and from behind the car door, withdrew his weapon.

Seeing the deputy's action, the FBI agent briefly turned on the flashing lights, letting the deputy know they were law enforcement. The deputy holstered the weapon and waited as the Suburban approached and parked.

Petronovich was about to exit the SUV when he looked at the driver and said, "We've got it from here. Thanks for the ride."

Volkov was out the other side, speaking to the deputy.

Petronovich identified himself, as did Volkov, showing their federal credentials.

Five minutes later, after a brief discussion, the deputy was driving away from the property. They both watched as the vehicle turned onto the main road.

Petronovich glanced to his left and noted the kitchen light had turned on. "Someone is up early."

Mike and Jason were early risers.

Mike was out at sunrise to tend the grapes and Jason was in his beat-up '55 Jeep along with Rosie, his Labrador companion no later than five a.m. The men walked toward the back of the house and lightly tapped the kitchen door.

Mike opened the door to find Petronovich and Volkov staring back with wide smiles.

Petronovich asked, "Do you have a couple of extra coffees?"

Mike stepped back. "I knew you two would show up like this."

Jason had been sitting in the dark at the kitchen table, reading the news from his phone. He stood and gave each man a handshake and hug. "I'm glad you're both safe."

Before long, even though there was very little noise, the entire house was up. Julie and Brenda came into the kitchen first, surprised, and happy to see their friends. Zach and Sam followed about a half hour later. Through all the commotion, Brenda and Julie made a large breakfast. While they were doing that, Vladi and Volkov gave Mike and Jason a summation of what had happened. The sensitive points regarding Naryshkin and his passing were made out of earshot of the women and kids.

The breakfast was over the top, with hashbrowns, eggs, bacon and French toast for the picky eater, Sam.

While they were eating, Petronovich broke the silence, "I've been thinking."

The moans and an "Oh, no," were immediate along with light laughter.

"What do you have in mind?" Jason asked.

"Well, Mike, Julie and kids have never been on a cruise." "Stop right there Vladi," said Mike. "We were on the seven-day cruise for at least two days, or so."

"Right, that's my point. Because of me, your vacation was ruined, not to mention putting all of you in danger and almost seeing Vasily leave this earth plane."

"That's a nice way to put it," replied Vasily as he looked at the kids. "So, get on with it, tell them what you're thinking."

"How about we do a cruise with all of us, on my dime? It would be a small boat like the one you were on, but this time, staying away from Mexico and Europe. We just came from the Mediterranean Sea, the Black Sea is part of it, so that's out. And Alaska is too close to Russia. I'm thinking of the Caribbean in the spring before Mike is swamped caring for the vineyard."

"That would be great, Vladi!" said Zach.

"Can we go, Dad?" Sam asked, looking at both Mike and Julie.

"I love the Southern Caribbean, especially Aruba and Barbados," added Brenda.

"Southern, it is!" said Petronovich. "Jason, Mike, Julie?"

Mike looked at both Jason and Julie, who nodded and smiled.

Then, Mike said, "Vladi, I swore I'd never go on another cruise. But what kind of trouble could we get into in the Caribbean? We're in!"